THE
SLAVERS

Other books by F. M. Parker

The Far Battleground
The Shadow Man

F.M. PARKER
THE SLAVERS

NAL BOOKS
NEW AMERICAN LIBRARY

A DIVISION OF PENGUIN BOOKS USA INC.
NEW YORK
PUBLISHED IN CANADA BY
PENGUIN BOOKS CANADA LIMITED, MARKHAM, ONTARIO

PUBLISHER'S NOTE

This book is a work of fiction. Names, characters, places, and incidents either are the product of the author's imagination or are used fictitiously, and any resemblance to actual persons, living or dead, events, or locales is entirely coincidental.

NAL BOOKS ARE AVAILABLE AT QUANTITY DISCOUNTS WHEN USED TO PROMOTE PRODUCTS OR SERVICES. FOR INFORMATION PLEASE WRITE TO PREMIUM MARKETING DIVISION, NEW AMERICAN LIBRARY, 1633 BROADWAY, NEW YORK, NEW YORK 10019.

Published simultaneously in Canada by Penguin Books Canada Limited.

NAL BOOKS TRADEMARK REG. U.S. PAT. OFF. AND FOREIGN COUNTRIES
REGISTERED TRADEMARK—MARCA REGISTRADA
HECHO EN DRESDEN, TN

SIGNET, SIGNET CLASSIC, MENTOR, ONYX, PLUME, MERIDIAN
and NAL BOOKS are published *in the United States* by
New American Library, a division of Penguin Books USA, Inc.,
1633 Broadway, New York, New York 10019,
in Canada by Penguin Books Canada Limited,
2801 John Street, Markham, Ontario L3R 1B4

Library of Congress Cataloging-in-Publication Data

Parker, F.M.
    The slavers/F.M. Parker
    p. cm.
    ISBN 0-453-00655-8
    I. Title.
    PS3566.A678S58   1989
    813'.54—dc19

Designed by Arturo D. Bull

First Printing, May, 1989

1 2 3 4 5 6 7 8 9

PRINTED IN THE UNITED STATES OF AMERICA

The Kids

Prologue—The Lost Valley

The Ice Age died.
The Great Desert was born.

THE COLOSSAL GLACIER, SOME FIFTEEN HUNdred miles wide and more than a mile thick, lay upon the continent for millennium after millennium. The mighty mass of ice thrust cold arctic winds far beyond its border, making the winters of the land long and the summers short, and causing torrential rains to fall and hurricane winds to blow.

Twenty thousand years ago, the earth began to warm and the glacial epoch waned. The great glacier began to shrink, retreating from its far-flung borders.

At one latitude on the sphere of the earth, the sun had burned directly down for billions of years. In this equatorial zone, the air become heated as in a furnace and surged heavenward in an unending tide. Reaching tremendous heights, the stupendous updraft split, half dashing south and half north. The northern segment, rushing through the frigid atmosphere at speeds exceeding two hundred miles per hour, hurried toward the top of the world. However, it grew weary before it reached its goal and plunged down toward the face of the earth.

During the glacial epoch, these dry, descending south winds would have mixed with the damp, cool surface air blowing from the north. Now, however, the land was warming as the millennia passed and the equatorial winds grew hot and parched with a prodigious thirst that could consume ten feet of water in a year. And the glacier's domination of the climate ebbed.

On a small mountain range twelve hundred miles southwest of the shrinking glacier, the pine forest began to die. The strong, boisterous stream that tumbled down a valley on the eastern flank of the mountain started to dwindle. The inland lake that filled the broad basin at the foot of the mountains grew shallower and drew back from its shores.

The glacier withered away to but a fraction of its original mammoth size. As it came close to death, the glacier completely lost its mastery of the rains that fell upon the land, and they diminished to rare thunderstorms. The harsh desert came stalking across the mountains and the valleys.

The stream on the mountain become weaker and weaker. Finally it became so feeble it could not maintain a surface flow, and it hid from the burning sun in the rock and alluvium of its channel. In one location near the lower end of the valley, the stream struggled to the surface and ran in view of the heavens for a mile. Then it sank back into the rubble, to forever creep blindly through the Stygian gloom of the underworld.

The pine forest died except for a patch of stunted trees in a cove on the cooler north side of the mountain. The cacti and desert brush and bunchgrass invaded the land, climbing to the very peak of the mountain.

The lonely inland lake continued to diminish under the

scorching sun. Then one year there wasn't enough water to last through the dry season and all the fish perished.

The desiccated, sandy bottom of the dead lake began to ripple, the fine grains of sediment rolling and tumbling under the prying fingers of the dry wind. Monstrous sand dunes came to life. Like waves of a dirty yellow sea, the dunes migrated to the west, lapping against the feet of the mountains and marching to the very mouth of the valley.

In some unrecorded and forgotten time, a wandering band of copper-colored men found the valley. They halted beside the short stretch of running water and killed the rabbits and gathered the seeds of the wild grass. But the food supply of the valley was small, and after a brief period, the men left.

Many years passed between the happenstance visits of the brown men to the valley. Once the valley lay lost and untrod by humans for three hundred years.

On a hot, windy day, a band of people with white skin and yellow hair trudged south along the narrow zone between the sand sea and the rocky flank of the mountain. The men drove horses pulling wheeled vehicles carrying provisions and farming equipment. Brave women and sturdy children journeyed with the men. They found the valley.

The leader of the band called his yellow-haired followers to him and pointed into the valley. "The soil is rich and there's water to irrigate our crops. This is the place where we shall halt and build our homes. There on that rise near the creek we shall consecrate land and construct a church where we may worship our God."

The nine men and their twenty-seven wives and forty-nine children went into the valley.

9

1

June 1877, Mexico City

THE OLD DUELING MASTER, LUIS CALLEJA, knew he would be dead in less than a minute and there was absolutely nothing he could do to prevent it.

They fought, the master duelist and his young adversary, with thin-bladed, two-edged swords, unbelievably sharp. The large drill hall rang with the harsh sound of steel striking steel as quick thrusting blades were parried and knocked aside. The hurried thud of boots as the men advanced and retreated across the wooden floor was a drumbeat to the battle.

Closer and closer to Calleja drew the threatening sword point of his opponent, the student Melchor Zaldivar. The master's own sword had grown heavier as the contest continued, and his aged right arm was failing to fend off the attacks with the swift, powerful strokes that had once come so naturally to it.

Sweat beaded on the master's face and his hand was slippery on the handle of his weapon. Every breath came

11

fast, scalding his lungs and rattling with a hoarse, sawing sound in his throat.

The dangerous blade of his opponent reached toward him again, coming within an inch of his chest before he could parry the thrust. His counterattack was weak.

A pleased smile began to play about the young swordman's mouth, and a cruel, deadly light came to life and glowed in his black eyes. He knew that victory would soon be his.

Now Calleja understood why Zaldivar had volunteered to be the first student for his exhibition with naked swords. He meant to slay the old dueling instructor. Calleja also knew the reason the man wanted to kill him, but that didn't make dying any easier.

"Halt! Enough," cried the dueling master, his words ragged with his shortness of breath. He stepped back and let the point of his sword drop. Perhaps Zaldivar would cease his assault when he saw the master's guard was down.

The smile of his enemy broadened with the knowledge of certain triumph.. "Never, Calleja. Today you die." Zaldivar bore in, his sword stabbing out to pierce the chest of the instructor.

Calleja jerked his weapon back into a defensive position. He swung the blade to block the incoming point and moved quickly backward. But the sharp tip of Zaldivar's sword, searching for a target, found Calleja's chest and brought blood even as the master shunted it aside.

"So be it," muttered the old man, so low that only he heard his words. Even as he gathered in the weakening strands of his strength for the last supreme effort of defense, he prepared his body and mind to take the death stroke from the sword of his foe. He would not cry out again.

Ken Larrway stood with the five other students against the wall and watched the two contestants come together with clashing blades. Each man stuck with his keen-edged weapon here, there, every time to be met with a parry by his opponent instantly followed by a return counterthrust.

The light in the big, high-ceilinged drill hall was growing dim, for the sun had dropped below the horizon, and deep gray shadows were forming in the corners. In the weak light, the swords moved so fast they were invisible. Only the ringing sound of metal hitting metal proved the deadly blades truly existed.

Luis Calleja was the greatest dueling instructor in all Mexico, perhaps in all the Americas. He had trained men in the art of killing for more than thirty years. In 1847 when the invading Americans made their final assault on Mexico City, Ken's father had been wounded in the storming of the Mexican power magazine, Casa Mata. The defenders captured the American and would have put him to death had not the young Mexican officer Luis Calleja stepped forward and stood with drawn sword over the injured American, forbidding the execution. Strangely, the enemies Calleja and Larrway had become friends over the months of American occupation of Mexico.

During the three years in the 1860s when the French under Emperor Maximilian had ruled Mexico, dueling had increased greatly, given impetus by the Frenchmen always so quick to anger and fight. Calleja had given instruction to many of the French generals and other high officers.

Ken had traveled to Mexico City—one of the great cities of the world, his father had said—to train under Calleja. This was the middle of the sixth month, nearly the end of the half-year Ken had allotted himself. At the beginning of July before the weather reached its hottest on the deserts to the north, he would return to his home in Los Angeles.

All Calleja's trainees were taught the use of sword, pistol, and rifle. Once the men became proficient with the three weapons, they began to specialize in that weapon that came most naturally to their hand. Ken's bent was strongly toward the pistol.

The duel between Calleja and Zaldivar had continued for a quarter-hour, an impossible time. Ken wondered why the master didn't call a halt to the contest. The session with unprotected blades was only to allow the student to experience the feeling of facing a weapon that could kill. And there were six students yet to go through the exercise.

The two duelists had been evenly matched at first. However, Ken saw the master was slowing and showing signs of exhaustion. Zaldivar gave no evidence of weariness. He seemed to be growing stronger, if that was possible, and a pleased expression masked his face.

Ken heard the dueling master call out for an end to the contest. Zaldivar smiled and, instead of halting, pressed his attack even harder.

"Ken, I believe Melchor intends to kill the master," said his companion Lucas Alamán in a hushed whisper. "The old man's strength is failing. In just a few seconds, it will be all over."

"No. He's not going to die." Ken's voice was brittle. He owed the dueling instructor nothing. But his father owed the man his life. It was time to repay that debt.

14

Ken stepped quickly to a table against the wall where his pistol lay. His hand snaked out and grabbed the revolver from its holster. He extended the gun, cocking the hammer as it rose. The pistol exploded, jarring the walls of the drill hall and rebounding back in an ear-shattering roar.

Zaldivar flinched back as the buzzing bullet tore past less than an inch from his nose. He spun, sweeping his sight over the students, seeking the source of the shot. His attention riveted on Larrway. Yes, the gringo would be the one. Only he would be so foolish as to try to stop a Zaldivar from doing what he desired. He raised his sword and pointed it at the *norteamericano.*

Larrway held his pistol and stared through the gray-black gunsmoke that swirled and tumbled in the disturbed air. His expression was cold and glacial as his eyes battled with Zaldivar's.

"You gringo bastard," hissed Zaldivar. He advanced toward Larrway, his sword rigid in his hand. "I'll run you through for that trick."

"If you come within reach of me with that blade, I'll shoot out both your eyes," Ken threatened, raising his pistol so that the black open bore of the weapon was aimed directly into Zaldivar's face.

Zaldivar looked at the revolver in the gringo's hand. Larrway wasn't a Mexican; he wouldn't be afraid of the power of the Zaldivar family. He had fired his gun to stop the attack on Calleja. But more than that, he would kill to protect Calleja and himself. The sureness of that purpose lay glinting in the blue orbs of his eyes.

Zaldivar glanced at the five Mexican students. They watched him expectantly, wanting to see what a Zaldivar would do when confronted with such a man as the American. There appeared to be a smirk on Alamán's face.

Zaldivar wouldn't forget that. Alamán would soon regret such an expression of disrespect.

Zaldivar spoke to Larrway. "You have interfered and taken a stand in a situation you know nothing about. For that you will never leave Mexico City alive."

The American's shoulders moved in the merest of shrugs. "Why don't you challenge me to a duel?"

"You can wait," said Zaldivar. He whirled upon the dueling instructor. "You killed a Zaldivar, my Uncle Antonio, four years ago. I watched you do it. When my father discussed how to dispose of you for that, I asked that you be allowed to live so that when I became a man I would have the pleasure of fighting and killing you. That time is now. Are you a coward, or do we meet?"

"Your uncle was an overbearing bully who insulted me. The duel was fair. I gave him his choice of weapons."

"All of that means nothing. He never had a chance against you. But I can beat you. Now, do we meet? Answer or show how much you fear the Zaldivares."

"I shall meet with you."

"Excellent. My second will call upon your second. Who will that be?"

"I need no second," Calleja replied. He knew he would never leave the dueling place alive. He needed no second to halt the contest should he be injured. "Have your second call upon me to make the arrangements."

"No," said Larrway. "I'll be Luis Calleja's second. The duel will be fought fairly."

"That's very good," said Zaldivar. He chuckled in a pleased manner. "I want you there when this old man meets his death."

"Perhaps you'll be the one to die," countered Larrway.

"That won't happen. Neither of you can kill me." Zaldivar turned, walked to the table, picked up his pis-

16

tol. With heels pounding the floor, he stomped from the drill hall.

The remaining five students retrieved their weapons. They left in a quiet group. Lucas Alamán cast a look behind and raised his hand in salute to Larrway.

"You are a fool, Ken," Calleja said harshly. "Why did you get involved by threatening Melchor?"

"He would have killed you," Ken replied, surprised at the man's anger. "Don't you want to live?"

"Oh, yes. But it will only be for a few hours. And now you will also die."

"I feel very much alive and I'm not afraid of Melchor." Zaldivar."

"Ramos Zaldivar is Melchor's father. He's a caudillo, a military chieftain, and one of the richest and most powerful men in all Mexico. He owns more than two million acres of land and rich gold and silver mines. It is also said Ramos deals in slaves, beautiful white-skinned women. He has wealth and is not afraid to use violence, so he is much feared. Melchor is nothing compared to his father. You must take your horse and leave immediately for California."

"I won't leave my father's friend to fight alone. He would disown me if I crawled home a coward."

"You're wrong. Your father was an officer in the American army. He knows there are times one must retreat in the face of a superior force. Ramos Zaldivar will carry out his son's threat. He must, for a man who practices violence mustn't allow violence to be used against him."

"Will Ramos Zaldivar challenge me to a duel, then?"

"I don't believe he will. Melchor likes to duel and so does his older brother, Martín. But that's a foolish game. Their father is wiser. He too dueled many times as a young man and has slain more than thirty men, but now

17

he rarely duels, and only against his most important enemies, those he cannot have murdered. Those are few now, for Ramos is a very great *pistolero* and swordsman. He's better than either Melchor or Martín, especially with a pistol. No, Ramos won't fight an unknown person; he'll send his men to slay you.

"Ramos has his own private army, the largest among the caudillos. It is supposed to have more than three thousand soldiers. To his army, he can quickly add his hundreds of vaqueros and thousands of peons as fighters. President Lerdo did not attempt to disband those private armies—nor has President Díaz. He knows that to move to crush one of the caudillos would cause others to band together, and that would plunge Mexico into another civil war.

"I think Ramos will send *pistoleros* to shoot you, and he will have no fear of punishment. You must leave tonight."

"Only if you go with me."

"I'm too old to start anew. And besides, I have agreed to the duel."

"Then we'll go together to the dueling place."

Calleja evaluated the young Larrway for a few seconds and then, with a scowl, turned away. He surveyed the darkening drill hall, letting his eyes roam slowly, fondly over the big room. He had spent thousands of pleasant days teaching eager men, young and old, how to defend themselves and have fear of no man. Those days were now gone forever.

"Walk with me to my home, Ken," said Calleja. "We have things to talk about." He slid his sword into its scabbard and led the way from the practice hall.

Without speaking, the young man and the old one walked along the cobblestone street. All around them the dusk of evening gathered. People passed by on the street. Some of the men recognized the dueling master and his student, and called greetings to them. A horse-drawn buggy rattled by, its iron-rimmed wheels echoing off the walls of the one- and two-story houses lining both sides of the thoroughfare. Within the homes, lights were being lit and rectangular windows began to glow with the soft yellow luminescence of candle flame. From the Zócalo, the Grand Plaza of Mexico City, a block to the north, came the sounds of the street vendors gathering up their wares at the end of the day and calling good night to one another.

Ken glanced through the gloom at the sad face of the instructor. The once vibrant spirit of the old man had gone out of him.

Ken spoke to him. "Haven't you kept any secrets from your students? At least one trick of the sword that will help you to beat Melchor?"

"No. I have always believed that the men who come to me to learn to use the weapons deserve to be taught all I know. I have no maneuvers to defeat Melchor and remain alive. He was an excellent swordsman when he came to me for training. As you were an expert *pistolero*. However, he had fought duels before and won, while you had never fired at a man. I helped both of you to become the very best. He can win against me. I have lost some of my strength over the years."

"Then you must defeat him early in the fight while you're still strong. Perhaps you should use a pistol. As the person challenged, you have the choice of weapons."

A pistol requires less strength and it's a very certain way to kill an enemy, if you are quicker. However, for months now, I have trained Melchor. I know he's both quicker and stronger than I am. I believe there is more of a chance that he may make a mistake if we fight with swords."

The dueling master was quiet for a long moment. Then he said, "I have waited these several years for Ramos Zaldivar to strike at me. Knowing him as I do, I always wondered why he didn't take his revenge."

Calleja looked directly at Ken. "We must plan what should be done whether I win or lose. In either event, you must leave Mexico City. If I should by some miracle survive, then I too will be forced to go. We must be ready to make a long journey immediately after the contest. You can return to Los Angeles, where you have family. I have powerful friends in Spain and will travel to Vera Cruz on the coast and catch a ship."

"I don't like running from the Zaldivares," Ken said.

"I agree it is a bad thing. And the Zaldivares may send men to follow and slay you even if you do escape from Mexico and reach California."

Calleja paused for a moment. Then he spoke softly, "I think the duel will bring death for me and a trap for you. Melchor knows you are more skilled with a pistol than he is. So he will not challenge you to a duel and let you have the choice of weapons. Instead, he will have men nearby to attack you, probably on your way back to your quarters."

Calleja studied the somber young Larrway. Seldom had he ever seen the man smile. Ken kept mostly to himself, sometimes practicing with Lucas Alamán. And practice diligently Ken did, every day, spending long hours in the drill hall or on the firing range in the hills west of the city. His skill was honed to the finest edge. Calleja judged him the quickest and most accurate *pistolero* he had ever taught. Ken was almost as good as Ramos Zaldivar. The difference in their speed couldn't be measured by a timepiece. Only by combat between them. The slower man would die.

Regardless of Ken's skill with a revolver, it was most unlikely that the son of Calleja's friend would see another sunset.

"It doesn't matter how you feel about the Zaldivares," Calleja said. "From now on until you are far away from their stronghold, which is all Mexico, you must always be prepared to travel swiftly and stay beyond their reach."

"Someone is waiting for you," Ken said, pointing ahead at a square-built man dressed as a vaquero and leaning against the iron patio gate of Calleja's house.

The man nonchalantly watched Ken and Calleja approach. He drew deeply on a thin cigarillo, and the hot coal gleamed like a bright-red ruby in the growing dusk.

A feeling arose from deep within Ken that the man meant him harm. He should be killed this very instant. That red spot of the cigarillo would be a perfect target. Then Ken let the thought go.

The man stepped away from the gate and his hand moved to hang close to his holstered pistol. Had he somehow read Ken's mind?

"It is Delgollado," said Calleja. He lowered his voice. "He is one of the best *pistoleros* in all Mexico. He is one of Zaldivar's soldiers. Never let him draw first on you."

"Señor Calleja, I'm Señor Zaldivar's second for the duel," said Delgollado. "He has asked me to make the necessary arrangements."

Calleja nodded shortly. "This is Ken Larrway. Speak with him. Whatever he agrees to is satisfactory to me." Calleja turned to Ken. "It is best to get these things over with as soon as possible. Set the contest for early tomorrow morning. But not before sunrise. Old men can't see so well in the dark. Come inside after you finish talking with Delgollado."

"Okay," replied Ken.

The old duelist lifted the latch on the gate and entered his patio. Ken faced the Zaldivar gunman alone.

2

MELCHOR ZALDIVAR RODE HIS HORSE ALONG the Belén Causeway, a stone-paved roadway raised above the broad marsh lying south west of Mexico City. He passed under the stone arches spanning the road and supporting an overhead aqueduct carrying water to the city. On all sides the huge valley that his ancient ancestors, the Aztecs, had called Anáhuac was filling with the deep dusk of approaching night.

He looked up at the big evening stars coming alive in the darker eastern sky. Spanish men had found the Aztec women excellent wives, and under these very same stars had started the lineage that had produced Melchor. It was good to live where your family began and to be very important.

His heart beat pleasantly as he contemplated the coming duel with Calleja. Winning should be relatively easy. Still, the contest could be dangerous. Unforeseen accidents could happen. One slip on the grass, a momentary drop of his guard, and the old duelist would run him through.

Zaldivar felt the bite of anger. It was because of the interference of that bastard gringo that Melchor must fight a duel before he could feel his sword cutting into the body of the murderous Calleja. Larrway would pay with his life for drawing a gun on him.

Melchor passed the foot of the two-hundred-foot volcanic hill called Chapultepec. He glanced up at the strong, stone-walled castle resting on top of the hill. The structure had been the resort of the long-dead Aztec princes. Later it had been used by the viceroys of Spain and later still by the French Emperor Maximillian as a residence. Most important, the castle was the site of the massacre of innocent young cadets by the savage Americans in that terrible time of invasion and occupation.

Melchor barely noticed the thick cypress woods, the place of many duels, at the north base of the hill. He touched his mount with the big, sharp rowels of his spurs and increased his pace across the dimly lit countryside.

He passed three ox-drawn wagons filled with wood from the hills. The woodcutters called out a greeting to the hurrying caballero. Zaldivar ignored the shadowy figures completely.

Without slowing, he sped through Tacubaya and took the private road up the slanting hill to the Zaldivar family hacienda, a large two-storied structure with many rooms and painted a brilliant white. It stood within a three-acre compound surrounded by an eight-foot wall made of stone and adobe. His father and he had lived there alone with their servants—until very recently.

As Melchor hurried toward the entrance of the family stronghold, a pleasant feeling of anticipation grew within him. The most enjoyable event of the day would soon begin.

He dragged the horse down to a walk as he drew close

to the gateway, then halted completely as a guard with a rifle stepped into the opening and touched the brim of his hat in salute.

"Good evening, *patrón,*" said the guard.

"Good evening to you, Oso." Melchor jumped down and tossed the reins of his mount to the man. "Keep the horse saddled. I have business in the city and will return there later tonight."

"Yes, *patrón.*"

"How many guards are on duty?"

"Two and myself," replied the man.

"Stay very alert tonight."

"Always, *mi jefe.*"

Melchor halted in the wide vestibule of the hacienda, removed his pistol, sword, and hat, and hung them on the tall lacquered rack near the door. A dispatch addressed to his father, lay on a low table. Melchor sliced it open with his knife. Something important might need attention and his father had not yet returned from business in Vera Cruz.

The message was from Jacobo Jiménez, Zaldivar's business manager in Torreón. Melchor began to read. Near the end of the message, he began to smile. Jacobo was asking Ramos to arrange for an auction of a golden treasure that he would bring to Mexico City in early November. Melchor replaced the message on the table. He already had a golden treasure.

He cleaned up, walked into the dining room, and took a seat at the long table lavishly spread with dinner for two. Immediately a male servant entered and poured him a piping hot cup of coffee. Melchor methodically placed two level teaspoons of sugar into the black liquid and began to stir. The servant remained motionless near the door, waiting. He knew the exact sequence of events.

"Ask the Señorita Anya to please have dinner with me," directed Melchor.

"*Sí, patrón,*" the servant responded, and hastily left. The man went down a long passageway and stopped at the bottom of a flight of stairs to the second-floor level. He took up a small bell from a stand and rang it softly.

On the floor above a large, dark-skinned woman rose from a chair and peered down the staircase. "What do you want?" she asked.

"The *patrón* wants the white woman," the man said. "Bring her at once."

The woman mumbled something the man couldn't hear and went off ponderously along the hallway to a door. She knocked roughly.

Melchor drank some of the coffee, savoring the flavor. It tasted immensely delicious after the evening's contest of skills with the dueling master. It was doubly enjoyable as a prelude to the meal about to begin.

He heard a sound and looked up. His pulse quickened. A young woman with striking white skin and yellow hair had come into the room. She stopped just inside the door.

"Good evening, Anya. Please be seated and have dinner with me."

"If you insist," said Anya Borgeson, coming forward.

"No, no. Not insist. I mean it as a most kind invitation. In fact, I have ordered every servant in the hacienda to obey your orders instantly. All that is here belongs to you."

"Everything but my freedom. That giant of a woman follows me everywhere about the house and I have no privacy. Neither she nor the guards will let me go outside the walls. I'm a prisoner, a slave to your every whim and command."

"That will change someday soon. For now, please sit down."

Anya went to a chair at the far end of the table and picked up a napkin at the plate. Once, shortly after she had been kidnapped from her home in Janos and brought hundreds of miles here to Mexico City, she had rejected an invitation to eat with Melchor Zaldivar and had walked out of the room. After three days during which every particle of food had been withheld from her, she had grudgingly accepted his request to eat with him. She reasoned that her strength had to be maintained, for one day she might discover a way to escape and then she needed to be strong to travel the long distance home. But in the meantime she shivered at the thought of him coming in the darkness to lie with her.

Melchor ate slowly, his eyes often upon the girl. He enjoyed observing her feminine movements, the curve of her fair cheek, and the swell of her young bosom.

Anya's blue eyes swept over the man in a challenging manner to show she was not afraid. Yet she knew she was.

He smiled in pure delight at the look in her eyes, and in his anticipation of the coming night with her. Soon she would be with child, and once it was born, she would not want to return north to Janos. She would willingly live here with him and share in his land and wealth. He had seen this happen with other white women after they had a child.

He lingered over the meal, drawing Anya into conversation. She answered in short Spanish sentences. He was pleased with her rapidly growing knowledge of his language. She was an intelligent woman.

Anya found a pause in the conversation and stood up. "May I leave now?" she asked.

27

Melchor would have liked to extend the pleasant time with Anya. However, he had men to see and plans to devise to kill an enemy. He arose and came to Anya. His hand moved up and he ran his fingers along her cheek. Her face was snow beneath his dusky brown skin.

"Good night, Anya. Thank you for the pleasure of your company. I have an early meeting in the morning. Perhaps after that we can go riding up into the hills."

Anya didn't reply. She turned abruptly away.

As she went to the door, Zaldivar intently evaluated her features. He was very pleased with what he saw. She was a rare jewel here in a land of dark women. She was worth the long journey and the danger of stealing her away from her menfolk. Still, if she continued to be stubborn and intractable, he would sell her as the Zaldivares had sold so many other white women. And there were more beautiful and young blond women in that strange town of Janos for him to steal. He walked swiftly to the vestibule, retrieved his pistol, and went out into the courtyard.

"Oso," Zaldivar called sharply, "bring my horse."

Ken woke before dawn and lay staring into the blackness. He recalled Calleja's warning that a powerful enemy would be plotting against him. If Calleja was right, this new day could be the most dangerous he had ever lived. He shoved the thought aside and buried it in a deep recess of his mind. Too much worry about dying could slow a man's hand on his weapon.

He climbed out of bed and lit a candle. The breeze blowing in through the open window washed coldly over his body and made the candle flame jump and flicker. He dressed swiftly into the clothing of a vaquero. Beneath his shirt, he fastened his money belt.

For a moment he looked about the one large room that had been his home for his stay in Mexico City. Then he started to gather his scant belongings for travel. There were actions that must be taken before the sun rose and the duel began.

He placed his American clothing on top of his blanket. To that he added a small quantity of food and extra ammunition for his pistol and repeating rifle. All the items were rolled into the blanket and then encased in a waterproof canvas and tied tightly with a cord. He picked up the bundle, a canteen, and his rifle from where it leaned in a corner. With a quick puff, he blew out the candle and left.

Ken circled the building to the stable in the rear. The black horse heard the man enter and it stood stock-still. It drew in a breath of air, identified the scent of its master, and nickered a welcome. A moment later the man's hands brushed the horse's muscular neck and withers in the manner of greeting both had come to expect over the years.

Ken began to saddle the long-legged horse. The mount twisted its head and nuzzled the man. Ken reached out and stroked its long bony jaw and soft velvety nostrils.

"Old fellow, we may have some hard riding to do today," Larrway told the horse.

The beast nickered back, encouraging its master to talk, for it liked the sound of his voice. But the man didn't respond and began to cinch the saddle securely into place. The horse sensed a tenseness in the man and stomped its iron-shod hooves on the ground in empathy.

Ken left the city and the three hundred thousand tired and sleeping inhabitants of that ancient place. He passed the great defensive fortress of Ciudadela on his right. A quarter-mile farther along, he entered the Garita de Belén, a large paved space at the base of a strong stone structure that guarded the causeway. This was the place where the tax collector demanded payment of a tariff on all goods entering the city for sale. The office of the tax collector was dark and there were no soldiers on duty.

Ken hurried onward, running his horse through the blackness of the Mexican night spread thickly over the aged Belén Causeway. He wanted to be first at the dueling ground.

Chapultepec hill took form ahead. On the top of the hill, the huge, three-story Chapultepec Castle blanked out a patch of stars. Ken pulled the horse down to a walk and guided it off the stone pavement onto an ill-defined dirt road leading to the thick cypress woods at the base of the fortified hill.

Ken halted on the border of a small meadow within the woods and tied his mount. For several minutes he remained motionless among the boles of the giant cypress trees and scrutinized the dark meadow. A fragile quietness lay everyplace and he felt a reluctance to break it. Still, men who would try to kill him might have already arrived and be hidden in the trees. They would have to be found.

He stole through the woods surrounding the meadow. In the top limbs of a tree a large bird took fright at his nearness and screamed out in a shrill piercing cry that ravaged the stillness of the morning. Ken heard the beat of its feathered wings for a few strokes as it darted away across the woods.

He moved on. In the east, a drop of dawn fought the dark sky. The aisleways among the large tree trunks became more visible. He stealthily completed his search and turned back toward his horse.

A man moved about in the clearing, circling slowly and

looking down at the ground. Ken recognized Luis Calleja and went directly to him.

"There's nobody in the woods," Ken said.

"Very good," said Calleja. He continued to walk about staring down at the ground.

"What are you looking for?" questioned Ken. "Have you lost something?"

"Before a duel, a man should know the surface he will fight upon. Whether there are rocks or low spots that might trip him and throw him off balance."

Ken heard the soft thuds of walking horses and the creak of wheels. He turned to look at the edge of the meadow. "Someone's coming," he told Calleja.

Three mounted men came into sight. Almost immediately a buggy with one man, followed by a surrey carrying only the driver, appeared at the edge of the woods. Ken noted the rear seat of the surrey had been removed. The dead or wounded would be transported in that space.

The cavalcade stopped on the perimeter of the clearing and the men climbed down. They glanced briefly at Ken and Calleja in the meadow and then began to assemble in a group.

Calleja looked over the gathering of men. He spoke to Ken in a low voice. "Melchor and Delgollado are there. The man talking to Melchor is his brother, Martín. I'm surprised to see him here. He manages the Zaldivar mines in San Luis Potosí and is seldom in Mexico City.

"The judge of duels is the man that came in the buggy by himself. He's very old and knows the dueling code as no other man. He's always asked to conduct the duels. The tall man that drove the surrey is Canosa, a surgeon. He's the very best with wounds. And an honest man. Those two men have seen more duels fought and men die than anyone else in all Mexico.

"Now, listen to me. Martín Zaldivar is very fast with a pistol, faster than Melchor. He's probably here to help Melchor carry out his threat against you. Watch him closely."

"Would they shoot me in front of the medico and the judge?"

"Certainly. They would probably call out to you just as they drew their weapons so that they could testify they had warned you. But really, they have no fear of being punished for killing an American. The wounds of the American invasion of Mexico thirty years ago are still raw and the actions of the officials may well be unjust."

Calleja faced Ken squarely. "Should you escape being killed this morning, hurry out of Mexico City and run for California. Watch for Zaldivar's fighters. There's a squad of mounted soldiers at his hacienda near Tacubaya. Nearly all of his remaining fighters are at Torreón protecting the Zaldivares' major land holdings."

Ken looked into the old man's worried face. "Thank you, Luis. I respect your judgment, but I think you're exaggerating the danger to me. After this morning's trouble is over, I'll ride to Los Angeles, and that will be the end of my fight with the Zaldivares."

The talk of enemies made Ken reflect upon his reason for being in Mexico. His family owned a well-located pier and warehouse on the oceanfront in Los Angeles. Until a year ago the competition between the pier owners had been fair and the Larrway investment quite profitable. Then a new group of men began to buy up the piers and warehouses. They were crooked men who under the cover of darkness damaged the Larrways' stored cargo and dock equipment. They were shrewd at their sabotage and the authorities hadn't been able to find sufficient evidence to arrest them. But there were other ways to

32

THE SLAVERS

stop an enemy from harming you. Ken had vowed to
challenge them to a duel. Calleja had helped him train
for that deadly game.

Calleja glanced at the group of men moving out onto
the meadows. He lowered his voice to a whisper and
spoke hurriedly. "Now, listen to me. As my fight with
Melchor nears the end, you must watch the other men.
Don't be surprised at anything that happens between
Melchor and me.

"I believe Martín is here to help Delgollado. They will
draw their weapons and try to kill you at the end of the
duel. So stand ready to fight."

"But you will win the duel and then we can kill those
two gunmen easily."

"I don't think I'll win. You must be prepared to fight
them alone. And it won't be a duel with rules. Don't give
them an even chance. Kill them as swiftly as you can."

"One last thing," Calleja said, looking into the face of
the young Larrway. "Take my horse if I die. He's a
strong runner and will outdistance any pursuit and keep
you safe."

The judge of duels called out loudly. "Calleja, Larrway,
are you ready for the contest to begin?"

──────────────●▶ **3** ◀●──────────────

CALLEJA IGNORED THE JUDGE'S CALL AND
stared at Tlacoc Mountain looming dark on the
eastern horizon. Many times he had arisen
early solely to watch the day come to the valley. He
knew that in August the sun rose over the second peak
from the south. This would be the last time his eyes
would enjoy that wondrous event.

As he watched, a thin golden curve of the sun sailed
up above Tlacoc Mountain and a spear of light stabbed
down into the valley. The meadow filled with the sun's
fire.

"It is time," called the judge, motioning for the men to
come close.

Calleja stripped off his jacket and dropped it to the
ground. He was dressed in the somber gray garments he
wore as an instructor. He approached the judge.

Melchor walked up from the opposite direction. He
handed his cloak to his second and stood clothed in white
silk.

The surgeon stood to the right of the judge. Martín

34

Zaldivar and Delgollado were on the other side. Calleja saw both men cast a glance at Larrway, measuring him, and then hastily look away. His young friend didn't understand the full danger that threatened him.

"Is there any argument I can make that will persuade you to forgo this duel?" asked the judge.

"No," Melchor said firmly.

"Then I must also say no," said Calleja. He felt no fear, only a great sadness.

"Prepare your weapons," the judge said.

Both men unhooked their scabbards from their belts. They drew the swords and tossed the scabbards at the feet of the judge.

"Shall this be a fight to the death?" asked the judge.

"To the death," Melchor said.

"To the death," echoed Calleja.

"So be it. Take your places there on the meadow," directed the judge. He pointed to a position near the middle of the clearing.

The two contestants moved silently to the spot. They stopped and faced each other with a distance of some six paces separating them. Both stood as motionless as the boles of the cypress trees.

Ken looked away from the combatants to check on Delgollado and Martín. Could it be possible Calleja was right and these two men would try to kill him after the duel? If Melchor won, there could be three pistols against Ken. Ken had never shot a man. Now he might have to try to kill two, perhaps three. A cold prickle of alarm ran along his spine. Luis, we may both be dead in a short time, thought Ken.

"Let the contest begin," cried the judge, and he clapped his hands with a loud, piercing sound.

The combatants met in the center of the meadow with

35

ringing steel. They cut and parried for half a minute, searching for a weakness in the other's guard. Then back and forth over the meadow they moved, now on the attack, now defending.

Ken heard the keen-edged swords whispering as they swiftly cut the air. He marveled at the skill of the men to detect the next stroke of the opponent's blade in time to fend it off before it did harm.

Calleja was fighting superbly, but he couldn't break through Zaldivar's quick sword parries. The younger man was playing with him and not yet pressing the dueling instructor to the limit. Time was on Melchor's side. Ken worried about his father's friend. Why couldn't he have held back from his students at least one sword trick that would save his life?

The minutes passed and a noticeable slowness came to Calleja's sword strokes. He was more on the defensive, often backing away from his opponent.

Melchor, feeling his adversary weakening, become bolder, attacking fiercely, his sword flashing in the sunlight.

Calleja was suddenly in full retreat, his sword strokes in very close, barely defending his chest. The battle was nearly over. Melchor sensed the impending victory and bore in on his enemy.

Then abruptly Calleja was no longer retreating. He lunged toward his opponent. Melchor thrust mightily with his sword. The sharp blade penetrated Calleja's chest and protruded half a foot from his back.

But at the same moment, Calleja's sword plunged into Melchor's body just below the rib cage and exited at the rear.

Melchor's eyes flared wide in immense surprise. The whites showed brightly all around the dark pupils. The old dueling instructor smiled a ghastly smile at him.

For a moment the two men held their grips on the swords, each, unthinkingly, helping to hold the other man's body upright. Then Calleja coughed harshly and bright-red blood spewed out his mouth in a red fog. His hand loosened on his weapon and he fell to his knees. He pitched forward, driving Melchor's sword into his chest to the hilt. His face plowed into the meadow grass.

Melchor fought to remain erect. He caught hold of the sword piercing his body and tried to pull it free. His strength wasn't great enough. He sank to the ground and began to quiver and moan.

Ken stood in stunned amazement. The old dueling instructor, knowing he was going to die, had deliberately exaggerated his weakness to draw Melchor in pursuit. Then Calleja had thrown himself on Melchor's sword so that he could get close enough to drive his own blade through his stronger opponent.

Calleja had been correct. He knew of no trick to kill Melchor and stay alive. But he knew a maneuver that would take his enemy into the world of the dead with him. Ken believed his father's old friend had used it partly to aid him.

Ken came out of his trance and pivoted, his hand darting to the butt of his pistol. He had forgotten Martín and the paid gunman. Were the two *pistoleros* preparing to kill him?

Martín and Delgollado were staring in shock down at Melchor. Then Delgollado recovered, whirling and reaching for the pistol in his belt.

Delgollado's motion woke Martín from his daze, and he too spun. His face was twisted with anguish and hate. "Kill the damn gringo," he cried. He grabbed for his gun.

37

Ken lifted his weapon from its holster, swinging the barrel up at Delgollado, who was the immediate threat.

He shot Delgollado in the center of the chest. The lead projectile broke the gunman's sternum and bore inward to the very core of him.

Hurry! Hurry, Ken's mind cried. You've got another enemy to fight. Ken twisted rapidly, rotating his six-gun.

Martín moved with incredible swiftness. His revolver rose to point directly into Ken's face.

Larrway threw himself to the left. As he fell, he extended his pistol. The black barrel came into alignment with the man's heart. Ken pressed the trigger. The two guns crashed at the same instant. Ken felt the brush of his enemy's bullet against his ribs. His own bullet tore a hole in the man's chest before Ken hit the ground.

Larrway sprang up, quickly looked at both *pistoleros* lying motionless on the ground, and hurried to Calleja. The surgeon came and knelt beside him and examined the dueling master.

"He's dead," Canosa said, and he went hastily to Melchor.

Ken pulled the sword blade from Calleja's body and hurled it angrily away with all of his strength. "You were right," Ken whispered to the dead, deaf ears. "They killed you and they meant to kill me. You couldn't save yourself, but you kept me alive."

"Melchor is still alive," cried Canosa in a surprised voice. "Somehow the blade missed all the vital organs. He's bleeding, but I may be able to stop that."

The surgeon extracted the sword and worked swiftly to staunch the flow of blood. "Missed his entrails and major blood vessels as well," said the surgeon as he continued to work. "He just may live. Astounding!"

A few minutes later Canosa halted his treatment of

Melchor. "That's all I can do at the moment. Let me see if either of the other two men are alive." He knelt by each fallen figure and his skilled hands and eyes examined them. "Both dead," he said.

The surgeon glanced at Ken and the judge of duels. "We must take Melchor to his home. It isn't far. The women there can help me treat him. We'll take Martín's body as well." His sight settled on Ken. "Will you come with me and help? Then we can take your friend's body home."

"How about that one?" asked Ken, gesturing at Delgollado.

"I'll take him to the undertaker in the city," said the judge. "I have room in my buggy if you and Canosa will load him."

The surgeon brought up the surrey and he and Ken placed the wounded Zaldivar on the cotton mattress on the floor of the vehicle. They laid the corpse of Calleja beside the man who had killed him, and Martín's body on the opposite side of his brother.

Ken and the surgeon carried the dead Delgollado to the buggy, laying him on the floor at the feet of the judge. The *pistolero*'s horse was tied to the tailgate. The judge climbed up into the buggy and sat down. He clucked to his horse and drove off toward the city.

Ken fastened the four saddle horses to the surrey and took a seat beside the surgeon. They went off among the trees in the direction of the road.

Canosa's face was crinkled and gullied with age. A sad look of disapproval lay heavy upon the furrowed countenance. He began to speak. Ken leaned toward him to hear the low voice.

"We Mexicans have inherited a monstrous legacy, this act of dueling. The Spanish were fond of it and the

French even more so. But we have gone beyond either of them, and now we always fight to the death. No mere wound will suffice to atone for an insult to our honor. And worse still are the paid *pistoleros* like Delgollado. These are indeed very bad times."

Canosa glanced at the young American. "You fought very well against Martín and Delgollado. It was a fair fight on your part. They had planned from the very first to kill you. But they were nothing compared with Ramos Zaldivar. You have slain his oldest son. Ramos will go mad at this. He'll come after you with many fighters to take revenge. If you want to live, you should leave Mexico City quickly and ride until you are safely in the United States."

"I'll go north when it suits me."

But Ken knew he would begin his journey very soon. To be trapped in Mexico City and hunted by an army of men would mean death.

"Madre de Dios, it is Melchor and Martín," exclaimed the guard at the gate of the Zaldivar hacienda. "Are they dead?"

"Martín is dead," said the surgeon, "and Melchor nearly so. Quickly, man, find me a place in the house where I can treat him. The jolting of the surrey has increased the bleeding."

"Yes. Yes. Follow me." The guard broke into a run toward the entrance to the house. He threw open the door and shouted loudly inside. "Ramón, Vicente, come and help." He turned back outside as Canosa brought the wagon to a swift halt near him.

Two men ran from the house. At a curt motion from the guard, they sprang to the rear of the surrey.

"Lift Melchor gently and take him inside," directed

Canosa. "Larrway, wait here," he whispered. "As soon as they remove Martín's body from the surrey, leave for Mexico City."

The surgeon spoke sharply to Ramón and Vicente. "Gently. Handle Melchor gently."

"Melchor's room is on the second floor near the rear," said Vicente as Melchor was carried into the vestibule.

"No. Not up there," said the surgeon. "He's bleeding heavily now and the rough handling on the stairway would make it worse. I have to stop it soon or he's going to die. And I must be able to see. Put him on a table down here someplace in the bright sunlight."

"The kitchen will be the best," said Vicente. "We have treated wounds there before."

"That's good," the surgeon said. "Lead the way. Move along now."

Ken jumped from the surrey and moved to the back to untie the two Zaldivar horses. It was dangerous for him to remain any longer at the house of the Zaldivares.

"Wait. Please wait. I wish to speak to you." A woman's voice called to Ken from the vestibule, in English.

Ken halted and turned to look behind him. A pale-skinned woman hurried through the open doorway. She swept a hasty, furtive glance back into the hacienda.

Ken stared in surprise. The woman, more of a girl and younger than he, was strikingly beautiful. Her eyes were blue and large and unusually round. He saw them open quite wide and become rimmed with fear as someone called out in a loud voice.

Anya jerked her attention back to the man she had called to. He gazed back, his youthful face regarding her inquisitively. He was dressed in the tight trousers, embroidered shirt, and tall boots of a vaquero. He had a

41

broad—brimmed sombrero in his hands. A big pistol showed in a holster on his hip. His clothing was all Mexican, but he had seemed to understand her English.

"You're an American, aren't you?" she asked.

"Yes, from California."

"Are you a friend of the Zaldivares?"

"No," responded Ken. A strange question from a girl who obviously was living in the Zaldivar home. "Melchor has just killed a friend of my father's."

Ken became silent in reflection. Luis had died in a manner that had allowed Ken to live. "The man was also my friend. There was no reason for them to fight except an old grudge Melchor had."

The girl smiled. "My name is Anya Bor—"

"Aiii! Get away from her!" The piercing scream cut through the girl's words. A large brown-skinned woman rushed from the house. She ran past the girl, striking her roughly in the ribs with an elbow, and placed herself in front of Ken. The Mexican woman raised her voice to a shriek. "Vicente! Ramón! Vicente! Ramón! Come quickly. There is a thief."

The girl was shouting something, but Ken couldn't make out the words through the other woman's shrill clamor. The girl realized she wasn't making herself understood, and her eyes filled with a lost, helpless look. That expression gave way to a look of fear that tightened her face into a mask. She tried to push past the Mexican, but the larger woman spread her arms, barring the way, and began to curse the girl.

Ken was flabbergasted at the brown-skinned woman's sputtering fit of rage. He didn't like the fear he saw on Anya's face. He thought of shoving aside the woman and talking with the girl. Still, he was in the Zaldivares' courtyard and didn't know the girl's relationship to the family. He hesitated.

Vicente and Ramón appeared, running swiftly from the house. A guard with a pistol in his hand came racing along the side of the building.

Ken twisted and put his back against the wall of the hacienda. He wasn't going to allow himself to be taken prisoner or harmed. He would disable the armed man first and then the others.

The woman shouted at the men and pointed at Ken. "He's trying to kidnap Melchor's woman. Kill him! Kill him!"

"Wait," Canosa shouted from the doorway. He raised two bloody hands toward the group of people. "I'm trying to save a man's life. I don't have time to operate on another wounded man. Larrway is not a kidnapper."

The surgeon moved close to Ken. "Larrway, it's best that you leave now. Take my vehicle and go. Take the body of your friend to his home."

Canosa spoke to Vicente and Ramón. "Bring Martín's body from the surrey and carry it inside."

The Mexican woman started to speak and the surgeon hastily interrupted. "You misunderstood the *norteamericano*. He helped me bring Melchor here where I could operate on him. You should be thanking him instead of trying to hurt him." Canosa's eyes jumped to Larrway. "Go! Do what I say. Get out," he ordered.

Ken, watching all the men near him, sidled toward the surrey. He cast a glance at the girl. The fear was still there, and a haunted look of hopelessness. Then the big brown woman moved to block his view completely.

Silently cursing, Ken climbed up into the wagon and drove away.

*   *   *

43

A cavalcade of eight horsemen met Ken on the hacienda's private road near Tacubaya. At an order from a man in the lead, the band of riders fanned out across the road and barred Ken's way. The leader, a man in his mid-forties wearing a short black mustache, guided his big roan close to the surrey and peered inside at the corpse.

"Luis Calleja?" the man questioned in an arrogant voice, his black eyes hard as glass marbles.

"Yes," replied Ken. He evaluated the tough *pistoleros*. Without being told, he was certain this was Ramos Zaldivar and a group of his men. They would shoot him in an instant if they discovered that he had slain Martín and Delgollado and that Melchor lay badly wounded.

"Who killed him?" asked Ramos, gesturing at the body in the surrey.

"Melchor Zaldivar."

The man smiled broadly. "Melchor always said he would do it. Who are you?"

"Ken Larrway."

"What was your part in this?"

"I was Calleja's second."

The Mexican studied Ken and checked the pistol on his side. "I think you're one of Calleja's students."

"That is correct."

"This fight between Melchor and Calleja, was it a fair and proper duel?"

"The contest between them was fair."

"*Excelente,*" Ramos said. He would make Melchor a captain in his army, the same as Martín. The young man had proved himself by planning and killing Calleja. The fighting strength of his two sons would be valuable in the coming war.

Ramos spurred his horse along the road toward the hacienda. His band of men fell in behind.

Ken watched Ramos Zaldivar ride away. There was no doubt at all in his mind as to who the man was.

4

"**D**AMN THE ZALDIVARES," CRIED CALLEJA'S OLD servant. Tears streamed down his face as he stared at the corpse of Don Luis. "Those murderous bastards have killed a great gentleman. He will have a funeral fitting a very brave man."

"He was brave indeed," agreed Ken. He went to the rear of the surrey and the two horses tied there. He began to loosen the cinch of the saddle on Calleja's gray mount.

"Don Luis told me that I should take his horse if he should be killed," Ken said.

"That is something he would do," said the servant. "He was a generous man."

Larrway laid the saddle on the fence of Calleja's house. He swung astride his black mount and glanced down at the still form of Luis Calleja. I'll tell my father that you saved his son's life, thought Ken.

He left, heading north and leading the gray horse on a short rope. Soon he entered the broad square of the Zócalo. He wound a course through the throng of native

46

vendors hovering protectively over merchandise displayed for sale in open stalls or spread on brightly colored blankets on the stone pavement. A tremendous variety of foodstuffs and manufactured goods were for sale: nuts, fruits, candies, clothing, and children's toys. One man was hawking a donkey, and another man a big black dog on a thick leash.

Ken passed the National Palace lining the whole eastern border of the Zócalo. On the north side was a dark stone cathedral with soaring towers and domes and crosses capping all the highest points.

He recalled his father's description of the victorious American troopers marching into the Zócalo and forming orderly ranks in front of the National Palace. The American flag was run up and General Scott gave a speech and appointed General Quitman military commander of the magnificent city. The Americans had remained in Mexico for months, ruling the country until a peace treaty could finally be negotiated.

Larrway hurried onward along the broad boulevard, San Juan de Aragón. Soon the mighty city was left behind. Ken raised his horse to a trot on the much-worn Camino Real, the King's Highway, winding its course across a broad flat plain. He passed through thousands of acres of growing corn, squash, cotton, sweet potatoes, beans, sugarcane, citrus fruits, and dozens of other crops. The road was crowded with vehicles loaded with the products of the land and bands of sheep and cattle on their way to market in the city.

Many people spoke to the young man dressed as a vaquero. Ken returned the greetings. They wouldn't have been so friendly if they knew he was a gringo and an enemy of the Zaldivar family. At the thought of pursuit by Zaldivar and his *pistoleros*, Ken touched his horse

47

with spurs. The willing animal broke into a gallop. Before noon he had entered the steep green mountains that surrounded the valley of Anáhuac on all sides.

He halted on a high saddle to rest his horses. His view wandered back to the basin. East of the city lay Lake Texcoco, its salty brine a brilliant turquoise. Beyond the city and forty miles south east, the snow-capped peaks of Popocatépetl and Ixtacihuatl soared more than three miles into the sky. A gray tendril of water vapor and volcanic gases, barely visible at the long distance, climbed from Popocatépetl.

The land was beautiful and had a very old civilization. But it had always been a place of violent deaths. The Spaniard Cortés invaded Mexico, slew thousands of its inhabitants, and stole shipload after shipload of precious metal and jewels. The Americans came and they too killed large numbers of citizens and tore away half the land of Mexico for themselves.

Even before Cortés, violence had occurred. Fifteen miles east of Ken were the ruins of the religious city of the ancient Aztecs, Teotihuacán. Two great pyramids, one more than two hundred feet tall, existed there. Cortés had found a large stone diaz on top of the largest pyramid. It was heavily stained with blood from human sacrifices made to Quetzalcoatl, the Serpent God.

Ken turned his back on the capital city and rode on El Camino Real into the heart of the mountains. He had traveled this very road on his way to Mexico City. Eleven hundred miles lay between him and the American border. The tremendous distance gave his enemies uncountable opportunities to overtake and kill him.

He halted in the edge of a black night and made camp off the road in a dense stand of woods. In the middle of the night he awoke to the thudding rumble of iron-shod hooves as several horses passed at a fast run. Ken sat erect and stared into the gloom. Were they some of Zaldivar's riders hurrying to Torreón to alert the private army? Had the pursuit for him begun so soon?

It was a long time before Ken found sleep, and then it was light and fitful.

"You're a liar," Ramos Zaldivar's voice lashed out at Anya. "The servants saw you speaking with Larrway. Tell me what you said to him."

"Nothing. I told him nothing," Anya retorted, gripping the arms of the chair and looking up at Zaldivar standing over her. "I tried to, but that big woman guard of yours got between us and yelled so loudly the man you call Larrway couldn't hear me."

Ramos didn't believe the woman. She had spoken with the American before Rosa had intervened. What had she said to him? What would he do with the information?

Anya started to rise from her chair. She would answer no more questions.

Zaldivar's hand snaked out and slapped her back into the chair. "I'll tell you when you can leave, you unfaithful bitch," he hissed.

Anya's fingers came up to her stinging cheek. Her voice rang out, "I'm a prisoner here. How can a prisoner be unfaithful?"

"I'm not Melchor," Ramos said. "Don't try word games with me. He wants you here, and here you shall stay. But in the future, any disobedience from you will bring severe punishment."

Martín was dead and lay prepared for burial. Melchor was as still as death in a room on the ground floor of the hacienda. Canosa had remained constantly with the injured man, cleansing the wound and applying poultices to prevent infection and the deadly gangrene. Ramos knew it would take a miracle for Melchor to live with a wound that pierced his body from one side to the other. Ramos didn't believe there would be such a miracle. He would lose both sons.

"If Melchor dies, I'll sell you to the lowest, meanest whorehouse in this city," Ramos growled at Anya. "They will chain you to a bed and there you will remain until you're so diseased you die. If Melchor dies, I'll take men and ride to Janos and kill every man, woman, and child."

Anya flinched at the horrible threat. She knew Ramos would do exactly as he said. She stared at him, her blue eyes burning with her hatred.

Ramos saw no fear in the American woman, only the hardening of her determination to be stubborn and contrary. She would continue to make trouble. His anger boiled. I'll make you afraid, he thought. He slapped her hard, and then quickly again.

It felt good to be hurting someone who had some association with the damnable, murderous Larrway. Too long Ramos had sat watching the corpse of one son, the second son dying, while his enemy was running north toward the United States. He slapped Anya again, very hard.

He smiled when he saw her wide eyes lose their focus with half-consciousness. Now she would be more obedient.

"I want this gringo Larrway dead," Ramos Zaldivar said. "You are to organize and lead the men in the capture." He stopped his pacing across the big room of the hacienda and stared stonily at Santos Tamargo, captain in his private army. "I would prefer him taken alive and brought here so I could stand him against that wall"—he jabbed a finger out the window at the wall surrounding the hacienda—"and personally shoot him. However, if he must be killed to be captured, then kill him."

Captain Tamargo stood at stiff attention. He'd never seen Zaldivar in such a rage. But never before had Zaldivar's family been so sorely hurt, and the one most responsible for the deed had actually come into the Zaldivar house. Making Ramos' anger greater, this Larrway had talked with the white woman Melchor was so fond of. What she had told Larrway was a very great worry to Zaldivar.

Ramos raised his big right hand. "I had Larrway right here and let him escape. Seven of my personal guards of *pistoleros* would have shot him on my command. Larrway knew what a bloody deed he'd done, but he sat there and stared back like an innocent. Now he'll try to get out of Mexico. I would go myself and hunt down the *norteamericano,* but I must remain here until Melchor is well. You will muster your company of soldiers. Leave fifty here to guard the hacienda. Take the remaining fifty and leave at once. Overtake Larrway. Trade horses as often as necessary.

"Station men at every town where Larrway might pass through or stop to eat or sleep. He's an expert with weapons, trained by Calleja, so keep your men in groups of no less than five. The bulk of our men are at Torreón. I'll prepare orders to Colonel Almonte that you may use all of them except the platoon guarding the shipments of gold and silver from the mines near San Luis Potosí. I don't want the *bandidos* to get that. Catch the gringo quickly and reassemble our forces before President Díaz can march against us."

"Larrway could go any one of several routes," said Tamargo. "It'll take many men to guard them all. May I use our vaqueros? Some of them are very skilled with guns."

"Yes. Stop at each ranch and take half of the riders. Be certain to select the men who are best with rifle and pistol. There will be thousands of other men helping you to find the gringo. I've had reward notices printed. They are already being carried north by three riders and will be posted in every town and village along El Camino Real.

"The notices give Larrway's description and state I will pay ten thousand pesos in gold to any man who captures him. And I will pay one thousand pesos in gold for information leading to his capture. You and your soldiers can also collect the reward if you should take this gringo. Here, read his description."

Tamargo scanned the reward poster. He felt a cool wave run over his body. He had read hundreds of such notices for wanted men, but never before had he experienced such a sensation. He felt certain it was an omen that he would collect the reward.

"It's a fortune, Señor Zaldivar," Tamargo said in amazement. "A man could buy a ranch and stock it with the best breed of sheep and cattle with that amount of money."

"It's surely large enough to catch the attention of the Federal Rural Police. They will help you catch Larrway."

"The *rurales* are over five thousand in number and stationed in most towns. They'll have the best chance to capture Larrway and collect the reward."

"I agree. So you and your men should ride very fast and get ahead of the gringo. Unless you're the one who catches him, you'll get nothing."

"Yes, sir. What of the revolution? Now that we delay our attack on Díaz, we must make new plans."

Ramos had also been speculating upon his scheme to

seize control of the country. "I'll put off the start of the revolution. But you must capture or kill Larrway quickly. I dare not wait long, or some of our friends may desert us. Do not fail me in this."

"I shall not fail you, Don Ramos."

Zaldivar accepted the promise with a nod. "After the gringo is dead, bring two thousand men to me here in Mexico City. Travel overland in small detachments so that Díaz and Castillo will not be alerted. You'll help me crush Díaz's army here in the capital."

Zaldivar knew that no single caudillo could defeat Díaz. For that reason, he had made a pact with the three strongest military chieftains in Mexico to join him in the revolution. They had taken Zaldivar's advice to remain neutral during the last war, and their armies weren't bloodied and weakened by many battles. With their thousands of soldiers added to Zaldivar's army, they would be invincible.

The caudillos were mustering their men this very moment, preparing to attack at the agreed-upon time. Zaldivar must speedily get word to them that they would have to delay a little longer. They wouldn't like that, but they would do it.

After Larrway had been killed, Zaldivar could call all the men to arms and march against the president's army. He would seize control of the key cities of the nation. The palace would be captured and Díaz taken prisoner. He would hang Díaz and his General Castillo in the Zócalo in front of the National Palace. A very pleasant thought.

"Suppose the American escapes us and reaches the United States?"

"The border means nothing. Select ten of your best men and have them change their uniforms for American

53

clothing. They must trail Larrway to his home in Los
Angeles. I want him dead." Zaldivar's voice rose. "If our
men must chase him to California, then tell them to kill
Larrway's family as he killed mine. Is all this perfectly
understood?"

"Yes, Señor Zaldivar."

"Very well. I'll write the orders to Colonel Almonte.
You must leave at once. There's still some daylight left
and you can travel several miles north before you make
camp."

Zaldivar seated himself at a desk and wrote hastily. He
signed the paper and put his seal on it. "Good hunting,"
he said to Tamargo, and handed him the document.

Tamargo would run Larrway to earth, as he had other
enemies. Once he began the chase, he never quit until
the contest was won and the prey captured or dead. He
had a sixth sense of what course the pursued would run.
The distance of the chase, one hundred miles or a thousand, meant nothing. Tamargo would be there waiting at
some unexpected ambush.

The captain was the very best horseman and fighter
Zaldivar had, and he was hungry, a hungry wolf with the
keenest hunting instinct. He had risen from vaquero to
captain of Zaldivar's army in a short three years. He
personally commanded the elite squad of troopers that
guarded Zaldivar and his private residence.

"If Larrway is killed, bring his head to me. I must be
able to identify him, so pack it in a barrel of salt or
tequila. Preserve it well."

General Agustín Castillo hurried along the marble cor-
ridor, nodded to the two palace guards at the door of
President Díaz's office, and entered. When the president
looked up, the general saluted.

"What is it, General?"

"Ramos Zaldivar, President."

Díaz's face tightened. "What is he plotting now?"

"He's mobilizing his army and half of his vaqueros. His Captain Tamargo and fifty of the soldiers he usually keeps in Mexico City are riding to the north. They left very suddenly. Cuadrado, our spy in Tamargo's unit, barely had time to send us a message before they rode out."

President Díaz rose from behind his desk and moved to the window to stare into the Zócalo. Mexico was just settling down after a bitter three-year war. Battles had been fought in most of the major cities. He had won only after many thousands of soldiers and civilians had died.

Díaz faced Castillo. "During the past fifty-one years, our governments have lasted less than a year on the average. We must stop the constant revolutions and centralize authority into a true, long-lasting national government. As long as the caudillos and their private armies exist, Mexico can never be strong. We must attack the largest, the Zaldivar force. If we should succeed in destroying it, then the others could be made to disband by threats alone." Díaz walked back to his desk and leaned across it.

General Castillo waited patiently, watching the broad face with the prominent nose. The president was a mestizo, a mixture of Spanish and Indian blood. It showed in his short body, still powerful in his late forties, and his dark-brown skin. The president focused his sharp black eyes on the general.

"Tell me all you know."

"Tamargo told his men that they have been ordered by Ramos Zaldivar to capture a *norteamericano*, a man named Larrway, who was involved in a duel with Martín and

55

Melchor Zaldivar. Luis Calleja and Melchor Zaldivar dueled this morning. Calleja died, but not before he badly wounded the young Zaldivar."

"I knew Luis Calleja," said the president. "A very skilled weapons instructor. It's too bad he's dead. Continue please."

"For some reason I don't yet know, Larrway fought Martín and one of Zaldivar's *pistoleros* at the dueling ground. Both men were very skilled with a pistol. Yet the gringo killed the two men in a gunfight immediately after the duel between Melchor and Calleja."

"The source of your information, is it reliable?"

"I questioned both Canosa, the surgeon, and the judge of duels. The information fits together. Something else will be of interest to you. The gringo helped Canosa take Melchor and Martín to the Zaldivar hacienda following the duel. Some of Zaldivar's servants and guards wanted to harm Larrway for talking to Melchor's woman, a very pretty *norteamericana*. Canosa stopped them long enough for Larrway to get out. Zaldivar was angry at Canosa for that. He's a vengeful man. But at the moment he needs Canosa. I fear for the surgeon after Melchor heals."

Díaz struck the desktop. "Canosa is too good a surgeon for us to lose. Perhaps we can save him from being killed. Send a message to Zaldivar. Tell him I'm pleased that my friend Canosa was able to help Melchor. We both must hope Canosa lives a very long time so that perhaps he can save one of us from dying of an injury." Díaz grinned wolfishly. "Ramos will understand my meaning."

"I'll attend to that," said Castillo. "Larrway has disappeared. Calleja's servant said he rode north. Zaldivar has offered a reward of ten thousand pesos for his capture.

The notices are already being posted along El Camino Real.

"Do you think Larrway is the real reason Zaldivar is assembling his men?"

"I believe so. But what he might do after he's captured the *norteamericano* is a dangerous unknown."

"I'm worried about the strength of Zaldivar's troops," said Díaz. "Our forces won the revolution, but the victory was narrowly won and our army seriously weakened. Many of our soldiers have now returned to their homes and farms. Our recruitment efforts to replace them are going slowly, and the training even more slowly.

"If Zaldivar plans to attack, never has the time been better for him to beat us." The president looked past Castillo out the window, and then back at the general. "The Zaldivar reward is bothersome. Our *rurales* will be enticed to try to capture this gringo."

"I think you're right. Every one of them will want that reward. And Larrway will probably resist arrest and may kill some of Zaldivar's men or our *rurales*. If we're lucky, he may shoot Zaldivar."

"That would not be good for us. Tell me about the gringo's fight with Martín Zaldivar. Who started it?"

"Canosa told me that he thought Martín had planned to kill Larrway. But Larrway was too quick in defending himself and Martín died instead."

"Canosa is an honest man. And it appears he has choosen to help the gringo. However, if the gringo kills another Mexican citizen, even if it is one of Zaldivar's men, we must execute him," said the president. "Especially if he should kill Zaldivar. Otherwise people may think I hired Larrway as an assassin to dispose of my greatest enemy."

"We must have current information," said Castillo,

"so I have sent orders to our army garrisons at Querétaro, San Luis Potosí, Torreón, Chihuahua, and Ciudad Juárez to increase their weekly reports to daily. They are to begin constant surveillance of the movement of Zaldivar's forces. The very best mounts will be assigned to the dispatch riders. We can have news from Torreón about Zaldivar's main contingent within two days. Our officers can receive our orders just as quickly."

"You have done well, General. There is only one other action I wish you to take."

"What is that, President?"

"Tell your colonels that you have been told by a spy that Zaldivar is planning an attack on our garrisons and the National Palace here in Mexico City. Tell them to double their efforts at recruitment and training and prepare to resist such an attack."

"Do you truly think that is what he plans?"

"It is a possibility. He has just returned from Vera Cruz. We know he met and talked with Alejandro Malespina. That caudillo has twenty-five hundred soldiers. We don't know what schemes and agreements they made. Also Zaldivar might make a mistake in his pursuit of Larrway and do something that I can condemn as threatening the national government. We can then march with our army and crush him while his forces are chasing the gringo and are scattered across the land."

"It would be a very strange thing if this lone gringo provided us the opportunity to destroy all the caudillos," said Castillo. He looked questioningly at Díaz. "And what shall we do about Larrway?"

"Have our soldiers and spies report his movements to me. I believe he'll fight Zaldivar's men, perhaps Zaldivar himself. Trained as he is by Luis Calleja, he'll certainly kill. In the end, he'll die, one way or another."

5

KEN CAME AWAKE WITH THE PALE FACE OF the moon casting its ghostly glow down among the trees. He arose at once and rolled his blankets. Without eating, he saddled and led his horses out from the woods to El Camino Real. He mounted his black and rode through the cold harshness of the pre-dawn light. The solitary flash of the polestar lay directly ahead of him.

All morning he journeyed on El Camino Real through short volcanic mountains covered with brush. Many other travelers came and went on the much-used highway. Once a stagecoach drawn by six trotting horses passed him with a jolting rattle. Ken kept his hat pulled low to hide as much of his light-brown hair as possible and to keep his gringo face in shadow.

Near noon the mountains pulled back until they were a couple of miles from the highway. Thinking anyone pursuing him would follow the main, traveled highways, Ken veered aside and trekked along the side roads connecting the farms tucked away in the valleys emptying out from the mountains. The people in the fields and on the roads paid him little attention. Now and then, when he passed close by, some folks greeted him. The younger men paid more attention to the two excellent horses than to Ken.

He ate the last of his food at noon. When the gray wave of twilight came stalking in, he began to cast about for a likely farm where he might purchase some provisions for the evening meal. Just when he decided he'd be forced to go without supper, an isolated farm came into view. He turned up a narrow lane toward the small adobe house.

An old man badly crippled in the left leg came hobbling out of the house and stood in the yard. A gray-haired woman came and watched from the doorway.

"Good evening, sir," said Ken. "I'm a stranger here and the night has caught me away from a town. Would you sell me some food?"

"I would," replied the old man. "But we have very little."

Ken pointed to the melon patch beside the house. "One of those melons and some bread would do nicely."

"Pick one to suit yourself," said the man. He turned to the woman. "Gertrudis, didn't you bake some fresh bread today?"

"Yes. And I still have a little boiled mutton," the woman said.

Ken walked into the melon patch and started to examine the fruit. The man came to the border of the garden and watched.

"Would you pick one for me?" Ken asked. "I'll surely get a green one."

"Certainly." The man went down a row of widespreading vines. He halted and pulled a melon. "This one will be ripe and sweet," he promised.

"I bet it will be," said Ken, smiling, and took the melon.

The woman approached with a half-loaf of bread and a bowl filled with chunks of cold mutton. She offered it to Ken. "This should fill a young man's stomach."

"Thank you very much. How much do I owe you?"

"Whatever seems fair to you," said the man with a sly look in his foxy old eyes. The gringo appeared to have money and would not be selfish.

Ken fished a silver peso from his pocket and offered it to the man.

"You're very generous," said the man. The woman nodded in pleased agreement.

"Then I'm happy," Ken said. "May I eat here?"

"I'll bring out a stool for you to sit on," the woman said.

Resting on the stool and leaning against the wall of the house, Ken ate, using his knife, and talked with the man. By the time he had finished, the evening dusk had chased the daylight from the land.

"It's too late for you to travel farther today," said the man. "You may stay here tonight. We have no bed for you, but there is a rick of freshly cut hay just there on the edge of the field. That will make a soft place to sleep, and your horses can be fed."

Ken glanced across the countryside full of night shadows. Not one neighbor's house was near enough to show a light. This should be a safe place to sleep.

"I accept," Ken said.

"That will be an additional peso," the man said.

"Good enough." Ken paid the man. "Now I'll say good night and go while there is still a bit of light left." He picked up his horse's reins and went off in the darkness.

He pulled some hay from the stack and spread it on

the ground as a mattress. He bedded down with a mound of hay at his head. At his side the horses began to chew contentedly on the fresh grass.

Ken felt the peacefulness of the farm and the two old people in the house. The thought of Zaldivar and his army pursuing him seemed unreal here. Maybe I'm wasting time on these side roads, he thought, and should follow El Camino Real. Still, he pulled his pistol and rifle close to his hand. He cocked his ear to hear any strange sound and went to sleep.

The marriage ceremony had begun. The senior elder of the valley conducted the ritual of the vows. The bishop of the church couldn't speak the words, for he was the bridegroom.

The bride stared past the shoulder of Elder Fiersen at the stained-glass window in the wall of the church. The monotone voice of the religious man was barely heard by a corner of her consciousness. She felt the presence of Bishop Blackseter beside her and the press of people in the church behind her. Every resident of the valley was present, crowding the pews and filling all the extra benches along the rear wall.

Nilo Wilander would be there in the back near the door. He had said he wouldn't come, but she knew he would. Her heart cramped with pain at the thought of him. She wanted to turn and tell him that she was sorry, that she had no choice. She was fifteen and of marriageable age. How could she resist the persuasion of her father and the proposal of the bishop, the revered leader of her religion? This most powerful man in the valley had come to her home to court her. He had said it would give him great pleasure if she would consent to marry him.

The bishop's first wife had given him permission to

take another wife. The permission was not unexpected. The first wife had given it fourteen times before.

Bishop Blackseter was the leader of the original founders of the settlement in the mountain valley. His land had first claim upon the water from the stream. In fact, his rights were superior to all others, even the elders who had arrived with him. He had half a square mile under irrigated cultivation and could support a sixteenth wife.

The bride's lips twisted ruefully at the thought. The wives in reality supported themselves. They and their children worked long hours irrigating and tending the crops. In the mornings, the women and the largest children, both boys and girls, went, like a work brigade, into the fields. Some of the younger children, after the morning session of school lessons and the noon meal were over, came and joined in the labor.

Elder Fiersen spoke in his ceremonial voice to the bride. "Ragna, do you, here in the house of the Lord, take this man to be your lawfully wedded husband?"

"I do," said the bride, still looking at the stained-glass window behind the senior elder.

She heard booted footsteps hurry from the church. Nilo would be leaving. She hoped he wouldn't do anything violent that would make him an outcast to the church and the valley settlement. The sound of Nilo's boots faded away.

Oh, Nilo! You're so young and handsome. But you have no land. The window became blurred in her vision. Tears welled up from their tiny salt springs and, overflowing, coursed sadly down her fair cheek.

Ken skirted the edge of the broad valley, riding beneath the morning heavens half-filled with great swirls of purple and pink and flaming scarlet. The soil underfoot, derived from the mineral-rich lava, was fertile, and nearly every level section of land was being farmed. The fields were alive with men, women, and children working in the coolness of the morning. By noon, the time of the siesta and rest in the shade, Ken was virtually alone upon the land.

In the evening on a rocky ridge that extended out from the base of the volcanic mountain Huichapán, the gray mount threw a shoe. Using the loose side of the shoe as a lever, Ken pried the piece of iron completely off. He turned directly toward Querétaro lying ten miles west. There would be a blacksmith in the town to reset the shoe.

Night had overrun Querétaro when Larrway finally entered the border of town. He decreased his pace and rode at a slow walk. His eyes swept the streets nearly abandoned in the darkness.

The murky side streets were left behind and Ken reached the main thoroughfare. He halted in the deep shadows beside a two-story building that appeared to be some sort of warehouse, and scrutinized the street. Oil lights lit the intersections of the business district of town. Two men crossed the street three blocks away and went into a hotel. A vaquero came along the sidewalk and entered the cantina near the hotel.

A single horseman walked his horse into the lighted section and stopped in front of a restaurant. Ken glanced through the window and then stared first one way and then the other along the street for two or three minutes, as if looking for somebody. He dismounted, tied his horse to one of the hitching posts, and went inside the restaurant.

Larrway felt his own hunger gnawing deep in the pit of his stomach. He had eaten nothing but half a melon in the morning twilight. As he contemplated food, a dog, carrying something in its mouth, came skulking out of the alley beside the restaurant. At least the dog had found something to eat.

The ringing sound of iron hammering iron pealed from a lighted, open-fronted building across the street from the restaurant. The hammering ceased, and a red glow joined with the yellow lantern light framing the opening of the building. Bellows creaked as they were pumped. Ken felt relief that a blacksmith was still at work.

Ken saw no sign of armed men that might be some of Zaldivar's soldiers. He knew there was a government army post just west of Querétaro and he had seen *rurales* on the streets of the town on his previous trip south. However, he shouldn't have any trouble from either of those groups of men. The town appeared harmless enough. Ken moved forward into the lighted street.

The blacksmith turned from his forge as Ken drew rein and swung down to the ground. He shoved a piece of metal that he held with tongs into the red coals, and came over to Ken. The blacksmith swept his eyes over the weary, sweat-streaked horses and the canvas-covered pack behind the saddle. His attention settled on the young rider with the dust thick on his clothing. The gringo had come a long distance.

Ken dug the horseshoe from his saddlebag. "This came loose. Can you reset it for me?"

The smith examined the shoe in the light of the lantern. "There's plenty of iron left. Yes, I can reset it."

"Good. Also, check all the other shoes on the horses. Make sure they're in good condition and the nails tight."

"I'll do that," said the blacksmith.

"How long will it take?"

"Only a few minutes. Say a quarter-hour."

"I'll return about then," said Larrway.

He left the blacksmith and went across the street to the restaurant. He looked through the open window. The establishment had only one customer, the rider who had come in earlier. He sat near the back in a dimly lit part of the room. His hat was low on his forehead. He was eating hurriedly.

If one man can eat with his hat on, why not a second? thought Ken. He threw one last, skimming look along the street and entered the restaurant.

The first patron was young. Dust lay heavy in the stubble of his black beard. As Larrway watched, the man raised his face and locked narrow, sniperlike eyes on him in a fast, hard evaluation.

Larrway nodded at the man and seated himself in the rear, two tables from him.

The cook came through a doorway from the kitchen. "What will you have?" he asked.

"Meat, beans, potatoes, bread, coffee, whatever is already cooked and you can bring me immediately."

"Like him," said the cook, gesturing at the first customer. "You want to eat fast and not enjoy my good food."

Ken didn't answer. He kept his blue eyes staring toward the front of the restaurant.

The cook went off with a slap of sandals on the dirt floor. A minute later be returned with a heaping plate of food and a mug of coffee. He slid the plate in front of Larrway and plopped down the mug. "Thirty cents," said the cook.

Larrway gave him fifty cents and waved him away. He began to eat with high relish.

Five horsemen came into sight on the street. Four

reined their mounts to the tie posts of the restaurant and climbed down from their saddles.

"See you in a minute," called the fifth man, and he continued on to the smithy.

A stumpy, heavily bearded man entered first, the others trailing behind. Their big spurs jingled icily. As the men seated themselves around a table near the door, they briefly glanced at the two customers on the opposite end of the room.

"Jorge, four beers for us and one for our friend to come," called the stubby man.

"In a minute," the cook called back from the kitchen.

Through slitted eyelids, Larrway cautiously examined the men. Each carried a pistol in a holster. All were dressed as vaqueros. Their clothing, trousers, shirts, vests, and sombreros had a degree of similarity, all being a shade of brown. The outfits were almost like uniforms.

As the group of vaqueros talked among themselves, the one facing the rear of the restaurant began to study the man near Larrway closely. The vaquero leaned and spoke to his comrades. They all twisted to stare across the room at the man.

"I believe you're right," the stumpy man said. "Let's see about it."

The four stood up and fanned out facing toward Larrway and the man near him. "Hombre, take off your hat so we can see your face," ordered the stumpy man.

The first customer became very still for a handful of seconds. Then he laid down his fork and shoved back his chair with a scraping sound. Slowly he rose to his feet. He made no move to comply with the order.

"I said take off your hat," repeated the vaquero. His hand swung closer to his pistol.

"What's going on?" the fifth vaquero called as he came from the sidewalk into the restaurant.

"Hurtado, we think maybe we got the *bandido* Matías Ortiz cornered here. He's got a five-hundred-peso reward on his head, put there by Zaldivar for robbing a gold shipment from the mines near San Luis Potosí."

Hurtado laughed coldly. "There's something more valuable here than Ortiz and his five-hundred-peso head. That other fellow sitting there so quietly is the gringo Larrway. The blacksmith told me so, and I agree with him now that I've seen him. He's got a ten-thousand-peso reward on his head. I say we take both of their skulls to Zaldivar."

A hoarse whisper from Ortiz reached Ken. "Are you this Larrway?"

"Yes," Ken said under his breath as he stood up. His sight was locked on the vaqueros. They were waiting for the leader, Hurtado, to give the order to strike.

"I think we're going to die," Ortiz said. "But let's not be the first. Help me shoot some of Zaldivar's soldiers. Shoot! Now!"

The room exploded with the crash of the bandit's six-gun. The man who had identified Ortiz backed up a step at the punch of the bullet. His bones melted and he fell.

Larrway was startled by Ortiz's sudden action. Then the four soldiers were grabbing for their pistols. Larrway's hand flashed up with his revolver. His first shot struck Hurtado, collapsing him with a thud to the floor.

To Larrway, the actions of his adversaries seemed abruptly slow, their bodies moving lazily. The room seemed completely silent, as if he had become deaf.

But Larrway's eyes saw everything, the faces of the

men wanting to kill him and the muzzles of their revolvers rising to point.

His hand, without a conscious command from his mind, cocked, aimed, and fired, and fired again. The soldiers shuddered under the impact of the bullets hitting them. They fell, scythed away by death. And then nobody was standing in front of Ken.

"Madre de Dios," exclaimed Ortiz. "I draw and shoot before you, and still you kill three to my two. No wonder Zaldivar has put a ten-thousand-peso reward on you. It would be most dangerous to try to capture you."

Larrway said nothing. A terrible worry chilled him. Why had he lost his hearing during the fight, and why had the pistol seemed to have a life of its own—to kill and kill? Worst of all, he had felt nothing, as if he'd been a mere bystander at the battle.

"*Bueno, bueno!* Oh, what a thing that was to see." Ortiz slapped Ken on the shoulder. "Now my head won't be pickled in salt."

Ken began to eject the spent cartridges from his weapon and to insert fresh ones. As he handled the clean, unfired rounds, a surge of joy rushed through him, the ancient atavistic joy of the warrior at still being alive and the battle won.

"Let's go," Ortiz said hurriedly. "There are many more of Zaldivar's soldiers in town." He dashed to the door and sprang out onto the sidewalk.

Larrway followed, finishing reloading and shoving the six-gun into its holster.

"Where's your horse?" asked Ortiz.

"At the blacksmith shop."

"Listen," said Ortiz. He cupped his ear in his hand and pointed down the main thoroughfare. "Several riders coming. They've heard the shots. It'll be Zaldivar's men

or the *rurales*. Either way it's trouble for us. There's no
time to get your horse. Take one of those." He began to
untie the soldiers' mounts and slap them away along the
street. "Maybe some horses running loose in the dark
might confuse whoever trails us."

Ken jerked the reins loose on one of the mustangs and
leapt upon its back. Ortiz spurred away. Ken followed.
With his limited knowledge of the land, his best chance
of escaping was to ride with the bandit.

The remaining mustangs broke into a run at Ken's
rear. Used to traveling as a group, the horses wouldn't
be left behind. In a few strides, they had pulled parallel
to Ken and held position at his side. The pounding,
iron-shod hooves of the running horses filled the streets
with sound and rebounded in multiple echoes from the
fronts of the buildings.

Ken looked behind. Through the dust mist raised by
the horses, he saw the blacksmith hurry up to a squad of
mounted men. The smith spoke to them and pointed
down the street toward Ken and the bandit.

Ortiz spun his mount around a corner and onto a side
street. He spurred his horse cruelly straight ahead.

A plan came to Larrway. He pulled his mount in and
dropped back a few yards. At an alley, he reined hard to
the side and darted into the black opening. Abruptly he
slowed his mount to a quiet walk. The hammering hooves
of Ortiz and the other horses faded away toward the
border of Querétaro.

Before Ken had gone the length of the block, he heard
the thunder of riders charging past the end of the alley.
The men were shouting out in a wild clamor to one another
like the blood roar of a hunting pack, deep and savage.

Ken halted and tied his mount to the fence of a back-
yard. On foot, he slipped through the shadows.

— ◆ 6 ◆ —

ON CAT'S FEET KEN ENTERED THE REAR OF THE blacksmith shop. He held his pistol ready as he scanned the interior. The smith was gone. Ken spotted his burly body among the other men across the street in front of the restaurant.

Swiftly Ken went to the gray horse. "Stand easy," he whispered as he lifted the horse's hoof. The iron shoe had been replaced. "Let's go, fellows," he whispered again, and untied the animals from the big wooden stanchion in the center of the smithy.

Ken leapt up on the black and, towing the gray, went out the rear and into the darkness of the back alley. Holding to the unlit streets, he worked his way north.

He passed a staggering drunk. The man shouted out to Ken. "Hombre, give me a ride on your other horse."

Larrway didn't respond or slow. At his rear, the man cursed him in a loud voice.

The town dropped away behind. The horses settled into a swift walk on the worn, dusty road. Ken listened closely for any sound, and his eyes moved restlessly searching for movement or a shadow that would mean danger.

His mount lifted its head and thrust its ears forward. Ken recognized the signal and pulled the animal to a stop. In the quietness, he heard horses moving on the road. He quickly went off to the side into the darkness.

A squad of five horsemen passed along the road. The sound of their horses' hooves faded and the quiet night came again. Ken reined his mount back to El Camino Real, wondering if the men had been searching for him.

As long as the night masked his movement, he would follow the highway, for that was the fastest route to San Luis Potosí. Before daylight, he would abandon the main traveled road and ride the back country.

Two hours later where the road cut across a wild, unpopulated section of land, Ken halted to rest the mounts. He sat silently, leaning on the pommel of his saddle and staring into the deep gloom.

He deeply regretted killing the Zaldivar soldiers. He had no argument with them. But reflecting upon the fight, he could think of no way he could have prevented it. He hoped there would be no more killing. He would avoid every town. Just to be left alone so he could return to California was all that he desired. Somehow he sensed that was not to be, and a deep, sad melancholy fell over him.

As Ken contemplated his situation, the moon sailed up over the mountains to the east. The huge, shining globe drifted across the sooty sky, gilding the roadbed and the brush and rocks lying on all sides in its silver rays. Long black shadows came to life behind the lone rider and his horses.

Ken spoke to the black and the gray, and the animals broke into a lope. The cayuses were as weary as Ken, but many miles must be put between him and Zaldivar's gunmen at Querétaro.

Late in the cold hours of the morning, the mustangs halted of their own volition and stood motionless in the roadway. Ken dared not completely exhaust them for at any moment he might need a burst of speed to save his life. He reined them off the road and down into a sunken place where they could not be seen. They were staked out on the end of rope tethers. Too tired to graze, they remained unmoving, resting.

Ken unrolled his bedding and found a somewhat level spot of ground. He kicked out some hollows for his buttocks and shoulders. He lay and watched the moon, already past its zenith, beginning its long slide toward the western horizon. The stars were brittle and far away. On the high ridge of the mountain above him, a wolf howled, wild and lonely, a weird and lovely sound. Ken went to sleep as the wolf cry died.

He awoke with a start. The moon had fallen halfway from the sky. He hadn't meant to sleep so long. Swiftly he saddled and mounted the gray and hurried north through the murk on El Camino Real.

The moon sank to lie on the left-hand horizon. And the dawn came, a silent explosion of red that fanned out across the eastern sky. Steep lava mountains took shape, coming out of hiding and rearing up in craggy peaks. The black shadows in the valley bottom started to shrink and die. Ken veered from the road and rode parallel to it some two miles distant.

The sullen red sun opened half an eye on the rim of the earth, and the day brightened. The gray sky turned blue. On the far-off King's Highway, a band of men could be seen riding slowly to the south.

Ken halted in a patch of tall brush and didn't stir until

the men had passed from view. Then he moved on. At the first hidden place with water and grass, he would stop for the day.

A broken, chocolate-hued lava mesa gradually crowded Ken back toward the highway. As he drew close, he saw a giant walnut tree, dead and barren of leaves.

A flock of ravens clung to the tree's limbs like the black boils of some awful disease. The birds' heads turned from side to side as they examined, with first one eye and then the other, some object hanging from a branch and swinging slightly in the slow wind.

One of the ravens took wing and glided down past the object for a better view. It landed just beneath the hanging thing, plucked something from the ground, and raised its head to swallow.

As Ken drew near, the flock of ravens took fright. Chattering nervously to one another, they dived from their perches, becoming airborne and climbing away on wide wings.

Ken jerked his mounts to a fast halt. He saw what the thing was that had so interested the hungry ravens. The body of the bandit Ortiz swung by its legs from a rope fastened to a branch of the tree. Ken recognized the corpse by the clothing it wore. The head was missing. Blood dripped in slow-congealing drops into the dirt.

Where were the men who had killed Ortiz? The surface of the ground was well-trod by horses and men. The freshest tracks led off to the south. Ken believed he had seen Ortiz's murderers, that group of men on the highway. Had he been a few minutes earlier, he too would have joined Ortiz on the end of a rope on the walnut tree.

Ortiz had fought and killed and ridden hard to prevent

74

his head from being pickled in salt. The poor bastard had lost.

Ken rode off swiftly toward the densely wooded slopes of the Sierra Guanajuato. Behind him, the hungry ravens turned and with loud squawking calls came diving back toward the corpse.

Captain Santos Tamargo led his squad of five men into Querétaro and along the dark street in the direction of their sleeping quarters. Sergeant Quillón was at his side, the four *pistoleros* behind. The men rode quietly, sullen and untalkative. All day they had lain beside El Camino Real waiting in a futile ambush for Larrway.

The captain and his full troop of men had arrived in Querétaro in the early-morning hours. They had ridden fast, changing mounts twice, and he felt certain they had beaten Larrway to the town. He had posted five soldiers to patrol the streets. Another five had been ordered to take up station north of town along the highway until deep night had fallen. He had kept five men himself and directed his lieutenant to proceed onward with the remainder of the troop.

The lieutenant would muster the vaqueros from the ranches and the soldiers at Torreón and position men at every major town and along El Camino Real. The pattern was to be the same as Tamargo had used at Querétaro, a squad of men north and one south of the town, and a third patrolling the streets.

Tamargo had taken his men back to the south some three miles from Querétaro. There, in a jumble of rocks above the highway, they had begun their day-long vigil. He wanted to be the first to intercept Larrway. The young gringo might not yet be aware he was being hunted and would ride directly into Tamargo's guns.

But Larrway had not appeared. Three times Tamargo and his band had swarmed out of the rocks and charged down upon a rider that could have been Larrway. Each time they were disappointed, and returned back to their hiding place, leaving behind a shaken rider, gradually recovering from the assault and glad the men had not been bandits.

A gunshot shattered the stillness of the street ahead of Tamargo. Instantly several more gunshots exploded, so close together they blended into one continuous roll of sound, ripping apart the fabric of the quiet night.

"Follow me," the captain shouted out to his men. He spurred his horse, the big sharp rowels raising long welts on the ribs of the mount. The band of men raced full-tilt toward the lighted length of the street half a dozen blocks farther along.

Tamargo saw several horses running down the street ahead of him. Some seemed to be riderless. That was strange. A man hurried out of the blacksmith shop and began to wave his arms over his head to halt Tamargo.

"I saw Larrway! I saw the gringo," the blacksmith yelled as Tamargo slowed. "He killed some of your soldiers. There he goes." The smith pointed at the horseman in the gloom on the distant street.

The captain jabbed his horse with the spurs again. The man worth ten thousand pesos in gold was only a quarter-mile away. He would not escape Tamargo.

Behind the captain, the blacksmith cried out in a shrill voice, "The thousand pesos are mine."

Tamargo lifted his head and smelled the dust in the air. It was like a good wine to him. He would soon be rich. Each time he caught a fleeting glimpse of running horses in the patches of yellow light thrown on the street from windows, he felt more certain of success in capturing the American.

"Keep a sharp watch," Tamargo called out to Sergeant Quillón riding beside him. Quillón was the best tracker in the troop, and if any one could find the trail, he would.

Querétaro fell away behind them. The hunted and the hunters rushed on beneath the silver moon. Tamargo saw he was not gaining, perhaps even losing ground. He raised his whip and began to lash his horse.

Tamargo saw three riderless horses trotting off at an angle from the course of the pursuit. He opened his mouth to order one of his men to investigate the animals. Just then a horseman crested a rise and became silhouetted against the sky. The captain kept his men with him and bolted onward.

Several times Tamargo lost sight of Larrway in the weak light of the moon. However, his steed, tracking the object of the chase with its night-seeing eyes, held to the route. Tamargo let the brute have its head.

A small mountain rose up out of the night, and the running horses passed it close on their right side. Tamargo began to think he knew where Larrway was heading.

The mounts started to slow. By the time they reached the broken, rocky land at the base of Sierra El Zamorano, the animals were plodding at a slow walk. Tamargo realized his tired horse no longer followed Larrway.

"Let's rest, Captain," called Sergeant Quillón. "We've lost him and we're hurting the horses. Come daylight, I'll find the tracks."

"Not yet. I believe I know where he's going," said Tamargo.

"Where's that, Captain?"

"La Mesa del Sordo."

77

"How could Larrway, a gringo, know about El Sordo and all its rough canyons and fields of brush to hide in?"

"I don't know. But that's where we'll find him. We will go on slowly and be there when daylight comes."

The horses carried Zaldivar's soldiers late into the night. When the moon shadows were long and black, Tamargo and his band had reached La Pileta, a flowing stream at the southern base of the Mesa del Sordo. The men dismounted stiffly and lay down to drink from the fresh water coming down through hundreds of feet of rock from the high tableland above them. The horses stood beside their masters. Men and animals slaked their thirst together.

"Find a place to rest," Tamargo told his men. "At first light, we'll look for a sign of Larrway."

"Captain, you're good at figuring out what men will do and then catching them, but you're betting against the odds. Larrway probably doesn't know this country and could go one way as well as the next."

"True enough. Let's sleep for a few hours. We'll know tomorrow if he's here."

The dark sky lightened to gray in the east. Captain Tamargo watched the patch of morning grow. He had risen early and sat on lookout on a high point on the side of the mesa.

Shortly, the golden orb of the sun floated up above the hulking bulk of the two-mile-tall Sierra de Zimapan. The bright sunrays drove the last lingering night shadows into the rocks and gullies and killed them there.

On the rocky land three-quarters of a mile west, a lone horseman came out of hiding from a side canyon of the mesa and moved off at a trot. That course would take

78

him close to El Camino Real and to the north side of the mesa.

Tamargo grinned mirthlessly. I have you, Larrway. He hurried down from his lookout to wake his sleeping men.

Ortiz spotted the horsemen the moment they streamed out of the shadow of the mesa. He silently cursed his bad luck and the skill of the trackers who had trailed him through the night. How had they accomplished that?

He ran his horse at a moderate pace. The day would be long and the mount's strength must be conserved. He checked the front. El Camino Real swung in near to the mesa foot some two miles ahead.

Ortiz glanced behind. The pursuers were flogging their horses. They meant to make a short chase of it.

"Hijos de puta," growled Ortiz. He began to whip and spur his cayuse. The beast responded with a spurt of speed. It ran swiftly along the base of the mesa. Warily it watched the myriad rocks jutting up from the ground, searching for safe spots to place its hammering feet so as not to trip and fall.

The horse made a wrong guess at an especially rough spot and its right front hoof plunged down between two rocks embedded in the ground. The hard hoof, driven with a force of thousands of pounds, became wedged, locked within the crevice.

The momentum of the half-ton of hurtling horse broke its anklebone with a sickening snap. Man and animal crashed down, cartwheeling end over end.

Ortiz lay for a moment trying to catch his breath. He was bruised and jarred by the fall on the rocky earth. His head rang. But his pursuers were very near. He rolled to his knees and struggled to his feet. He grabbed for his pistol. The holster was empty.

* * *

"Kill him! Shoot him," shouted Captain Tamargo to his men. He yanked his revolver and rode straight for the man rising from the ground.

The first bullet spun Ortiz around. Before he could fall, three more flying chunks of lead tore into his body. His dead face smashed into the hard earth.

Tamargo reined his excited horse up beside the slack, crumpled body. He began to laugh. The reward was his.

But the laughter died. The beard of the dead man was black, and so too was the hair protruding from under the sombrero. Larrway's was brown. Tamargo leapt down and kicked the body over onto its back. The eyes of the corpse were black.

The other soldiers had drawn close and sat their horses, watching. Sergeant Quillón stepped down and studied the corpse's face.

"Surely not Larrway," Quillón said. "But it seems I should know him." He snapped his fingers. "It's Ortiz. It's Ortiz the bandit. He's wanted by Zaldivar. There's a five-hundred-peso reward for him."

Tamargo cursed harshly. He punched his fist into his other hand and stomped up and down. Somehow, during the night, Larrway had turned aside and escaped. Damn the American's luck.

How did Ortiz fit in with Larrway? Tamargo would return to Querétaro and talk with the blacksmith. He needed to know as much as possible about Larrway. The captain wouldn't be fooled again.

He ceased pacing. "That tree"—he pointed to a dead walnut tree—"is close to El Camino Real. Hang Ortiz there so that all travelers can see what we do to bandits.

Cut off his head. We'll take that. Five hundred pesos will pay us for the night's riding.''

Tamargo watched his men tie the lariat to Ortiz's feet and hoist him up on a limb of the tree. Sergeant Quillón pulled his knife and began to saw on Ortiz's neck.

7

ALL DAY KEN REMAINED ON LOOKOUT AT HIS hidden camp in the forest on the east side of the Sierra Guanajuato. He stared across the shimmering valley at El Sordo, blurred and distorted by the rising heat waves. The King's Highway ran along the base of the mesa, but was far beyond the reach of his vision.

His weariness lay heavily on him, and now and then he would doze off. Sometimes he would dream of Anya. Then he would snap awake and hastily look around. He didn't want to lose his head as Ortiz had done.

The fireball sun rolled slowly up its ancient sky path and down the opposite side. Ken saw not one human throughout the day. In all that time only once was the total aloneness around Ken broken, and that was when a small bluebird swooped in to land on a dusty spot beneath an adjacent tree. It scooped, fluttered, and rolled in the fine, dry dirt, bathing in the brown dust. The bird shook itself, flaring and flicking its feathers to rid itself of the dust. Then it launched upward, wings stroking in rapid beats to climb the soft ladder of air.

The sun sank and shadows grew like ghosts among the trees. Ken stirred himself, rode down from the mountain, and intercepted the King's Highway. Hunger moved in the pit of his stomach, growling and arguing with him for hours as he trotted the horses north.

All night he journeyed at the base of the long chain of mountains forming Sierra San Migueleto. He was drawing near to San Luis Potosí and several times he heard horses or rattling vehicles coming along the road. He always hurried to the side out of sight until the travelers passed.

When the dawn began to unfurl its pale light across the cloudless sky, he found a deep, narrow valley on the northern face of the mountain. At a spring that watered a meadow of an acre or so, he halted and made a hungry camp.

San Luis Potosí, a town of approximately seven thousand people, was nestled in full view in the valley below Ken. The waste dumps of half a score of gold and silver mines made dark-brown wounds on the green hillsides above the town. Occasionally a wagon, miniaturized by the distance, came down a winding road to the town. He saw several bands of men riding on El Camino Real both north and south of the town. How many of those men searched for him, to take his head and collect Zaldivar's reward of gold?

The day waned and stalking night came swiftly. Lights flamed alive in San Luis Potosí. Then as the night grew old, the lights began to die, flickering out one by one. When the town was totally dark, Ken made his way down from his hiding place. Torreón lay 350 miles of hard riding away, across a high, desolate plain sparsely inhabited. Ken must have provisions to traverse that hostile stretch of land.

* * *

Under the pressure of Ken's shoulder, the flimsy rear door of the dark restaurant came open with only one complaining rattle of a lock breaking. He entered and stood quietly. The hollow silence told him the room was empty.

He lit a candle and hastily began to assemble a supply of food. He found a loaf of bread and some cooked meat and part of an apple pie left from the day's menu. He ate ravenously, wolfing the food and washing it all down with some sweet milk he found in a crock.

A small quantity of fruit and canned goods was taken from a skimpily stocked pantry. He crammed the items into a burlap sack and tied the end.

He left five silver pesos on the countertop and retreated, closing the broken door as best he could. He laid the sack across his mount's neck and rode from San Luis Potosí by a side street.

Ken picked up the dark highway and, with his ears cocked, urged his mounts northward. He looked into the safe blackness all around him. The need to conceal himself as he traveled had made Ken a lonely, nocturnal animal.

Ramos Zaldivar galloped his horse through the darkness lying densely on El Camino Real. The stalwart beast carried him past a string of six cinder-cone hills, then through the sleeping village of San Marcos, and began the long climb to the high pass between Ixtacihuatl and Cerro Telapón.

Ramos' hate boiled and seethed. He felt the fire within him and he cursed the gringo Larrway who had killed his son Martín.

However, Ramos had one bit of good news: Melchor seemed to be recovering. The surgeon Canosa had come in the afternoon, examined Melchor, and given him a tonic. Shortly thereafter Melchor had called for his father and they had talked, the very first time they had done so to any extent since the duel with Calleja. Melchor had eaten a small quantity of food and then had fallen asleep.

Feeling somewhat more at ease about Melchor's health, Ramos had seized upon the opportunity to ride to Vera Cruz. The military chieftain Malespina was an impatient man and would require a direct personal discussion with Zaldivar before he would delay the planned attack on the governmental forces. Further, a delay meant a new battle plan had to be designed with Malespina.

Ramos touched his horse with spurs and held the brute to a grueling pace, mile after mile. A man on horseback, by changing mounts frequently, could ride to Vera Cruz from Mexico City in a day and a half, and still take a short rest at Zacatepec near the midpoint.

He traveled without his squad of personal guards, and his clothing was that of a common vaquero. His saddle had no silver inlays. He wanted no attention drawn to him. This trip to Vera Cruz must be made without anyone knowing of his absence from Mexico City.

In the small hours of the night, the sky became very black and mostly obscured by the mountains that crowded in to tower over Zaldivar. A cold wind came tumbling and moaning down from the huge ice fields on the crown of Ixtacihuatl. Zaldivar pulled his serape from his bed roll, dropped it over his head, and hurried onward.

The walls of the mountains retreated and El Camino Real angled downward. The icy winds from the peaks of Ixtacihuatl were left to the rear, giving way to a warmer breeze blowing in from the sea, lying two hundred miles to the east.

Zaldivar didn't let the tiring horse slow, but drove it

on with whip and spur. In the morning hour just before daylight, he halted at a friend's rancho and changed mounts. After extracting a promise from the man that he would tell no one of his visit, Ramos raced off.

The night weakened and in the east dawn cut a hole in the darkness. With the day's first sunlight, the chill begin to lift off the earth, carrying with it the night's dew in little gray lines of vapor.

At the town of Texmelucan lying at the base of the three-mile-high Sierra La Malinche, Zaldivar swapped horses again. With the fresh mount, he took the rougher but shorter route north around the giant mountain to the sea.

Zaldivar set the steed at a ground-devouring gallop. He felt his weariness, and his head was light and woozy. He dozed off and on, holding his seat on the horse by instinct.

In the long shadows of evening, Zaldivar reached Zacatepec. He went directly to his cousin's house, a cowardly man who had little ambition and had refused to join Ramos in his plans to become ruler of Mexico. In fact, Ramos had never mentioned the thought to the man again after that first discussion years before.

The cousin gave Zaldivar a corner bedroom where the wind had easy access for a cross draft that would keep him cool as he slept. Zaldivar was up and astride one of his cousin's best horses while the sun was still far below the dark horizon.

He sped down the slanting stretch of El Camino Real leading to Vera Cruz on the sea. The hot breath of the tropical lowlands near the coast met him as he swept down the mountainside. Before the night could fling its thick, dark curtain over Vera Cruz, Zaldivar rode into the city. He went directly to Alejandró Malespina's walled fortress south of the city and overlooking the Gulf Of Mexico.

"Please come in, Señor Zaldivar," said the servant, and bowed very low. "I'm certain Don Alejandró will want to see you immediately." He took Zaldivar's hat. "This way please. Don Alejandro is in the rear courtyard with his officers."

The servant moved aside to allow Zaldivar to enter, then hurried ahead to lead him through the large and lavishly furnished house.

A redheaded woman rose from the shaded veranda on the side of the house. She had seen the rider enter the gate and tie his mount at the entrance. As he'd drawn closer, she had recognized him, and her blue eyes flared. On silent slippered feet, she walked swiftly to intercept Zaldivar. She wished she had a gun so that she might shoot this hated man.

Zaldivar saw the woman approaching, and slowed. He stared at her and couldn't help it. She was still the most beautiful female he had ever seen. To look into her large sky-colored eyes, set far apart in an amazingly white face, was like being kissed. Once he had owned her, for just a short time after buying her from the captain of a pirate ship. Zaldivar had not asked the pirate where he had obtained such a rare creature, but he had often wondered what the answer might be.

Zaldivar had been negotiating with Malespina for some five years to join him in a war to gain control of the nation. As part of the final agreement, Zaldivar promised Malespina he would be given the next white-skinned woman that came into Zaldivar's possession. This lovely female had been that woman. Malespina kept her locked away here in his seacoast hacienda. His Mexican wife was in another hacienda north of the city. Malespina was a reckless man to keep two women in the same town.

The blue-eyed woman came close to Zaldivar. She began to curse him. Her voice rose to a strident screech and the curses were the lowest and vilest Zaldivar had ever heard. Malespina would beat the woman for such an outburst. She must know that. Still she raved. Her eyes became wild, crazy. She spat at Zaldivar.

The frightened servant broke into a run. Zaldivar found himself speeding his own steps. The woman screamed an insane stream of curses at Zaldivar's retreating back.

Ramos came out into the sunlight in the rear courtyard. He was glad to be out of the shadowy hacienda and away from the woman.

Malespina and his colonels and captains sat at a long table under an awning. A map was spread before them. Malespina was pointing at something on the map, but he was staring at the entrance to the hacienda.

Surprise registered on Malespina's face as Zaldivar and the servant burst from the house. Then his features became controlled. He sprang up from his seat and came forward to meet Zaldivar. The officers became silent and watchful.

"You may go," Malespina told the servant, and motioned him away. He took Zaldivar by the arm and steered him out of earshot of the officers.

"What brings you to Vera Cruz? It is dangerous for you and me to be seen so often together."

Zaldivar didn't want to antagonize Malespina to such an extent that he would withdraw and not assist in the revolution. The man commanded a powerful force of men, second only to Zaldivar's among the caudillos. The man was easy to anger, but this was more than compensated for by his high quality as an officer, a leader men willingly followed into battle.

"My son Martín has been killed and Melchor badly wounded," Zaldivar said.

"You have had a very great loss," said Malespina. "How did this happen?"

"Martín was killed in a fight with an American. Melchor was wounded in a duel. I wanted both of my sons to join with you and me in the revolution. I can never have that now, but I must have at least one son be part of this important undertaking. I wish Melchor to have time to heal before we begin the war."

"Martín would have been a brave warrior. So will Melchor, but I see no need to wait for him to recover from his wound. The war will be long, probably months. Melchor can become strong and have many battles to fight."

"He can't travel and I dare not leave him at the hacienda. The moment we start the revolution, Díaz would surely take him prisoner and threaten him with harm to control me."

Malespina's countenance was stony. He stomped the ground and glanced at his officers, who stared openly at the two chieftains.

"How badly is Melchor injured? How long would we wait?"

"His wounds are quite serious. Luis Calleja, the dueling instructor, ran Melchor through with a sword. It may require a long period before he's able to travel. He may yet even die. Though he seemed improved when I left to ride here."

"We must not delay too long," Malespina said. His dark face became darker. "Many of my men have already assembled. The attack is scheduled to begin in four days. Are you certain that Melchor can't travel?"

"It would finish killing my son to move him."

"And what of the American who killed Martín, and Calleja? Have you taken vengeance on them?"

"Melchor killed Calleja. I have sent Captain Tamargo in pursuit of the American."

"Come. Let's discuss this situation," said Malespina. "My officers must help us decide."

Zaldivar and Malespina and his subordinates talked for more than two hours. They agreed to delay the start of the revolution. Then they discussed tactics, modifying the original positioning of the armies and the timing of the sequence of attacks on the national army.

"With surprise on our side, my men can take Díaz's garrison of federal troops here in Vera Cruz," said Malespina. "Then I'll send a detachment of soldiers marching north as if we intend to capture Jalapa. That should draw General Castilllo and most of his army from Mexico City. The presidential palace will be left with but weak protection. I'll continue north for three days. At that time Castillo will be certain of my plans. Then all my forces will quickly return to Vera Cruz and hold the city to prevent any supply of arms or foreign soldiers from landing to assist Díaz."

Zaldivar clapped Malespina on the shoulder. "I'll take Mexico City and make Díaz a prisoner. Then my soldiers will march south to help you to defeat Castillo. We will catch him between us and completely destroy him. Our friends in the northern part of the country will have their armies assembled and will attack at key points. The revolution can succeed."

"I ask one favor," said Malespina. "Don't execute Díaz until I can arrive and see him die."

"It is agreed," Zaldivar promised.

8

MOUNTED ON ONE OF MALESPINA'S FASTEST
horses, Zaldivar rode to the edge of Vera
Cruz. He reined to the right onto the waterfront road and followed that winding, sandy way. Dusk
had fallen by the time he reached the stone-paved quay
between the row of large warehouses and the Bay of
Campeche.

Zaldivar halted at the office at the end of his warehouse near the docks. As he tied his mount, he scanned
the waterfront. The sea breeze blowing along the quay
carried the damp smell of saltwater and the multitudes of
odors from the docks and warehouses full of merchandise
from half a hundred foreign countries.

More than thirty ships were berthed at the half-score
of piers extending into the sea. A few of the vessels were
tall-masted, graceful clipper ships. There were some
schooner-rigged coastal men. Most of the vessels were
squat, broad-beamed steamships.

Some of the steam-powered ships had their boilers
fired. Three of the sailing ships had sailors moving on

deck and in the rigging in preparation to catch the evening tide. Zaldivar heard the men calling to one another as they worked.

An elderly man came from Zaldivar's warehouse and locked the door behind him. He saw Zaldivar and hastened his step toward his employer.

"*Patrón*, good to see," called the man.

"And you too, Facundo," Zaldivar greeted the man who managed his shipping business in Vera Cruz. "I came to the city to attend to a personal matter and thought I would stop for a brief moment to speak with you. Are there any business problems you wish to discuss?"

"No, *patrón*, there are no problems. The warehouse has just this day been emptied of our export merchandise. Everything sold at a handsome profit. Tomorrow I'll go among the foreign ships and buy the best goods to refill our warehouse. However, I'm most pleased that you have come at this particular time."

Facundo drew close to Zaldivar and lowered his voice. "There are some beautiful items that you may wish to purchase. Captain Gunther has them aboard his ship, the *Louisiana Witch*."

"I don't want to take time to examine any goods, no matter how special they might be."

"I have already inspected them. They are very lovely things."

"I don't know this Captain Gunther. Tell me about him."

"I don't know him either, so I have asked questions of the ships' captains that I trust. They tell me Gunther is a mean man, and unpredictable. He was in the slave trade in a large manner for several years. Since the Civil War in the United States, that business is no longer profitable, so now he transports arms for revolutionaries and many other types of contraband. He kidnaps women and sells them."

"How did he know to come to you with his offer of women?"

"I asked him that when I went with him to inspect them. He said that Captain Spencer of the *Evangeline* told him. That much is true at least, for I checked with Spencer. Shall we go aboard Gunther's ship so that you may see the merchandise?"

"I am interested in seeing these females, but we must hurry. If they are satisfactory, then I'll negotiate a price and you can make the actual payment and take possession of the women. Take three *pistoleros* with you and make the transfer in our warehouse. Watch this Captain Gunther very closely. He may try to steal the money and not deliver the women."

"I understand the danger," replied Facundo. He guided the way across the quay and along one of the piers to its seaward end. He pointed at a clipper ship. "That is Gunther's vessel."

"It looks very fast," said Zaldivar.

"And quiet, as a smuggler's ship should be. Let's see if the captain is aboard and will see us."

At the top of the gangway, an armed seaman barred the Mexicans' way. "What do you want?" he demanded in English.

Facundo answered in the same language. "Tell Captain Gunther that Don Ramos Zaldivar is here to see the special cargo."

The seaman peered closely at Zaldivar, then spoke to Facundo. "He doesn't look rich enough to buy that cargo."

Zaldivar understood the man's words. He spoke angrily in Spanish, "Tell this gringo bastard if he does not go instantly and inform the captain that I'm here, I'll leave."

The seaman had understood Zaldivar's heated statement, and his hand moved swiftly to touch his pistol.

Zaldivar's hand moved even more quickly. His fingers curled around the butt of his revolver and he half-drew it from the holster. His temper was short, for he was immensely tired and worried about his son and the revolution. Killing this ass of an American would be a pleasant diversion. Here in Vera Cruz among his friends, Zaldivar would be applauded for the killing of the insulting man.

The seaman's sight dropped and he swung his hand away from his weapon. "Stay here," he growled, and walked away from the gangplank.

Lampshine spilled out onto the deck as a hatchway was opened. Then the hatch closed and the evening dusk settled again over the ship.

As Zaldivar and Facundo waited, dusk became early night. Water began to gurgle around the pilings of the dock as the tide turned and started to flow out of the bay. The ship tugged at the lines holding it to the shore, and it groaned as it rubbed against the hemp fenders.

A sailor went aft on the opposite side of the ship and lit an oil lantern hanging on a rope stretched between two masts. Finishing that task, he vanished down a hatchway. A short moment later he reemerged with another man and both went forward.

"I don't like this,' said Zaldivar. "I think it best that we leave."

"Look, Don Ramos," said Facundo, pointing. "The women are being taken to the captain's quarters."

Two women accompanied by a sailor had left a forward cabin near the main mast and were proceeding along the deck. Both women glanced at the two Mexican men near the gangway. They entered the same portal used by the gangway guard.

Almost immediately a tall man came out of the same entryway and crossed the deck. Zaldivar saw a revolver and a knife on his belt.

"Welcome aboard the *Louisiana Witch*," said the man in moderately good Spanish. "I'm Sanderson the first mate. Captain Gunther's waiting. So too is the merchandise. Facundo, did you tell Señor Zaldivar how beautiful the women are?"

"I told him there are women for sale," Facundo replied briefly.

"Good. Now, Señor Zaldivar, you can see them for yourself. Follow me, if you will?"

"Wait for me on the dock," Zaldivar directed Facundo. Don't come aboard unless I personally tell you too."

"Yes, Don Ramos," responded Facundo.

"He should come too," Sanderson said. "I'm sure the captain would want to see him again."

"Facundo, do as I say." Zaldivar's suspicion was growing that things were not as they seemed. In the event a battle started, he didn't want the unarmed old man in the way. But still, this might be nothing but a simple purchase. He would soon know.

Facundo looked at Zaldivar. He saw the wary glint in the *patrón*'s eyes. He spun around and went down the sloping gangway.

Sanderson walked off across the deck. As Zaldivar trailed behind, he looked about the shadowy ship. He touched the pistol in its holster, a comforting feeling. He entered the cabin with the first mate.

A storm lantern hanging on a brass gimbal fastened to the bulkhead lit the interior of the cabin. A large, bearded man—Captain Gunther, judged Zaldivar—sat in a wooden chair bolted to the deck. A pistol was stuck in his belt. The gangway guard stood beside his captain. Why was the guard still here? The two women were against the far wall. The first mate took a position on Zaldivar's right a few feet distant.

Zaldivar checked for other exits from the room. A second hatchway was in the bulkhead on his left. A porthole was open in the same bulkhead, and the fingers of a breeze poked through to flicker the flame of the lantern.

Zaldivar scanned the women swiftly. Both were truly beautiful, the pale beauty of the fair Scandinavian woman. However, the expression on their faces was not that of kidnapped women being sold into slavery, but rather one of watchful expectation. But expectation of what? Were they willing partners in what was brewing? Zaldivar's nerves tightened, strumming with a mounting warning of danger.

Gunther rose from his chair. The fight to take the rich Mexican's money would begin in a second. However, he hesitated in giving the signal to spring the trap. Zaldivar had examined everyone in the cabin with one quick sweep of his sharp black eyes. He had visibly tensed, coiling like some great spring. A trace of a hard smile thinned his lips, and the smile was increasing as if he were amused and, knowing what was about to happen, welcomed it.

Gunther knew he had cornered not a rich, fat merchant, but a tough, fearless man aware of the threat and ready for the fight. The captain extended his hand. If he could once catch hold of the Mexican, he wouldn't let go and the fight would be finished. "Welcome aboard my ship, Señor Zaldivar."

Zaldivar knew from the positioning of the men that the enemy's plan was for the first mate standing on his right to strike him down while the captain held his attention. He stepped forward as if to take the offered hand. As he moved, he whipped his pistol from its holster and slashed savagely down upon the captain's hand. Bones crushed under the heavy iron weapon. He slammed the captain on the side of the head. The man fell.

Zaldivar spun, swinging his pistol toward Sanderson. The first mate's revolver was nearly from its holster. The man's face took on a startled look, which swiftly changed to one of fear as Zaldivar's pistol came to point directly between his eyes. Zaldivar shot him through the bridge of the nose.

The guard frantically yanked his six-gun from his belt and fired. Zaldivar was already hurling himself aside and the bullet tore a hole where he had been an instant before. He burst the guard's heart with a speeding projectile of lead.

Zaldivar lunged for the nearest woman. Intent upon taking her hostage, he almost missed the man suddenly at the porthole with a rifle. He should have known that the captain would have a backup plan to kill him should he by some lucky chance be close to escaping.

Zaldivar flung a shot from his pistol at the man. The bullet hit the edge of the porthole, shattering the wooden coaming into a score of splinters and flinging them like a handful of darts into the man's face. Bellowing in pain, he fell away from the porthole.

The women bolted for the hatch that led to the deck. The first one jerked the portal open and both sprang outside.

Zaldivar raced after the running women. He caught the slower one from behind and clamped a viselike arm around her ribs. Slowing only a fraction, he lifted her, kicking and screaming, and ran on toward the gangway.

Two sailors charged up from the darkness on the fantail of the ship and positioned themselves between the Mexican and the gangway. They carried no firearms, but each held a long-bladed knife in his hand.

Zaldivar continued to advance. He raised his pistol and carefully shot the sailor standing on the left. The sailor staggered backward, tripping over the safety cable at the edge of the deck, and vanished into the void separating the ship from the pier.

Zaldivar motioned with the barrel of his gun for the other man to move aside. He would have enjoyed shooting the fellow, but he might need the bullet before he could reload. The sailor hastily obeyed.

Zaldivar hurried down the gangway and reached the darkness of the dock. Facundo sped up to him.

"Take her to the warehouse," ordered Zaldivar. "Get some men and come help me. I've taken one of the American's women. Now I'm going to take this ship."

Facundo grabbed the woman and dragged her away. Zaldivar started to reload his pistol.

Above Zaldivar, men ran with pounding feet up to the top of the gangway. They gathered there and shouted at one another, questioning what had happened. Gunther's voice roared across the ship and all the men became quiet.

"The Mexican has one of the women on the dock. Get her back. Kill the damn greaser."

Zaldivar lifted his pistol and aimed it up the gangway at the lighted deck of the clipper ship. Methodically he shot the first two men coming down the narrow walkway, tumbling them into the sea. The remainder scattered back from the edge of the ship.

Zaldivar jumped behind a pile of crated goods on the

dock. The gangway was a path of death. He had the Americans trapped on their own ship.

A rifle began to fire blindly from the ship down onto the dark pier. Good, thought Zaldivar, that will bring me help even faster.

Gunther shouted and the firing ceased. Silence held for minute, then Gunther called out something Zaldivar couldn't make out.

Chains rattled as a windlass took up slack and the gangway began to rise. The hawsers holding the ship to the dock were loosened and tossed into the water. The tall clipper ship began to inch away from the pier, drifting on the outwash of the tide.

The jib sail of the ship unfurled, caught the wind, and filled. The bow of the clipper pivoted toward the open sea. Men scampered up the rigging and the reefed mainsail dropped and bellied with the wind. The ship gained headway, sliding off into the night lying thick on the Bay of Campeche.

Zaldivar's laugh floated on the breeze out over the bay. He hadn't captured the ship. But he had killed some Yankees and had taken a beautiful white female captive, a valuable prize that would sell for many thousands of pesos in gold.

He had one more Yankee to kill . . . Larrway.

— ❧ 9 ❧ —

ANYA STOPPED AT THE OPEN DOOR AND PEER-
ed into the darkened room. She saw Ramos
Zaldivar sitting motionless beside the bed and
staring at the face of his son.

Ramos had returned from Vera Cruz four days before.
He had flown into a wild rage when he saw Melchor's
thin wasted body, pallid face, and skin stretched tightly
over angular bones. He shouted at Canosa and threatened him for his failure to bring Melchor to health.

The surgeon had spoken quietly to Ramos and then
left, returning to his office in the city and his other
patients. Still, once each day he drove out in his buggy to
examine Melchor and treat him with poultices on the
wound and tonics to take internally.

Anya felt sorry for the good physician. She believed
Melchor would die regardless of what skill Canosa might
possess.

Ramos' head snapped around and his black eyes stabbed
at Anya. As if reading her thoughts, he snarled at her in
a fierce voice. "You hope Melchor will die. But he won't."

100

Anya backed away from the terrible hatred in the man. She whirled about and hurried off along the passageway.

Behind her, Ramos' voice climbed higher. "Rosa, lock that yellow-haired bitch in her room. Don't let her out until I tell you to."

The large woman came hastily out of the shadows at the end of the hall where she had been standing. She lumbered forward and grabbed Anya by the shoulder. Roughly she propelled the girl onward and up the staircase to the second floor.

A cruel smile stretched Rosa's lips as she hurled Anya into her room with such force that the girl was thrown from her feet. Since Melchor's injury, Rosa could do what she wanted to the white girl. The key rattled in the door and the bolt slid into its locking socket with a solid *thunk*.

Ramos reached out and touched the arm of his son. He now knew why Melchor had appeared so much recovered on the day he had left and ridden to Vera Cruz. Canosa had given Melchor a large dose of laudanum. The potent narcotic had provided the brightness of eye and sense of well-being.

Even though Zaldivar had been fooled by the laudanum, he hadn't reprimanded the surgeon for it because Melchor's pain was very great. And the body could heal itself while stupefied with the drug.

Ramos spoke to his son. "Melchor, you must get well. We have enemies to kill and a nation to conquer and rule."

Melchor stirred as if he'd heard his father. His eyes opened and his mouth worked. Ramos quickly bent forward.

Melchor screamed out from his unconsciousness. He

screamed again, his voice rising to an unbelievable peak of pain.

Ramos jerked back. His anguish soared and he trembled with rage. He exerted all his willpower to stop himself from rushing from the hacienda to saddle his fastest horse and speed north to help Tamargo capture Larrway. His hand balled into a fist. Dios! Dios! How he hated the American. If Larrway had not prevented Melchor from killing Calleja during that first fight, the old master would never have had time to plan the strategy that so grievously wounded Melchor. Then the gringo, with his own hands, had killed Martín, Ramos' strong, steady son. Larrway would have the worst possible death for his deeds.

Ramos left Melchor's sickroom and went outside to the courtyard. He circled the hacienda and walked to the armory, a long, squat structure made of two-foot-thick stone walls in the rear of the compound. The building held sufficient arms and ammunition to equip a thousand men for battle.

As Ramos surveyed the rifles and pistols and crate upon crate of cartridges, he reflected upon his scheme to become ruler of Mexico. His permanent army of three thousand men and his vaqueros and peons could be assembled quickly. They would be the nucleus around which the dissidents and revolutionaries that always resisted every Mexican government would come flocking. He thought the Mexican people saw revolutions against the government as something inevitable. He knew the revolution against Díaz's government was inevitable.

Ramos took several boxes of cartridges for his pistol and went back outside to the courtyard. "Vicente," he shouted. "Bring some targets. It's time to practice again."

"Sí, patrón," Vicente called back. A moment later he

102

came from the rear door of the house with a sheaf of paper bull's-eye targets in his hand.

Anya heard the pistol shots and went to the window. Ramos and the always obedient Vicente were at the firing range in the far corner of the compound. Vicente had fastened a target to a thick wooden plank set against the wall.

She watched the marksman shoot. As always, standing at a distance from the target Anya thought impossibly long, Ramos slowly drew his pistol and fired at the target. Five times the gun crashed. At a gesture from Ramos, Vicente trotted to the target, attached a new bull's-eye, and returned with the used one.

Ramos methodically reloaded the empty chambers of his pistol as he waited on Vicente. Then critically he examined the placement of the bullets in the bull's-eye. He drew the pistol more swiftly for the next round of shots. And ever more quickly with each succeeding five-shot series. Until his hand was a blur of motion as the pistol rose from his holster and sent the series of five bullets hurtling at the target.

Anya had heard Vicente and the guards discussing with awe Zaldivar's mastery of the pistol. They said he had killed many men in duels and had never been wounded. Lately the guards had begun to talk of something new. Zaldivar had always been a violent man. Now that violence had become intensified and nearly constant. All the inhabitants of the hacienda talked in whispers and tried to stay out of the *patron's* path as they went about their duties.

Since the trip to Vera Cruz, Zaldivar hadn't attended to his many business interests. Instead, he spent long hours in Melchor's sickroom. At times, for some unknown reason, he would suddenly rush from the house to the stables. Whipping and cruelly spurring his horse, he would race from the courtyard and speed off along the road. Hours later, he would return, his mount covered with sweat and blood from the sharp spurs and trembling with exhaustion. Immediately Zaldivar would fling the saddle on a second horse and rush away again. Even a third mount would sometimes be ridden nearly to death. Once or twice Zaldivar had come back with the saddle on his shoulder, the horse left dead, its heart burst on a steep grade or its leg broken in a boulder patch.

At the end of his wild rides, Zaldivar would come into the hacienda, shout for absolute silence, and throw himself upon his bed. He wouldn't reappear for a day, and oftentimes longer.

Ramos heard the rattle of iron-rimmed wheels on the stony road leading up from Tacubaya. He walked to a place where he could see past the hacienda toward the front gate.

A light wagon drawn by a trotting team of horses swept through the entrance. The guard merely waved at the driver dressed as a vaquero.

Zaldivar recognized the soldier, Fuentes, one of Tamargo's elite squad of one hundred guards. He saw the barrel sitting upright and fastened with ropes in the rear of the vehicle. A single barrel brought swiftly to him could mean only one thing: a barrel of salt, Larrway's head.

"Vicente, go get a hammer and pry bar to open a barrel," Ramos shouted, and hurried out to meet the wagon.

Fuentes spotted Zaldivar coming along the side of the hacienda. He reined the team of horses in that direction

104

and brought the vehicle to a stop near the man. He pulled a paper sealed in oilskin from inside his shirt.

"Señor Zaldivar, Captain Tamargo said I should bring you this message and that barrel in the back of the wagon." Fuentes held out the paper.

"I have been expecting it," replied Ramos. He yelled to Vicente just turning the corner of the house. "Hurry your slow ass."

"Señor Zaldivar, do you want to read Captain Tamargo's message?" asked Fuentes.

"In a moment," Zaldivar said.

Vicente ran up with tools in his hands. Zaldivar, with a curt motion of his hand, directed Vicente up into the wagon.

"Get the lid off the barrel," Ramos said.

Vicente jumped into the bed of the vehicle and began to knock and pry the wooden slats from the top of the barrel.

When the barrel was half-open, Ramos vaulted up into the wagon bed and shoved Vicente aside. "Get out of the way. Let me see."

He plunged his hand down into the white grains of salt filling the barrel. His seeking fingers felt the hair and the round dome of a man's skull.

Ramos locked his fingers in the hair and began to pull. His heart speeded its beat. Dios, but it was grand to have your worst enemy dead and his head in your hand. My sons, you have been avenged.

The head came free of the salt, spilling a gallon of the crystals like a shower of snow onto the wagon bed. Ramos vigorously shook the object to remove the clinging salt, and it rained down, white and red. Clots of salt bound with congealed blood.

Ramos lifted and rotated the head to look into the

face. Red-stained salt streamed from the open mouth as if the head was vomiting blood. One eye was closed. One black, sunken eye stared at Ramos.

"This is not Larrway's head," Zaldivar shouted. He exploded with a paroxysm of curses and started to savagely beat the head against the side of the barrel. "That stupid bastard Tamargo has killed the wrong man."

Ramos flung the head at Vicente. "Take this and feed it to the dogs."

Vicente fumbled in catching the head, not wanting to touch the object. It struck him in the chest and fell to the wagon bed, then rolled to the ground.

"Do what I say," Ramos growled at Vicente. He faced Fuentes. "Let me see Tamargo's message."

Zaldivar ripped off the waterproof covering and swiftly read the brief communication. He crumpled the paper into a tight wad and dropped it.

"Damn Tamargo. He wastes my time with such an unimportant bandit." Zaldivar stormed off across the compound.

He drew his pistol as he approached the firing range. The hammered iron weapon was a feather in his hand. He began to shoot as he walked, and the bullets, every one, went true as if drawn by a magnet to the bull's-eye.

Fuentes left Zaldivar's hacienda, glad to be gone from the half-crazed man. He drove directly to his brother's small house in Mexico City. It was time to forgo his disguise as Fuentes and become his real self, Emilio Cuadrado, lieutenant in Díaz's national army.

The house was empty and he wondered where his brother and sister-in-law had gone. He ate cold food and slept through the afternoon and into the evening.

In the early darkness, Cuadrado dressed himself in

ragged peon clothing with a battered straw hat. He left the house by the rear door and went quietly down the alley.

He walked leisurely among the hundreds of strollers on the street. On the far northern end of the city, he turned and went east to the shore of Lake Texcoco. A man with a boat for hire rowed up to the pier when Cuadrado motioned to him. Cuadrado paid the man to transport him south for two miles and reland him. Confident now that no one followed, he wound his course back west toward the street where General Castillo lived.

In the darkness of the rear patio of the general's hacienda, two soldiers sat on a bench near the entrance. A bright spot from a burning cigarillo showed and Cuadrado smelled the smoke of the tobacco.

The soldiers saw Cuadrado in the street and immediately sprang to their feet. They brandished their rifles.

"Halt," one of the soldiers called. "Don't come closer. This is General Castillo's home. He has said that he expects no visitors. Only robbers or people who would harm the general would come stealing about at night."

"I'm not a bandit, nor do I wish the general ill," said Fuentes. "I must talk with General Castillo."

The soldier peered closely at Cuadrado and marked the peon clothing. "Go away. We do not bother him for such a person as you."

"Stubborn bastards," mumbled Cuadrado. Yet he was glad the general was so well-guarded.

"What did you say?" growled one of the soldiers. "Did you curse us?"

"Certainly not. Tell the general that Cuadrado is here and wishes to talk with him. If you do not do this, he will have you flogged when he finds out I was here and you forced me to leave."

F.M. PARKER

The soldiers whispered to each other, all the time warily watching Cuadrado. Finally one called out to him.

"Come close so we can see if you are armed."

One soldier held his rifle against Cuadrado's spine while the second thoroughly searched him. "No weapons on him," said the man. "Keep him here while I tell the general."

The soldier went into the house. He shortly came hurrying back. He shoved his comrade's rifle from Cuadrado's body. "This man is known by the general and is to be treated as a friend."

"You are becoming wise," said Cuadrado.

"We apologize most sincerely to you, Señor Cuadrado. Please enter. General Castillo is waiting in his study."

Cuadrado went into the house. He removed his hat and moved down the hall. He had been here before to report and knew the way.

"Lieutenant Cuadrado, very good to see you," said the general. "Come in and be seated. You have important news?"

"You instructed me to report on any sighting of Larrway by Zaldivar's soldiers."

"Then the American has been found?"

"Not exactly. I've been riding with Captain Tamargo. In Querétaro we heard shooting. A blacksmith told us that he had seen Larrway and that the man had killed some of Zaldivar's soldiers. We gave chase, running most of the night. In the morning we caught and shot a man. However, he wasn't Larrway, but a bandit named Ortiz."

"So Larrway was not in Querétaro?"

"He was there. I'm certain of that. The blacksmith gave a good description of him. The American helped Ortiz shoot the soldiers and then they both escaped.

108

Somehow during the chase, Larrway turned off and we didn't see it."

"How is it that you're in Mexico City and not with Tamargo?"

"The captain took Ortiz's head for the five-hundred-peso reward. He ordered me to bring it to Zaldivar. I've taken the opportunity to come see you and get any new orders you might have."

"Very little has been seen of Zaldivar lately. But you did see him?"

"Yes."

"What did he say and do?"

"I brought the head of Ortiz in a barrel of salt. When the barrel was opened and Zaldivar saw the head it contained wasn't Larrway's, he became awfully angry, almost like a madman."

"Did you see any sign that he is preparing for a new revolution?"

"His best fighters are mustered and armed. At the moment they are pursuing the gringo. I'm certain of that fact."

"Will they go back to peaceful work when that is accomplished?"

"I don't know. However, I've seen Zaldivar's supply of weapons at Torreón. He could equip an army of thousands. Tamargo has spoken of Zaldivar's rich mines and the fertile soil of his ranches. Money would be no problem if Zaldivar wanted to put an army in the field. He is very dangerous to President Díaz."

"You are correct, Lieutenant. He is the most dangerous caudillo in all Mexico. What orders do you have from Tamargo?"

"I am to ride north to Chihuahua and join him in his pursuit of Larrway."

"Do exactly that. Stop at Torreón and see if all the weapons are still in Zaldivar's armory. I must know immediately if he starts to arm additional men. And, Lieutenant Cuadrado, be very careful. Zaldivar would give you a very bad death if he should suspect that you were one of my soldiers."

"Yes, sir. Long live President Díaz!" Cuadrado rose and started to walk across the room. He slowed and faced about. " General, those two guards at the rear entrance would recognize me if they should see me again."

"I understand your concern. I'll transfer them to our garrison at Vera Cruz tomorrow."

"Thank you, General."

Castillo sat looking at the door where the young officer had disappeared. The general had fought in seven revolutions and many battles. Now, as an old soldier, he sensed the omens, the events drawing together that preceded and led to war. If war was inevitable, then he should strike first. With surprise on his side, the weakness of his army might not be fatal and he would win.

The general drew pen and ink to him. He began to draft orders for the commanders of his garrisons to hurry their preparations for war. Come morning, he would discuss the orders with the president. He shivered with revulsion at the thought of more slaughter of the good people of Mexico. But if he could defeat the caudillos, Mexico could have peace for a hundred years.

10

THE SIXTH NIGHT AFTER LEAVING SAN LUIS Potosí, Ken came off of the barren, rocky plain. The next night, he climbed up and over Sierra de Jimulco and came down into the Bolsón de Mayran, a dry basin from which no water escaped to flow to the sea. When the morning stole in, he could see Torreón and the Río Nazas, and far away to the west the Sierra Madre Occidental.

He had eaten nothing during the last two days. His horses had fared better, finding some grazing during the daytime rest. Water had been obtained by locating the stagecouch stations, and then, during the cover of darkness, stealing in with his horses to drink and fill his canteen from the dug wells or the stagnant, foul-tasting old water in the rain barrels.

Ken swung west, intending to avoid Torreón, the stronghold of the Zaldivars. He crossed the Río Nazas two miles from Torreón. Beyond a low, miles-broad water divide, the Bolsón de Mapimí was reached and Ken began the long trek over its sandy wasteland, the Llanos Tepalcates.

Two days into the windy plains Ken found a sheepherder's shack. He rested his mounts at the edge of the yard and scrutinized the house. The roof of the small structure sagged dangerously, and the adobe walls were crumbling, their top edge thin as a board. The weak walls seemed unable to support the weight of the roof.

Ken surveyed the flat land of the Llanos Tepalcates stretching away in every direction weary mile after weary mile. Only the desert brush huddling together in widely spread clumps broke the interminable sweep of the great plain. It was strange that there wasn't one sheep in sight. Still the plain contained sinks, depressed areas large enough to hide a band of sheep. Often these places were the location of the most grass and browse.

Ken rode in slowly, his eyes scanning the house. Nothing moved except a small dust devil spinning up dirt in a brown funnel. He stepped to the ground.

The huge black dog burst around the corner of the shack. It slowed half a second, its head rising, questioning. Its keen hunting nose caught the alien scent of the human invading his master's domain. The dog roared a deep-chested bellow that changed to a savage growl. It launched itself across the yard. Ten feet from the intruder, the dog leapt for his throat.

Ken snatched off his big hat and thrust the open side out. The dog saw the object suddenly in its way, but it couldn't stop. Its head went into the hat.

Ken clamped a viselike hold on the dog's neck. The momentum of its body jerked man and animal down in a struggling tangle at the feet of the horses.

Ken fought the beast on the dusty ground. Fierce primeval growls escaped his throat, mixing with the snarls of the animal. The dog tried to tear free, its clawed feet digging at Ken and the earth. Ken twisted mightily on the muscular brute and managed to turn its back to him. He locked the dog between his legs and applied pressure, compressing its rib cage. His hands squeezed ever more tightly on the sinewy, straining neck and closed off the air passage in the throat.

Gradually the dog's frantic struggles slackened and ceased. Cautiously, Ken released his hold on the animal's throat. The beast lay limp, its red tongue protruding far out from between its long white teeth. Its lungs quivered, sucking in a small draft of air. The dog took another weak breath.

Ken sprang erect and hurried to his horse. Swiftly he took a stout cord from his saddlebag and returned to the dog. The beast was trying to rise, and its head came up and its glazed eyes tried to see. Ken threw a loop around the pointed head and tied the wicked jaws together. The four feet were bound tightly. The dog was growling deep in its chest as Ken finished and stepped back.

He ducked his head and entered the one large room that made up the house. A fireplace occupied a corner. A raised wooden frame covered with several woolen fleeces was the bed. Two stools stood by a tottering table. A poor man's home.

He drank deeply of the cold water in an olla hanging from the ceiling joist. The liquid, cooled by the evaporation through the porous walls of the container, was the finest water he'd had in many burning days. He took a breath and drank again.

He ate heartily of cheese, corn bread, and cold boiled beans. The food was satisfying and gloriously filled his empty stomach.

He went to the doorway. The two faithful horses must be watered and fed.

Ken halted in midstride, stooped, and partially stood

in the doorway. A Mexican, rail-thin and bearded, stood in the center of the yard. He aimed a large-caliber musket directly at Ken's stomach. He said not a word, his finger tight on the trigger.

The Mexican's eyes flicked down at the dog lying on the ground and then hastily back to Ken. "Did you hurt my dog?"

"No," Ken replied. He started to step forward from the door so he could straighten.

The man's eyes squinted and his pressure on the trigger increased.

For a chilling second, Ken thought the man would shoot. At the close range of twenty feet or less, the musket would blast a cave in Ken's chest.

"I've killed a thousand coyotes and ten sheep thieves with this old gun," said the man. "And five Americans in the war of '47. Do you want to be the sixth American to die?"

"No, and there's no reason for you to shoot me. I mean no harm. I was just hungry and ate some of your food. I'll pay."

"How did you manage to tie my dog? He's a mean one."

"We fought and he lost. I could've shot him, but I didn't. He was just protecting your property."

The man's fingers relaxed a bit on the trigger of the musket. "Why are you here?"

"I got lost from El Camino Real."

"You're a liar. No one could get lost from such a well-used road. Now tell the truth."

"I'm coming out where I can stand straight," Ken said, and stepped into the yard. "The truth is I don't want to be seen by Ramos Zaldivar's soldiers. They would try to kill me."

A shrill, cackling laugh broke from the man. His beard split and a mouthful of broken teeth showed as he laughed loudly. He lowered his musket. "Zaldivar's soldiers are after you, eh? Well, he's got a lot of them and he owns nearly every acre of land around Torreón."

"So I've heard."

"But he doesn't want this worthless desert. That's why I'm allowed to graze my few sheep here. This land is so bad that I can't make enough money to even support a wife.

"I saw your tracks coming from the south. So you must be trying to get back to the United States. Where did you start from?"

"Mexico City."

"I was once in Mexico City when I fought you Americans." The man peered closely at Ken. "You speak the Mexican lingo very well. Now I haven't talked with anybody in a month or more. Will you talk with me and tell me what is happening in the capital? Then you can sleep some before you leave for the border at Ciudad Juárez or Presidio. Either one is a very long ride. Perhaps two weeks or so."

"I'll tell you what I know about the city," Ken agreed.

"Excelente. Come and put your horses in the shade under the lean-to at the rear of the house. My well is weak and makes little water, but I think we can pull up enough for them to drink their fill."

The man leaned down and released the dog with a few cuts of his knife. Then he cursed it into a cowering lump on the ground when it growled and started for Ken.

"The dog doesn't like you, gringo." The Mexican walked past Ken to lead the way toward the back of the house.

He looked over his shoulder. "You wouldn't shoot a man who has absolutely nothing of value, would you?"

"I only shoot men who try to take my life."

The man grinned through his whiskers. "That seems like a worthwhile reason."

11

KEN TRAVELED THROUGH THE CONGEALED darkness of the Mexican night toward Chihuahua. The black wall seemed to have a palpable density that the horses had to push aside as they moved. On the western horizon, a thin horn curve of moon lay dying. Wind moaned a dismal dirge across the barren land. He smelled the dust in the air and his raw eyes burned with it.

Ken was starving. A damn bad way to end a long night of hard travel.

Leaving El Camino Real miles south, he had held two miles east and had allowed the narrow, desert mountain range Santo Domingo to come in between him and the highway. In that way he was hidden from any enemies that might be waiting on the edge of the city.

He passed the north end of the Sierra Santo Domingo. A half-hour later he crossed the dry, sandy bed of the Río Chuviscar. When he topped the bank he stared into the night. Chihuahua, a city of thirty thousand people, should be directly ahead at the base of the Sierra Azul, Blue Mountain.

Some faraway lights feebly broke through the night. Early-rising citizens had lit their lamps. In the dusty darkness, the glowing candle flames were weaker than the lights of distant fireflies.

Ken spoke to the horses. They lengthened their strides.

In the last minutes of morning dusk, Ken entered Chihuahua, coming in among the dwellings along a little-used path.

He knew the city moderately well, for he had stopped there for three days during his journey to Mexico City. He had wandered the town, encountering many other Americans. Presidio was barely a hundred miles north-east and El Paso only two hundred and thirty miles north, an easy ride for the hard-assed gringos.

Nearly every one of the Americans was a rogue, a scoundrel—thieves and killers who had drifted south away from the U.S. marshals in New Mexico, or had been driven west from Texas by the tough Rangers.

A large Mexican army garrison and a sizable number of *rurales* were stationed in Chihuahua to maintain law and order. The rowdy and sometimes murderous Americans primarily frequented ten blocks of cantinas, brothels, and shabby hotels and boardinghouses on Martínez Street. There they could drink, gamble, and bed the whores. As long as they fought only among themselves and didn't commit murder, they were rarely bothered by the officials. However, if a Mexican citizen was harmed, the soldiers and *rurales* marched into Martínez Street and took ruthless retaliation against the offenders.

Ken guided his steed through the town toward Martínez Street. There, among the white faces, he thought he could safely purchase the provisions he had to have for his journey to the United States without his identity being discovered.

The day brightened as a red sun rose on the dusty horizon. The streets were filling with men and women hurrying off on private errands or to their places of employment. In a block of warehouses, Ken passed an American wagon train of fifty or more vehicles. The cargo of manufactured goods was being unloaded and laid out in a long, open-sided building. A large sign stated that an auction would be held at 9 A.M.

Ken entered Martínez Street and halted at the first livery stable. An American came from the rear of the building.

"What'll it be, fellow?" asked the man.

"Give each of my horses a gallon of grain and all the hay they can eat," Ken told the liveryman. "Brush and clean them. They've earned good treatment."

"I'll do that. The cost will be a half-peso each."

"Will you watch my belongings for a little while? I want to get something to eat."

"Sure. Put them over there near the wall. They'll be safe. I'm not going anywhere until noontime."

"I'll be back before then."

Ken placed his gear where the man had indicated, and walked off along the thoroughfare. His sight roamed over the people, many of them American, but also a number of Mexican men and women.

Though the day was still young, the heat of the sun was already filling the shallow canyon of the street. The wind was increasing in intensity, gusting briskly and here and there boiling up the dust in little yellow clouds. One of the waves of dust washed over Ken and he grabbed the wide brim of his hat and closed his eyes for a few seconds.

The cloud of grit passed and he moved on. He would find food and a bath, in that order. Then he would buy enough supplies to last him to El Paso. His clothing badly needed washing, but he would forgo that, as he didn't want to wait for them to dry. To linger in the town would be dangerous.

He entered a small cantina on the shady side of the street and took a seat at an empty table. Several Americans at breakfast cast curious looks at the gringo in the filthy, Mexican vaquero clothing. They soon lost interest and went back to their food.

Ken ordered steak, eggs, coffee, milk, and a pitcher of water, then sat wearily back. His swollen, bloodshot eyes burned and itched, and he felt totally exhausted. However, in four or five days he would be in Ciudad Juárez, and then all he had to do was cross the Río Grande to El Paso. He would be safe from Zaldivar there.

The food came. He ate leisurely, chewing every bite thoroughly and savoring the taste of the food in his mouth. Finally he finished the last tidbit and went outside to find the bathhouse.

The two American horsemen halted at the public bulletin board, the wooden wall of a building that stood tight against the edge of the sidewalk. The scores of pieces of paper tacked to the boards fluttered and rattled in the wind like a nest of tiny, angry rattlesnakes.

Dokken reined his dusty horse off the street and up on the sidewalk beside the wooden building. He reached out to still the dance of one of the pieces of paper. A Mexican coming along the sidewalk gave the gringos a sour look and circled out into the street to pass. Dokken ignored the man and began to scan the writing on the notices.

"God-a-mighty, Dokken, can't you wait to read those posters until we wash the dust off and get some grub?" Lambert said in an aggravated voice. "We've just rode two hundred miles through some of the meanest country in God's world. I need to sit in the shade and drink a cold beer."

"Stop grouching," Dokken said. "From a few minutes of reading these public notices, I'll know all that's happening—when the next fandango is, the next bull-fight, what's for sale, and who's wanted by the local law."

"I still say it can wait. Tomorrow is plenty soon enough for that. We know where the best drinks are and where the prettiest woman are waiting. And besides, nothing changes fast in Chihuahua."

"Look, Lambert, here's another one of the wanted posters on that American Larrway we saw in Ciudad Juárez. I wonder what he did in Mexico City that makes him worth ten thousand pesos to Ramos Zaldivar."

"Must have been damn serious. But we wouldn't have a chance of collecting that reward. The *rurales* will catch him long before he reaches Chihuahua. They're experts at that. In fact, they've probably already caught him. Anyway, we've got a pocket full of wanted posters for Americans that we think may have come south for their health. Finding those fellows and dragging them back to the States will take all our time."

"None of them are worth a tenth of what this Larrway is," Dokken said. He jerked the poster off the wall and thoroughly read it for the second time.

He'd find this Larrway, he knew it. Once discovered, a youngster such as the notice described should be easy to take. Ten thousand pesos would make Dokken very rich, even after he gave Lambert a share of the wealth. He folded the paper and put it into his pocket.

"Let's go," Dokken said. "I've got a feeling I'm going to find a lot of gold real soon."

Ken left the street and went into the bathhouse. The room was narrow and deep with wooden tubs arrayed in two lines of ten along the walls. Sheets, which had once been white but were now extremely dirty, hung on cords to enclose each tub and give some degree of privacy. At this early time of the day, the establishment was empty. Good, thought Ken, I have the place to myself.

He paid the attendant, a young Mexican, a quarter-dollar and took the offered towel. "Fill that far tub near the back door with four full buckets of hot water," Ken said.

"*Sí, señor.* I have water just outside. Please wait. It will take only a minute for me to fix your bath." He picked up a bucket and trotted out the back of the building.

As Ken waited, two Americans armed with pistols came inside. They were tough-looking men, dirty and raw-boned. They nodded curtly to Ken, but didn't speak.

The attendant motioned to Ken. "*Señor,* I have put four buckets of hot water in the tub as you ordered. If you want more water, the charge will be *cinco centavos* a bucket."

"Thanks," said Ken. He walked to the tub and drew the curtain on all sides. His pistol was unbuckled and laid on the bench near the tub. Using soft soap scooped from a dish of it on the floor, he washed his head and face and climbed into the water.

His eyes closed and he rested. He heard the attendant carrying more water and pouring it into tubs. In between

122

the splashing buckets of water, he heard the two Americans talking in muted voices.

"Your baths are ready," Ken heard the young Mexican call out.

"In a couple of minutes," replied one of the Americans.

Ken continued to lay soaking for a few seconds. Then abruptly he sat upright in the tub. Why would the men allow their bath water to cool? What was so important that it had to be done at this very moment?

For many days, Ken had been constantly on guard against enemies that he knew hunted him. Was that never-ending worry now making him overly suspicious?

"Damnation," Ken said, angry at his lack of ability to enjoy the bath. He rose from the tub and, dripping water, peered out between the curtains.

The two Americans were talking earnestly together. One extracted a folded piece of paper from his pocket and spread it out. The second man cast a quick glance in Ken's direction and then leaned to read the writing on the paper held by the first man.

Ken threw a look at the bath, tempted to climb back into the warm, pleasant water, but the paper the men studied could be one of Zaldivar's reward posters. There had been a calculating expression in the second man's face when he had looked toward Ken.

Hastily Ken started to pull on his clothing. The cloth stuck to his wet body, and his progress was slow. He finished and sat on the bench and yanked on his boots. As he picked up his pistol, footsteps sounded nearby in the aisleway between the tubs. Ken jerked the belt holding his pistol tight about his waist.

The curtains were roughly snatched aside. The two Americans stood in the opening.

* * *

Dokken looked closely at the young man. He was certain this was Larrway. The man had given himself away when he had cut his eyes at Lambert and Dokken with that questioning expression of whether he'd been recognized. Dokken had seen that look before from hunted men.

"What do you want?" Ken's voice was strained with anger. His heart thudded and he could feel it pounding in his temples. Why couldn't he be left alone?

"Never get angry." Ken heard Luis Calleja's warning in his mind. "Concentrate all thought on your enemy. Plan how you will defeat him."

Your training may not be enough to save me this time, Culleja, thought Ken as he watched the two Americans. The men appeared unconcerned about what action he might take. Instead, they calmly evaluated him as if he was no threat to them, but rather already a prisoner—or dead.

The confidence of the men worried Ken. Just how skilled were they with the pistols so handy on their belts? Which man was the quicker and the one Ken should try to shoot first?

"You look familiar," said Dokken.

"I don't know either of you," Ken replied. "We've never met."

"I didn't say we'd met, only that you look familiar. Lambert, show him that wanted poster we've got."

Lambert held up the piece of paper Ken had seen them studying. "Take a good look at this," Lambert said.

Ken kept his attention locked on the two Americans. This could be a trick to catch him off guard.

"Doesn't that describe you exactly?" asked Dokken.

"Your name's Larrway and you're worth ten thousand pesos in gold."

"You've made a mistake," said Ken in a quiet tone. "My name's Tolliver."

Dokken heard the lie in the soft voice. He saw a hard glint come into the young man's eyes and the subtle shift of his body to a stance tensed to fight. Dokken recognized the preparation for battle and the willingness to gamble with death. He had seen it too many times to ever mistake what it meant. He hadn't expected such a calm, controlled reaction. Had he made an error in how they should take Larrway?

Then his confidence in his skill with a gun returned. The kid should be easy to kill.

"We don't believe you at all," Dokken said. "The description fits you too well. Lambert and me, we intend to collect that reward."

Dokken's hand plunged down for his pistol.

I'm glad you two men didn't have your pistols drawn when you opened the curtains, thought Ken. He pulled his revolver with a lift of his hand. The gun fired as it came level.

Dokken's chest exploded with pain. Every rib seemed to shatter. He was hurled backward. God! How could a man be so quick with a gun? Blackness caught Dokken like a thunderclap.

Ken rotated his gun toward his second foe. The man's hand was moving, touching the butt of his pistol, beginning to grip it. The man's action seemed amazingly slow to Ken. Perhaps he didn't have to die. Ken shifted his point of aim away from Lambert's heart. He fired, sending a bullet skittering across the man's ribs.

Lambert was spun violently around. He fell with a choked cry. His pistol fell to the floor with a clatter.

Ken grabbed up both revolvers and tossed them into the water. He leaned over Lambert, staring into the pain-stricken face. "I've let you live. Don't come after me again," Ken warned.

He hurried through the rear exit and turned right along the alley. The bathhouse attendant was pressed tightly against the wall near the huge tub of heating water. He watched Ken with fear-filled eyes. Larrway checked the man over swiftly to see if there was any danger in him.

The man shook his head. "I saw nothing," he said in a choked voice.

"Good. Now don't move for three minutes and I'll not come to hunt you," warned Ken.

The attendant hastily nodded his understanding.

Ken ran up the alley to its intersection with the street. He immediately slowed and then strolled nonchalantly out onto the thoroughfare. He pulled the broad brim of his hat down and, staring straight ahead, walked at a leisurely stride up the winding street. He went two blocks, turned, and returned to Martínez Street. The livery stable was a block ahead.

His identity had been discovered by the two Americans in less than an hour after his arrival. How many other men were at this moment looking at him and making comparisons with the description written on the reward poster? Zaldivar had created a thousand enemies for Ken.

He peered out from under his hat, examining the people on the street. Some were looking off through the dust and wind in the direction of the bathhouse. Most continued on about their business. No one was looking at Larrway. A shooting on Martínez Street wasn't a novelty.

He heard the bathhouse attendant call out behind him.

"Two Americans have been killed. Hurry. Somebody get the *rurales*."

Without speaking to the man in the livery stable, Ken saddled the gray horse and left leading the black.

On the edge of town, the dust was driving the vendors from the plaza. Lugging their wares, they streamed away on the side streets. Ken steered clear of men who might be aware of the reward. He headed toward two young women, one carrying fruit, vegetables, and prepared food in a flat basket on top of her head; the second carried water in two gourds hanging on woven straps over her shoulders.

Ken called out to the women and rode close. They flashed big black eyes at him while he filled his saddlebags with food and his canteen with water. He paid and reined his mount into the wind.

El Paso lay four, maybe five days' travel to the north. He was within striking distance of the safety of the border.

12

THE GALE-FORCE WIND ARRIVED ON THE MAP-
imí desert with a whistling roar. It killed the
giant dust devils that played on the super-
heated surface of the sand sea, collapsing their spiriling
loads of dust and blowing it horizontally in a hazy yellow
mist.

Streams of sand formed and flowed in crooked, mean-
dering rivulets around the feet of the great dunes and
continued up and over the twenty-foot crests, to fly
onward like spume from the peaks of ocean storm
waves.

The sand sea, awakened once more, began its migra-
tion. Its combers, composed of the ancient detritus of the
long-dead lake, moved off to the west toward a desolate
desert mountain range of black lava rock.

"Madre de Dios," exclaimed the Zaldivar soldier. "I'm
drowning in dust. Captain Tamargo, I don't believe the
gringo Larrway will travel in such a storm."

"Patience, Ochoa. This is just the kind of storm he
would travel in. Or at night. For that reason, no one but

128

us will capture him. Don't think of the dust. Think only of the golden reward."

Tamargo looked at the four men scattered around him between the two tall sand dunes. He had selected the very best *pistoleros* and horsemen from his elite personal command. Hankerchiefs covered their noses and mouths, and their sombreros were pulled low on their foreheads. The men, all except one, stared back at him with squinted red eyes.

The last man, Sergeant Quillón, stood leaning against his horse. At the moment the tracker's eyes were closed and his skinny body slack. He appeared asleep, a very false impression, for no one was more alert or ready to ride and fight than Quillón.

Tamargo turned back to watch El Camino Real winding through the sand dunes approximately one hundred yards away. After Larrway's escape at Querétaro, Tamargo knew the man wouldn't be trapped easily. Therefore, the captain had halted only a few brief minutes at San Luis Potosí and other towns to change mounts and renew provisions. At Torreón he had given Zaldivar's instructions to Colonel Almonte, then issued his own orders to the soldiers and vaqueros for their pursuit of the gringo. Now Tamargo and his men lay waiting at the most probable location to intercept and capture Larrway along the entire route from Mexico City to the American border. That was the sand wasteland of the Bolsón de Mapimí.

The land of sand dunes stretched sixty miles east to west and nearly thirty miles from north to south. El Camino Real crossed close to the middle of the vast expanse of dunes, where the area of sand was necked down to only a narrow, twenty-mile distance. Travelers riding to the north would pass through the wasteland on this section along the King's Highway.

"Come, Larrway, come," ordered Tamrago in a whisper not heard by the other men over the sound of the wind. "Be like other men. No, not like other men, for then you would have been killed before you reached this point. Just make a mistake this one time and travel in the daylight where I can see you."

As Tamargo watched, the curtains of dust parted on El Camino Real, whipped aside by a fickle gust of the wind. A man with two horses, braced against the storm, rode north on the highway.

"That's Larrway, Captain," Sergeant Quillón called through the storm. "The chase begins."

Tamargo nodded. "Mount up," he ordered his men.

Larrway left the broad stretch of stony ground north of Chihuahua and rode into the sand dunes on the Mapimí desert. He saw the storm front destroy the awesome, writhing pillars of the gigantic dust devils. Immediately, a mountainous surf of dirty yellow dust rolled toward him. He was reminded of the thick winter fog that sometimes came in off the California ocean, and a pang of homesickness touched his heart.

The wind buffeted him and snapped the brim of his hat up and down. The sun overhead became a hazy red disk through the choking dust. Sharp grains of sand sprang up from the ground into the air and bit his face like tiny stinging bees.

Ken tied his bandanna over his nose and mouth. He screwed his eyes nearly shut and looked into the keening banshee of the wind. The furious howling and the twisting, swirling sand shapes in the storm seemed to fill the desert with some undefined menace. A chill ran along his spine.

A powerful blast of wind staggered the horses. They

tried to turn their heads from the brunt of the storm, but Ken reined them back to the northern course.

The steeds had traveled all the long night to reach Chihuahua. Then, after only a short stop in the town to eat and drink, they had covered another fifteen miles. Now they fought against the swift, turbulent river of wind. Worse still, there would be no place to rest them in the dust so thick that a man could reach out and catch a handful of it.

The horsemen came like black specters from behind the high sand dune of Ken's right. They plunged their mounts through the billowing dust toward him. The bang of exploding rifles and pistols rose above the roar of the storm. A bullet burned the tip of Ken's ear.

He spun the gray horse away from the attackers. As he did so, he threw a loop of the black horse's lead rope around the horn of the saddle. He raked the gray with spurs. Both horses bolted away with the wind.

Ken leaned low over the neck of the gray. He yelled a loud, piercing call at the horse. The great brute understood the primal challenge. It lunged forward in a flat-out, dead-streaking run. Its long neck extended and the pointed ears thrust forward. The strong legs stretched, every step reaching for the longest piece of distance possible.

Behind Ken the pursuing horsemen were wavering, indistinct forms in the leaping dust. He counted five riders. More shots rang out from their guns. Their shouting voices were heard for a moment before they were sucked away by the roaring wind.

The lead rope to the black horse became taut and hard beneath Ken's leg and he glanced to the rear to see what was holding the black back. The animal was limping. One of the bullets had struck it.

The gray horse was being slowed by the injured black. Ken judged the mounts of his enemies were fresh. They would surely run him down if the race continued for long.

Ken tossed off the coil of lead rope from the pommel and released the black. God! He hated to lose his old companion. But the gray now ran easier.

Ken positioned himself over the shoulders of the straining horse to help it carry its load most easily. He slapped the horse's neck. The space separating him from his foes began to increase.

The magnificent gray beast ran on and on, its powerful legs swinging, carrying its master into the afternoon. Ken touched the reins only rarely, to guide the steed around an especially tall dune. His pursuers fell away behind and became lost to sight in the dense, blowing dust. But Ken knew they were still there, close, riding hard, following his tracks before they could be blown away by the wind.

As the miles fell away, the gray became lathered with sweat. Its pumping breath began to rattle in its throat. The rattle grew steadily until it became a hoarse, sawing sound. Froth dripped from the horse's gaping mouth.

The driving legs slowed. The race was finished. The horse had given its heart.

Ken's anger boiled through his veins. Damn Zaldivar's men to hell. The sons of bitches had shot his black horse, then chased the gray until it was ready to fall. They would kill Ken for the promised gold. It was time they died instead.

He spurred the staggering mount on between two long, tall dunes. He circled the snout of the dune on the left and reined hard to bring the horse back along the side of

132

the sand hill. Halting, he grabbed his rifle from its scabbard and leapt down.

Ken scuttled up the steep side of the dune. The rumble of running horses reached him as he neared the top. He might be too late. He leapt to the crest.

Below him a string of horsemen raced by in the shallow valley between the dunes. The lead rider was already past Ken and fast disappearing into the dust.

The rifle jumped to Ken's shoulder. He aligned the front and rear sights of the gun on the second rider, tracked the swiftly moving target for two jumps of the horse, and fired.

The man rocked to the side as if hit by an invisible hammer. He fell from the back of his mount, rolling in a cloud of new yellow dust.

Ken instantly levered another cartridge into the firing chamber. He swung the rifle to point at the next man in line. The shot knocked the rider from his saddle.

The fourth man saw his comrades fall. He swerved his mount abruptly to the right and jabbed it hard with spurs up the nearly vertical side of the adjacent dune. Ken fired at the rider's back.

The bullet passed through the man and struck the horse in the neck. A deadly blow. The cayuse reared up from the slope of the dune, held there a moment pawing at the red sun, then fell heavily backward upon its rider, crushing the air from his lungs in a short, high wail.

Ken whirled to the last enemy. The man had reversed direction and was racing into the masking dust.

Ken lifted his rifle. The pursuit must be broken so badly that he could continue safely on to the border. He sighted down the long, iron barrel of his weapon at the center of the rider. He knew, with the assurance that only truly competent marksmen ever know, that his bullet would go exactly to the point of aim he intended.

Yet he held his finger from pressing the trigger. Maybe he had killed enough of his foes.

The rider plunged on into the screening dust of the storm and was gone.

You came to slay me for gold, but still I let you live. Go tell all the others that I'm tired of running. That death awaits all who come hunting me.

Ken dropped swiftly down the back face of the dune to the gray horse. The exhausted beast stood with splayed legs and drooping head. It did not look up as Ken picked up the reins.

Carrying his rifle and leading the tottering horse, Ken moved off with the wind, wading the rivulets of sand that coursed in all the low swales.

The darkness came and mixed like ink with the clouds of yellow dust. The last lingering memories of the heat of the day leaked away into the sky. As the high desert cooled, the wind slackened and finally died, the sand ripples lying motionless across the desert.

The sand sea grew completely silent around Ken and he halted to listen to the quietness. It was so enjoyable after the uproar of the storm. Without the wind, the dust fell back upon the earth. The stars became visible, bright and hard and close to the desert.

Ken drank deeply from his canteen, then poured the remainder of the water, nearly a half-gallon, into his hat. He held it out to the gray horse. The thirsty animal sucked up all the water with one long, noisy pull. It looked up at the man, questioning, wanting more.

"That's all, old fellow," Ken said. Gently he ran the horse's ears through his hands, as he had so often done

134

to the black horse. "You ran well today. Calleja was right. If you'd been rested like the horses of Zaldivar's men, they never would have caught you."

Ken loosened the cinch and dropped the saddle to the ground. Selecting a level spot on the sand, he spread his blankets and lay down.

Ken's head was woolly with his fatigue, and sleep came at once. The gray horse stood quiet, a weary sentinel over its young master.

In the deep reaches of Ken's sleep, the dreams came. The men he had fought and killed rose like phantoms from the sand. Each was calling out, cursing him with the most awful profanity.

The swearing voices began to jumble and garble one another to such an extent that Ken couldn't make out one word. As he watched the angry men in his dream, he felt a great and heavy sadness at the deaths he had caused. Worse yet, he knew not one, nor had he any enmity for the many men who had perished before his gun.

The phantom men faded away and Ken saw again Anya. She was crying out to him in a fright-filled voice, but the bellowing shouts of the big brown woman drowned her out. Ken jerked awake with the frightened face of the girl in his mind. What was she trying to tell him? That she was in trouble and wanted his help? Yet, when he had had the opportunity, he had ridden away without finding out the truth.

Ken finally went back to sleep. But often Anya's voice rose up in his remembrances, begging, haunting him.

The tumbling dust clouds hid Larrway as his running horse drew away from his pursuers. Captain Tamargo

135

began to worry when he lost sight of the American. He looked to the side at Sergeant Quillón racing swiftly near him across the dunes.

Quillón was leaning far forward over his horse. His stare was fastened upon the string of tracks in the sand. He raised his whip, trying to drive his mount to a faster speed.

Tamargo had ridden many times with the tracker after outlaws. Always they rode in a daring, headlong chase, and always the wanted man was run down and captured, or killed if he fought. Tamargo thought they might be making a mistake this time by running so hard after Larrway.

The gringo had safely traveled a thousand miles, avoiding uncounted ambushes and an even greater number of enemies. He had been snared one time. He had proven himself a deadly fighter and broken free. Five dead men had been found behind him.

Larrway, like the wolf that had once felt the bite of a trap's steel jaws, wouldn't be caught so easily again. If caught, he would be tough to kill. Tamargo thought Larrway would try to outdistance the soldiers, but failing that, he would halt and lay an ambush of his own for those who threatened him.

Tamargo considered ordering Quillón to slow and be more cautious. However, he hesitated, not wanting the huge reward for Larrway's capture to slip from his grasp. Never again would such an opportunity present itself. A plan came to him.

The squad of men entered a zone of large dunes and Tamargo slowed his mount by a slight tightening of the bridle reins. He gradually fell back. The tall dunes offered excellent places for Larrway to pull an ambush. Let Quillón and the other men forge ahead. Then, should

Larrway actually be waiting, they would be the first targets of his gun. Tamargo would have time to draw back and devise a new plan to capture the American. The captain dropped into last position with a satisfied grunt.

The horses grew hot. Sweat formed on the straining animals and clotted foam was flung from their heaving flanks.

The string of soldiers came to an area of dunes that were low, elongated hills. They poured into a hollow between two of the ridges of sand.

Tamargo heard the spiteful crack of a heavily charged rifle. Ochoa pitched from the saddle and rolled on the ground. In a fraction of a second the next man in the line of riders crumpled and fell from his running horse. The ambush had happened fast, the perfect trap.

Tamargo yanked the reins of his horse into his lap and brought the animal to a sliding stop. He spun the horse and began to whip it back the way they had just come. He threw a hurried look behind.

A man with a rifle in his hands stood in the wind-driven dust on top of the southerly dune. Larrway. The gringo fired at the soldier who was trying to drive his mount up the steep face of a dune. The horse and its rider tumbled back into the hollow.

Captain Tamargo bent low and drew blood from his horse with his spurs. He knew that he was still well within rifle range of such an expert marksman. He braced himself for the strike of the bullet that would kill him.

No shots came. Then Tamargo's horse, lunging powerfully, carried him into shelter behind a dune.

Tamargo continued on into the storm for three hundred yards. In a swale between two sand hills, he jumped

F.M. PARKER

down and hobbled his mount. The beast must not be
blown away with the wind.

Tamargo yanked his rifle from its boot and scrambled
up the slope of a dune and down the back side. He
trotted through the whistling wind and the hissing, tumbling dust. Now, Larrway, you will be the one to die with
a bullet through your heart.

As he neared the ambush point, Tamargo slowed and
came in warily. Quillón had escaped. He would be stalking Larrway. He and Tamrago would catch the gringo
between them.

Tamargo squinted into the gritty lash of the storm.
Three dark forms lay scattered along the gully bottom.
One was the large mound of the dead horse on top of its
rider. Dust had already built long, narrow drifts of sand
behind each of the bodies. Not one man moved or made
a sound.

Tamargo checked the range to the place where the
rifleman had stood while he shot, and then looked at the
nearness of the bodies. Larrway was astoundingly accurate and quick with a rifle. Quillón had escaped only
because Larrway probably hadn't gotten into position
quickly enough to shoot him before he rode past. But
how had he himself escaped? He had been an easy target. Had the gringo's rifle jammed? Perhaps sand had
blown into his eyes. For whatever reason, Tamargo had
ridden safely away with his life. His luck was running
strong.

The captain circled the killing ground, always keeping
a tall ridge of sand between him and the corpses. Southwest of the ambush point in a somewhat protected place,
he discovered one horse track nearly full of sand. Though
he searched diligently, he found not the slightest trace of

additional signs. Tamargo was disappointed. He had hoped to fight the American.

"Captain Tamargo, this is Quillón. Don't shoot." The tracker emerged on his horse from the dust-filled air south of Tamargo. "Larrway didn't stay here long," the sergeant said. "I found tracks downwind from here for about a quarter-mile or so before I lost them."

"Good. Let's see to our men." Tamargo led off, retracing his steps to the ambush point. They went from one crumpled body to another.

"All dead," said Tamargo. "I'll mark this place and we shall return later for the corpses."

Taking Ochoa's rifle, Tamargo climbed the tallest dune to its peak and drove the long weapon halfway into the sand. His bandanna was fastened to the stock so that it flapped and fluttered in the wind. The place would be easily found, if the storm didn't blow so long as to bury the marker with smothering sand.

Tamargo retrieved his mount, and he and Quillón turned away from the brunt of the storm. Larrway wasn't going to be taken by a group of men. But two expert marksmen could trail him and shoot him while he camped, or from a safe distance with a rifle. Tamargo and Quillón would be those men. And they wouldn't have to share the reward with anybody else.

The captain stared down the dusty windcourse, watching the rivulets of sand pursuing one another in neverending currents.

Larrway had run with the wind throughout the chase. The captain didn't think he would change that pattern. He spoke to his horse and the animal started off with the storm pounding its rump. In a day, or maybe two, with Quillón's help, he would find the American's tracks. And then he would find the American.

139

13

THE EARTH REVOLVED AND THE COLDEST moment of night arrived upon the Mapimí desert.

Boom! The large sand dune near Ken emitted an earth-jarring drum sound, as if a giant cannon had fired from within the center of the mound.

The dune adjacent to the first responded with a mighty bass boom. Two others drummed out in deep bass voices, then half a dozen, and immediately scores more. The explosions of sound rippled outward over the wasteland in an ever-widening wave.

The gray horse stomped the ground and whinnied in a shrill, frightened voice. It began to tremble and yank at its tether.

Ken jumped from his blanket and hurried to the horse before it could break free. He hugged the muscular neck and talked in the beast's ear. The horse quieted and its trembling subsided. Its head came up and its ears flared as it listened to the strange, unearthly sound. If the man wasn't afraid, then why should it be? Still it pressed close against the man.

140

The symphony of drums continued minute after minute. Each dune possessed its own rhythmic cadence, booming out to the night sky once each second or two.

Ken's ears vibrated with the incessant but not unpleasant harmonic booming of the world's largest bass drums. He placed his hands over his ears to soften the volume, but the sound came through the very earth itself to enter his body.

He wondered what musical magic of the dunes caused the orchestration of sound. Perhaps it was some kind of internal shifting or settling of tons of sand inside the dunes so recently remolded by the wind storm and cooled by the night. Had he and the horse somehow triggered the avalanche of sound?

The booming gradually ceased, as if the unseen drummers had grown weary one by one. The last lonely boom echoed far off to the west.

Ken didn't return to his blanket. He climbed to the top of the dune that had started the noise and watched the frozen waves of the vast sand sea become gilded with the bright colors of the morning sun.

He ranged his eyes to their limits out over the wasteland, scouring the dune tops for the movement of an enemy. Nothing stirred to be caught against the rising sun. He saddled and rode slowly in the direction of the range of black mountains many miles to the west.

Lorca lay across the neck of his horse, pinning the animal to the ground. The horse's legs were tied with a knot that could be freed with one jerk. Beyond a few feet, man and horse were completely hidden in the tall stalks of ripe wheat.

Lorca had crept into the field in the dark hour before

the coming of the dawn. The trained horse had lain down at his command. Now Lorca patiently waited.

He chuckled softly to himself in anticipation of the swift action that would soon begin. Everything was planned and ready. His two comrades were hidden in the rocks at the mouth of the valley. They would protect him from pursuit if the men with the many wives chased him with guns.

For two days Lorca had concealed himself in the lava boulders and cactus on the side of the mountain and spied upon the comings and goings of the people of Janos. At the moment the villagers were asleep. Their tiny settlement consisted of a large church, two other common buildings, and fifteen houses, ranging from small to quite large. All the structures were grouped on a long bench on the north side of the valley above the creek.

Lorca watched the faint light of a false dawn come and then shortly die, allowing the night another few minutes to hold the valley captive with its darkness. Then, in the clear desert air, the true daylight came swiftly. The broad sea of sand dunes lying three miles to the east, turned silver, bringing the morning sun from the distant land of Tejas, the land the Americans had stolen from Mexico and now called Texas.

Men came from several of the houses and began to harness teams of horses in the corrals. Soon they were driving the teams off to various fields where they had ceased work the evening before. Other men came outside and, shouldering shovels and picks, went toward the creek at the upper end of the fields. Lorca had previously observed the men laboring there to strengthen the diversion dam that shunted water from the creek into the long canals that fed the irrigation ditches.

Women appeared outside and children followed them,

some complaining, but most dashing about and shouting in high good spirits. One of the bigger girls, more of a young woman, began to sing. Lorca didn't understand the English, but the lovely soprano voice with its full, round notes greatly pleased him.

Lorca widened the narrow opening through the stalks of wheat so he could better scrutinize all the girls. However, his eyes always came back to the one singing. He couldn't see if she was pretty. But the sun had made her yellow hair pure gold.

The women and children came along the paths on the borders of the fields. The singing girl in her lively mood had moved to the lead of the group that came in Lorca's direction.

The girl drew closer and Lorca saw her face was very lovely. He chuckled, almost loud enough to be heard. He couldn't stop himself. Such good fortune was his, that the girl should walk right to him.

Two men with rifles in their hands came from the small house at the extreme edge of the village. They picked up saddles from where they rested on a pole fence and carried them toward a corral of horses.

Lorca's mouth tightened. He recognized the two men. They had ridden out the previous morning to tend a small herd of forty or so cows that grazed on the scant stand of bunchgrass growing on the mountainside. Those two hombres would soon be mounted and could give pursuit.

The corral gate opened and the men galloped out and began to climb up and around the mountain to the south. Lorca relaxed. He chuckled again, without sound this time, for the girl was near enough to hear him.

Lorca reached out and tugged the knot loose on the rope binding the horse's feet. The animal sensed the freedom. Its half-ton body surged erect. Lorca sprang up beside it and yanked himself into the saddle.

The girl stopped instantly with the other women. They stood shocked, frozen into statues at the sudden appearance of the horse and rider so close in the wheatfield.

"Run! Run," an old woman screamed. "Run for the house. He's a bandit."

Other women and children took up the warning cry. All of them pivoted around and broke into shrieking flight toward the village.

The paths became clogged, the faster runners crowding the slower. People veered aside, scattering like a flushed covey of quail into the fields.

Lorca spurred his mount, and like a large predator, he bore down upon the girl that had sung so sweetly. The distance separating them closed swiftly. A scared young boy darted into the path of the charging horse and was knocked down and trampled.

The girl heard the swelling sound of the horse's thudding hooves and the child cry out. She threw a frightened glance to the rear. The bandit was leaning out to the side and reaching for her. She swerved steeply to the right.

Lorca reined his mount hard in a short half-circle and sent it again at the girl. He greatly enjoyed the game. So intent was he upon his pursuit of the golden girl that he no longer heard the shouts and screams of the women calling for help.

The girl zigzagged and doubled back in a determined effort to escape, but each time she changed directions, the nimble-footed horse cut her off. Then the girl made a desperate sprint for the village, her hair streaming out behind.

Like an arrow, the horse darted forward beside the running girl. Lorca stretched out a long arm, clamped a

144

hold on the long hair, and pulled the girl toward him. His other arm reached down, caught her beneath the arms, and scooped her up. Swinging her onto the saddle in front of him, he spurred the horse to the top of its speed in the direction of the open end of the valley.

The beast hurtled across the wheatfield, the thrashing hooves sending the ripe kernels of grain flying like bird shot from a gun. The horse leapt an irrigation ditch and raced over the baked surface of the desert above the irrigated land.

Two miles later, Lorca reached the mouth of the valley and turned south onto the broken land lying between the sand dunes and the mountain.

Two horsemen came from behind a ridge of lava and fell in at Lorca's rear. One of the men shouted out happily at him.

"Bravo, Lorca! Bravo! You have made us very rich."

The two men pulled their rifles and followed after Lorca at a distance of a couple hundred yards. Lorca relaxed. All was safe.

Lorca slid onto the horse's rump behind the saddle and lifted the girl into his vacated seat. He wrapped his arms around her slender body to hold her from falling from the galloping horse.

The girl swayed against the man with each lunge of the horse, and Lorca's blood warmed at her touch and coursed more swiftly through his veins. He felt an irresistible urge, and his hand rose to fondle the firm young mound of the girl's breast.

She cried out and grasped his fingers and tried to wrench them away from her. But Lorcas's hard-muscled hand gave not a bit and he chuckled deep in his chest at her struggles.

The girl turned to plead with her captor to leave her

alone. Until this moment she had not looked at him closely. She shrank back at the sight. The bandit's eyes, within inches of her own, were black and oily and sunken deeply into their sockets like those of a skull. She whirled back to the front without speaking. Her muscles stiffened. She tried to shut her mind to the hand kneading her breast.

Lorca's laugh faded and he became very quiet in the wonderment of the thought of how it would be to have five, eight, maybe twenty such white and gold women as wives. He had heard the men of the valley had that many. He knew a man would never grow tired of loving them.

However, as much as he would like to keep the woman, he was not a rich man, and sell her he must. He had already made the agreement with Jacobo Jiménez, Zaldivar's man who was waiting in Chihuahua.

The thousands of pesos Lorca would receive would be sufficient to last him a very long time without working, and to buy him women as he needed them.

He looked behind at his two cohorts. It was a good thing they would reach Chihuahua today even if it would be very late for if they had to spend the night on the desert, he might have to fight his companions to keep the girl safe. And they were very strong fighters.

Lorca's hand slid down the smooth, flat plain of the girl's stomach. It was a very long ride to Chihuahua.

The terrified cries of the women and children raced up the brush-covered mountainside and reached Joakim Wilander and his brother Asael. Both men instantly stopped and twisted to look down into the valley.

To their horror, they saw a group of villagers running in pell-mell flight toward the houses. One girl had been cut off from the other people by a horseman, and he was closing swiftly to catch her.

"That's Johanna!" shouted Joakim, recognizing his sister across the distance by her blue dress. "She needs help. Ride, Asael, ride!"

He spun his mount and with reckless speed tore back down the steep slope of the mountain. Asael spurred hard behind him.

Joakim saw the horseman in the wheatfield catch Johanna, lift her up in front of him, and speed away, angling south along the edge of the valley to pass at the longest possible distance from the men of the village.

The brothers struck the valley bottom and hurtled along the road beside the creek.

"A bandit took Johanna," Joakim shouted out to a group of men running up the road in the direction of the houses.

Joakim and Asael rushed on. At the edge of the sand dunes, they turned along the trail of the kidnapper. To Joakim's surprise, he saw far in the lead three horses and riders. The danger to Johanna had escalated. It might be impossible for Asael and him to rescue her from that strong a force. The calvacade ahead rode around a cactus-studded point of the mountains and were lost to sight.

The brothers charged onward. As they drew near the spot where the Mexicans had disappeared from view, Joakim's eyes scoured the rocks and cacti.

Something moved, just a flicker. Joakim reined hard, drawing his brother with him in the beginning of a wide circle that would soon have them safe far out in the sand.

A crash of distant rifle shots erupted. Asael's horse staggered and fell. Asael hurled himself clear, rolling on the sandy ground. The horse tried to rise, then collapsed, kicking away the last flutter of its life.

Bullets sang their deadly whining songs around Joakim as he whirled his cayuse and spurred it toward Asael. He braced himself in the saddle. Asael reached out and grabbed his brother's arm. He ran two steps beside the speeding horse, then vaulted upward. He swung onto the horse's rump behind Joakim.

Joakim spurred his mount savagely. Asael gripped the horse with his legs. The stalwart beast bunched its legs beneath it and lunged away, carrying the two men.

The sound of rifle fire fell away behind. Joakim began to think they would be able to ride clear of the hail of bullets.

His mount stumbled. Still, for a moment, it seemed to catch itself, holding its footing, running on. Then it sank to its knees and slid on the sand. The two men were thrown, spilling across the ground.

"Asael, are you okay?" called Joakim, climbing erect on wobbly legs.

"Barely. What bad luck. Twice a horse has been shot out from under me." He climbed painfully to his feet.

"You mean good luck," Joakim said. "You could've been killed. But I believe the Mexicans were shooting at the horses. They are the larger targets." He hurriedly checked the place where the rifle shots had come from. Men came out of the rocks and went behind the point of the mountain. A few seconds later, they reappeared mounted on horses and rode off at a swift gallop. Joakim saw a flash of Johanna's dress, then all that was visible was a string of fresh dust.

He yanked his rifle from the dead horse and examined the firing mechanism. He sighted down the barrel. "Everything seems in working order," he said. "Let's go get your gun."

"Why didn't the bandits finish us off?" asked Asael as they ran.

"They didn't want to risk their necks by coming back to fight us out here in the sand dunes where we'd have as much cover as they did. They killed our horses and put us on foot. Now they think we'll just go home. They're damn wrong."

They came to Asael's horse. Joakim caught hold of the saddle pommel and heaved powerfully, partially rolling the horse onto its back. Asael pulled his rifle free of the scabbard.

Joakim spoke to his brother. "Go get some men from Janos. Hurry. I'll trail the kidnappers wherever they go. Bring me a horse."

"They'll ride off and leave you. Or hide their tracks in rocky ground and you'll lose them."

"Not this time. We've never been so close to them. I'll keep up with them as best I can. If they make a mistake, I'm going to shoot the hell out of them."

"Don't let Johanna be hurt," cautioned Asael.

"I'll try not to let that happen. Now run. You're only about four miles from the village. Bring eight or ten men. No more than that. Someone needs to stay with the women."

"We don't seem to be much protection for our women," Asael said in an angry, disparaging voice.

"No more talk. Run like you've never run before. Watch for the signs I'll leave for you."

"Good hunting," said Asael. He broke into a swift run to the north across the sand dunes.

Joakim took the undamaged canteen from the dead horse and slung it over a shoulder. Trotting, trailing his rifle, he ran along the tracks of the horses that carried his sister away.

14

THE GRAY HORSE CARRIED LARRWAY ACROSS the forlorn stretch of desert dunes toward the range of lava mountains. The gray plodded slowly. It was weak from the hard chase of the day before, and now the lack of water. At times Ken climbed down and walked to relieve the mount of the burden of his weight.

He often checked behind for foes in pursuit. But only he and the horse existed in all the lonely, solitary world of the yellow sand sea.

The miles slid past beneath the weary feet of the horse and a valley became visible, cutting into the stony flank of a mountain. Ken set a course that would take him directly to the valley, the most likely place to find water in this desert land.

As Ken drew near the mountain, he could make out a small green area on the floor of the valley. He hoped it was a meadow. A tiny, darker green dot in the center of the plot might be a tree. A grassy meadow in a desert meant water was probably available close to or at ground surface. If the tree was a cottonwood, that also meant water because that species loved to keep its feet wet. But a cottonwood's long, probing roots could reach down forty, fifty feet to obtain the life-sustaining liquid.

Ken came off the desert in the heat of the midday sun. When he drew closer to the valley, he judged with more certainty that the green area was indeed a meadow. He began to climb the bouldery alluvial fan, debris dropped there during those rare times when the creek flooded. He lost sight of the meadow for a quarter mile behind a curve in the stream channel.

Ken came once again into sight of the meadow. As he halted to survey the terrain lying before him, the shrill cry of a woman startled him. He skimmed a quick look ahead.

A gnarled, old cottonwood tree, leaning at a precarious angle, grew in the center of the meadow. Three horses were tied beneath the tree. A Mexican lay in its shade. A second Mexican and a young woman, with astounding white skin, stood near a pool of water where a spring gushed up from the earth. The man was playfully splashing water upon the woman. He glanced up and looked at Ken.

The man under the tree arose. Another man climbed down from a lookout on a high ridge of rocks. Both walked to stand near the edge of the spring. From their leisurely, unconcerned movement, Larrway knew they had observed his approach for some time.

Lorca and his men had quickly ridden to the south between the base of the mountain and the desert. In the hot middle of the day, the leader veered to the side and guided the way into the mouth of a shallow valley.

"The caballos must be rested," Lorca called out, "and there is water just up ahead." They had halted the first pursuit of the men from Janos. An hour or more would be needed for the farmers to organize and again chase him and his companions. There was time to rest for a short period before they began the long, hard ride over the sand desert to Chihuahua.

The Mexicans stopped their sweating horses beneath a large cottonwood tree near a spring that gushed up and flowed for fifty feet or so across a small meadow before it vanished back into the dry earth. Lorca swung the girl to the ground and jumped down.

"Pascual, let the caballos cool a little and then water them. Alvaro, climb up on that ridge of rock and watch for our enemies."

Lorca caught Johanna by the hand. "Come, little white dove, let's drink the cold water of the spring. That will be very pleasant on such a hot day as this."

He drew Johanna with him to the spring. "Drink," he ordered.

Johanna lowered her hot face into the water welling up from the ground. She raised her head and shook off part of the wetness.

Lorca drank beside her, sucking noisily at the water.

"A lone rider is coming from the east," Alvaro called from his perch on the ridge.

"How far away?" asked Lorca.

"A half mile or less."

"Come down and stand with Pascual and me when the rider gets close," Lorca said.

"All right," Alvaro replied.

Lorca wondered who the man might be and why he was in such a remote place. However he felt no alarm. There was nothing to worry about from a single rider.

He idly began to splash water at the white girl. She drew back in fear of him, and also in anger. Lorca laughed. If I could but think of a way, I would keep you, he thought.

A few minutes later, Lorca saw the unknown horseman come into view down the valley. He dried his hands on his pants and loosened his pistol in its holster.

He stepped close to Johanna and clamped a hold on her arm. "Silence," he said in English. "Don't talk." He squeezed her arm roughly and she cried out with pain.

"Silence!" he hissed.

Lorca raised his voice and called out to the unknown vaquero. "Ho, *amigo,* what are you doing in such a nowhere place?"

Larrway lifted his hand and touched the brim of his sombrero in greeting. For a brief moment he looked at the girl and saw the expression of fear on her face. He didn't like that. He swung his attention and concentrated all of it on the Mexican men.

"Hombres," he said, endeavoring to speak Spanish without an accent, "I'm looking for water for my horse." He stepped down to the ground. It was too late to retreat. Besides his tongue was dry and thick in his mouth from his thirst, and the horse was ready to drop. He must have some of the precious water bubbling up just a few yards away. Even if he had to kill for it. He moved toward the men and the woman.

Lorca's face hardened with suspicion as the stranger advanced on him.

"Go somewhere else for your water," ordered Lorca in a hostile voice. "This is but a little spring and we have first claim on it."

"My horse must have water now, and this is the only water within miles as far as I know," replied Larrway.

Lorca's anger boiled up hotly. The man was a nuisance and interrupting his enjoyment of the girl.

153

"Go back the way you came from," Lorca said.

"I can't do that. I'm headed to Cuidad Juárez," Larrway said.

Lorca noted something odd about the man. Wasn't there a gringo accent? And his skin, though heavily burned by sun and wind, was much too light in color.

Johanna also heard the American tongue in the man's speech. His eyes were not black but some shade she couldn't yet determine because of his distance. She needed help to escape from the bandits. He might be her last chance. Her heart hammered hopefully. Would the man have the courage to stand against the kidnappers? She started to call out her plight to him.

Lorca sensed the girl's decision to speak. He squeezed hard on her arm. She winced with pain and her hands flew sideways, fluttering like white wings.

Larrway felt the wolf rise in his heart at the ruthless treatment of the girl. She was trying to ask for his assistance. He believed the girl at Zaldivar's hacienda had attempted the same thing, and he had left without giving her help. I won't make that mistake this time, thought Larrway. He concentrated on the man holding the girl, but watched the other two Mexicans from the corner of his eye. Three guns were against him. Should all of them be drawn at one time, then he would die. To survive, he had to kill the leader quickly and then bluff the others, if that was possible.

Lorca's glittering black eyes stared out from their deep sockets. Gringo, you are but one man, and we are three. I'll show you that I can do what I want. He squeezed harshly again on the girl's arm. See, gringo.

A heartbreaking whimper came from deep within Johanna. At the pitiful cry, an icy rage ran through Larrway.

He drew his pistol and shot the man through the bridge of the nose.

Johanna felt the bandit jerk under the horrible impact of the bullet hitting. His hand fell loose from her arm. She cowered down, dodging to the side, thinking the American might shoot the bandit again.

Before Lorca's body hit the ground, Ken shot the man on the right. He was driven backward and down with a bullet to the chest. The last man stood stunned as Larrway's gun rotated to point directly at him. He hadn't yet begun to draw his weapon, not believing that one man would attack three.

Ken knew the Mexican was his to shoot, and should be shot for what he had done. But he held his finger from pressing the trigger of his pistol.

Johanna saw the American wasn't going to slay the bandit. She feared for the future with the man alive. He would come again to Janos and carry her away.

"Kill him! Kill him," she screamed at Larrway. "He has to die."

"The fight is over," Larrway said in a flat, tired voice. "I don't want to kill another man."

"Then give me your gun and I will," Johanna cried. "You don't know what it is to be kidnapped." She moved toward Lorca's body and reached for his gun.

Larrway ran forward, lifting his hand to force the girl to stop. He couldn't allow her to kill the man.

A thunderous bolt of pain exploded in Ken's skull. The sickening vibrations of the blow careened around his brain. He thought the bones of his head were flying outward. Pain tore at his nerve endings, singeing them with torturous agony.

Earth and sky spun giddily across Ken's vision. His eyes went out of focus. He felt himself falling. All the

155

blackness of all the nights of the world squeezed into his head. He crashed to the ground.

Ken never heard the rifle shot that knocked him spinning. Nor the second shot that pierced the bandit's neck, half severing his spinal cord and flinging him to the ground where he flopped and cavorted like a maimed crow.

Johanna paced the floor waiting for Bishop Blackseter to arrive. She looked at Joakim sitting near the door and also waiting. His face had never lost its troubled expression since he had come out of the rocks and discovered that he had shot the man who had saved his sister from the kidnappers.

"It was not your fault," Johanna said to Joakim, trying to lessen his self-reproach. "You couldn't have known."

"He's dying," Joakim said, his voice hoarse with his sorrow and fear at what he had done.

"The bishop has the healing power. He'll lay his hands on this man and bring him to health. Just wait and see."

"I don't think so, Johanna. He hasn't moved since he fell yesterday. The long, jarring ride being held on the horse also hurt him. I don't think he will recover."

Joakim's stricken eyes evaluated the blanket-covered form of the unconscious man on the bed. The bullet had struck him on the right side of the head above the temple. When Joakim had run up to him immediately after the shooting, the white bone of the man's skull lay exposed, the skin torn apart and flung back by the horrible power of the speeding rifle bullet. Then the blood had come.

Elder Nystrom, the person with the nearest skill to a physician in the valley, had cleansed the wound and sewed the flaps of skin and flesh back together. He had shaken his head sadly. Head injuries made the most unpredictable wounds.

Nystrom had spoken to Johanna and Joakim. "The sooner he comes to consciousness, the better, for that will mean less damage has been done to the brain."

"Bishop Blackseter is coming from the church," Johanna said. The bishop always went to the holy place to pray before he practiced the laying on of hands to heal. Johanna hoped he had made a good, strong prayer.

Bishop Blackseter halted at the door and removed his hat. He glanced inquiringly at Johanna and Joakim. The Wilanders were the most stubborn and unruly family in all the valley. They were very hard to endure, sometimes resisting some of the tenets of the church. The bishop clenched his teeth. Nilo Wilander, one of the three brothers, had run off with the bishop's new bride before he had lain the first night with her.

"Have you thought about your request of this morning?" Blackseter asked. "Do you still want me to try to help the stranger?"

Joakim nodded. "Please come in. I think he will die without some help to heal."

"Very well. I will lay on the hands. But I promise nothing."

The bishop placed his hat on the table and dragged a chair near the man's body. He folded back the bedcover, baring the young man to the waist. The fellow was much younger than the bishop thought he would be after hearing the tale of the killing of the bandits. He was hardly more than a boy. He was leanly sinewed, almost gaunt, with his bones showing through his skin.

"Come close and lend me your strength," Blackseter said.

Brother and sister dragged chairs close so that their knees touched the bed.

Bishop Blackseter reached out and laid the palm of his left hand on the man's heart. His right hand, cupped, was placed over the grievous head wound.

"Make no sound," said the bishop. He closed his eyes and leaned forward over the stranger.

For many long hours the battered brain in the bullet-damaged skull had hung in a cold pit of liquid black and fought to remain alive and heal itself. Now it sensed a wave of potent, life-strengthening energy flooding through it. It drew back from where it hovered near the bottom of the pit and began to surface toward full consciousness.

With the awakening of his brain, Larrway felt the pain. Oh, God! The pain. His skull was broken open and someone was pouring molten lead into it. Larrway's body trembled with the intensity of the agony.

The mind reached out through the pain to test the remainder of the body, and found the heart beating weakly and the lungs moving feebly.

The brain struggled to override the damage done by the horrible wound. It ordered the body to live.

The heart gathered strength and the blood increased its sluggish pace in the arteries. The lungs inflated, sucking deeply of the air. Ken came to complete consciousness in one swift surge up from the cold black hole.

The bishop felt the man's life force build and build, swiftly, geometrically. Never had he sensed such strength, such vitality in a man.

He looked at the worried countenances of the Wilander brother and sister. "He will not die," the bishop said.

"Oh, thank you," cried Johanna.

"I did nothing," said Blackseter, and believed it.

158

"Whether a man lives or dies lies within himself. This man is immensely strong."

The bishop felt movement in the man's body and quickly looked down. A pair of blue eyes stared up at him with a hard, questioning expression.

"Who are you?" asked Larrway. He reached up and brushed the bishop's hands from his body.

Bishop Blackseter studied the alert eyes of the man. How improbable this was, one minute unconscious and the next fully awake. More than that, threatening. He's even stronger than I originally thought. An undecipherable worry came to life in the bishop. Somehow this young man was going to have a great impact on the bishop's settlement of Janos. What was that impact going to be?

Ken scrutinized the broad man with the large hands, a man who would be very strong in a fight. Why had his hands been on Ken? Who was he? Ken rolled his eyes and saw the girl who had been at the spring. The one who had wanted to kill the third bandit. Had she?

"Where am I?" asked Ken.

"You are in Janos. Where we live." She swept her hand to include the older man and a much younger man beside her. "And where many others live. My name is Johanna Wilander. This is Bishop Blackseter, and this is my brother Joakim. What is your name?"

"I've never heard of Janos," Ken said, ignoring the question and scanning the yellow-haired people. Were they friends or enemies? It was strange to find blonde people in this land of brown-skinned, black-eyed inhabitants.

"What happened to me?" asked Ken.

"I'm what happened," Joakim said. "I shot you. I was crawling up on the bandits while they rested at the spring.

I saw you ride in and thought you were one of them. I'm very sorry."

"And the man I didn't kill?"

"I shot him. He's dead," Joakim said.

"How far and in what direction are we from the spring?" Ken felt disoriented.

Joakim reflected a moment and then spoke. "About twenty miles north from the spring."

"You brought me a very long ways."

"Yes. And with each step we thought you would die."

"What is your name?" questioned Blackseter.

Ken decided the people were friendly. "Ken Larrway," he answered. He noted no recognition of the name.

"Welcome to Janos," Blackseter said. He picked up his hat and moved to the door.

"Thank you, Bishop," Johanna said.

"My thanks too," said Joakim.

"I did nothing that requires thanks," responded the bishop. He left the house.

Ken looked quizzically at Johanna and Joakim. What am I missing about what has happened here? He let the question go.

"I'm very thirsty," Ken said. As he thought of water, he quickly asked, "What about my horse?"

"The gray is being well taken care of," Joakim replied.

"I'll get you a large drink," said Johanna. She went hurriedly from the room.

Joakim reached and touched Ken on the arm. "I'm glad you're better. Thank you very much for helping Johanna."

"Like the bishop said, I did nothing that requires thanks," Ken said.

"She's the first girl we have ever gotten back from the

160

bandits. We wouldn't have done it this time if you hadn't helped."

"Women have been kidnapped from your village before?"

"Several times, but we'll talk later about that. You should rest. Here is Johanna with your water."

Ken propped himself up on an elbow. The pain in his head soared, but it was tolerable. He drank long and deeply, glassful after glassful from the pitcher of cold water.

His arms began to tremble from weakness. He wasn't as strong as he thought.

"I think I'll rest now," Ken said to Johanna and Joakim. "May we talk when I wake up?"

He went to sleep as they nodded agreement to his question.

15

KEN LAY AND LOOKED OUT THE OPEN DOOR at the honey-yellow morning that filled the valley of Janos. He had woken a few minutes earlier, but hadn't stirred, content to merely watch the simple, gentle happenings within his view.

At the edge of the yard, a flower bed was crowded with red hollyhocks turned upward like a thousand open throats to the blue sky. A hummingbird, a half-ounce of blurred movement, flitted from one flower to the next. The bird hesitated for a bare second to perch on an unopened flower bud. Its brilliant orange-red throat patch and the iridescent brown of its back and sides rivaled the rainbow.

Then in a wink, the tiny hummer was airborne, the soft feathers of its wings stroking the air at sixty beats per second as it hovered over a hollyhock. Its needle-billed head, designed to reach deeply into flowers, flicked from side to side as it appraised the depth of the blossom. It dipped its slender bill down inside the flaring petals and drew up the sweet nectar. Filled with the offering of the

162

flowers, the hummingbird vanished so quickly it seemed to leave, just for an instant, a small void there in the space above the hollyhocks.

A songbird began to warble in a delightful series of trilling notes from the roof peak of the house. Ken smiled, and the smile expanded to a laugh, and he basked in the peacefulness around him. How wonderful this all was after the hard travel and the battles that had lain between here and Mexico City.

He sat up and swung his feet to the floor. At the change in position, pain rose in his bruised head, throbbing with each beat of his heart. Swiftly the pain faded to only a trivial reminder of his wound, then even that ache disappeared. Like all young animals, the tide of his life ran strong and vital, and he was healing cleanly and quickly. At the feeling of his growing healthiness, he sensed a greater awareness of life than he ever had before.

His clothes, freshily washed and ironed, and his money belt were on a table nearby. His pistol hung in its holster on the back of a chair. Someone had cleaned the dust from the weapon and he saw a thin film of oil on the iron. Even his boots had been brushed free of dust. Ken silently thanked the unknown person who had shown such thoughtfulness.

He pulled on his trousers and went to open the second door of the bedroom. A living room lay before him. The furniture showed much use. He could see the corner of the kitchen beyond the living room. All the walls were made of stone and adobe, and painted white. Everything was immaculately clean.

Barefooted, he crossed to the front door and went outside. The valley, flanked by two lava ridges, stretched away to the east. Near its mouth, it broadened to nearly two miles in width. The flat bottomland had been broken into scores of fields from just below the village to some two miles downstream. Many people—perhaps every man, woman, and child in the village, thought Ken—seemed to be working in the fields. Beyond the valley was the vast expanse of the yellow sand dunes, extending farther than the eye could see.

The village of Janos was made up of a score or so houses constructed in a single line. Some of the homes near the middle of the town were quite large, with a peculiar pattern of apartmentlike segments, each with its own door. The segments appeared to be of different ages, as if new ones had been added over the years to the original house. The smallest homes were located on both ends of the village. All the structures showed the high skill of the builders, having straight, plumb walls and precise square-framing of the doors and windows.

A magnificent white structure, very large with a high peaked roof, sat all by itself on a rise of land above the village. A great tall steeple adorned the crest of the roof. Wide double doors stood open to give unhindered entry. A heavily trod path led up the slant of the land from the village to the door.

Ken looked up at the mighty black mountain that loomed over Janos and crowded the sky. Its topmost peaks stabbed upward in gigantic pinnacles so high the rocky crags could be nothing except the home of hermit eagles. A small grove of pine trees filled a cove on the north side of the mountain. The creek that had carved the valley headed in a deep cleft between its two largest pinnacles.

The shrill, happy cry of children erupted and Ken looked in the direction of the sound. Very young boys and girls streamed from a square building in the center of the town. The children broke into groups and ran off yelling in play. Ken saw the pale gold, almost silver hair of the tykes. A woman came from the building and gazed down across the valley at the people in the fields. School recess had begun.

The creek had been dammed at a point opposite the town. The water was diverted into two main irrigation canals, one going north and the other south. Ditches forked off the main canals and ran on the contour of the slope, traversing the higher edge of each field. Ken could see the sheen of reflected sun rays from the water in some of the fields. Men and women with shovels went along the ditches to evenly spread the precious liquid and irrigate the crops.

Directly in front of Ken at a distance of four or five hundred yards, a man, driving a horse-drawn, iron-wheeled mower, was cutting a field of fifty acres or so of ripe wheat. He had made a few passes around the border of the yellow grain.

Several women and many children walked behind the man and gathered up the mowed wheat. Using some of the wheat reeds as ties, they bound the grain into sheaves. The sheaves were then stood together on end to support one another in shocks. Each shock was capped with a layer of wheat that acted as a little thatch roof angled downward to shed rain.

Ken watched the industrious people work. Now and then, when the wind was to him, he heard the higher-toned voices of the women and children calling out to one another in good spirits.

At the schoolhouse, the teacher rang a bell and the children came running in quick obedience. They formed a line in an instant, and their tinkling voices became quiet. At a signal from the teacher, they dutifully marched back inside.

Feeling content in the serene valley, Ken went searching about the house. He thought of the people as he walked. The Wilanders seemed like kind people. But the older man, Blackseter, didn't appear amiable, and there was a tenseness between him and the Wilanders. Ken wondered what had caused that.

He found an enclosed bathing place with two tubs of water and a mirror at the rear of the house. He washed himself and shaved off his sparse, youthful beard.

He fully dressed and, feeling wonderfully clean with the fresh clothing against his skin, found a seat in the warmth of the morning sun. For a long time he sat without moving, without blinking, speculating upon the nature of his unpleasant deeds, the killing of so many men. Then he would consider and reflect upon what different actions he could have taken. Each time he could think of nothing else he could have done without letting his enemies slay him.

Ken ceased his introspection and watched the people in the fields. He began to ponder his future, but soon his eyes become heavy-lidded and he lay back and slept.

Ken snapped awake at the crunch of gravel beneath a foot. His hand stabbed down for his pistol. He rolled away from the sound, leapt to his feet, and stood, braced, taut.

A girl stared startled-eyed at him. She was poised on her toes, ready for flight.

"You scared me by moving so fast," she said in a trembly voice. "But then, I'm the one who woke you from a sound sleep. I'm sorry about that. I should have called out to you." She tossed her head as if the movement would erase the previous event and put everything right.

Ken relaxed. He recognized the girl the bandits had held prisoner at the spring. His hand came away from his side. There had been no pistol there. The gun still hung on the chair in the house. Careless of him.

He smiled at the girl, enjoying the surge of pleasure that came to him as he looked into her blue eyes framed by the blond hair protruding from under her bonnet. She was fourteen or maybe slightly older. Small freckles, like tiny rust spots, were sprinkled across her nose and the upper part of her cheeks. Ken didn't remember the freckles.

The girl untied the ribbons of her bonnet from beneath her chin and pulled the head covering off. She twirled it playfully and took a step toward Ken. "You were sleeping so soundly this morning that we didn't want to wake you for breakfast. Are you hungry?"

"Starved."

"I thought you would be, so I came to make an early lunch for you. The others will eat at the regular noon meal."

"I'll help you, if I may."

"You can watch. Come along."

As Ken followed after the girl, he glanced back at the people in the fields. They still toiled diligently at the crops. The man was continuing to mow the wheatfield with the clanking machine. The women and children were falling behind in their task of shocking the grain.

Far away on the southern horizon a line of thunderheads was being born. Wind and rain would be extremely harmful to the ripe grain, knocking it from the heads to be lost on the ground. Hail would be devastating.

Ken ate until his stomach was full, and then beyond that until gorged. Finally he pushed back his plate. Never had he consumed such delicious food.

He looked at the girl sitting across the table from him, and smiled at the lovely picture she made. "That was the best meal ever," he said.

"Well, after not eating for at least two days, I would think anything would taste good."

"That's not the only reason the food was good," Ken said. The flavor of the meal had been much enhanced by the presence of the beautiful Johanna.

"And what other reason was there?" asked the girl. Her eyes were totally guileless.

"The peacefulness and freedom of the valley," responded Ken, taking the conversation off on a tack different from his true thoughts. "You must be very happy here."

Johanna's happy countenance faded. She lifted her delicate fingers to her face in a gesture of reflection. "I know no other home, and it is peaceful most of the time. But freedom? Everyone is not as free here as you might think."

"You mean the bandits. Yes, they are a threat."

"More than bandits restrict the freedom of some of us."

Ken looked questioningly at Johanna. Some worrisome thing moved below the surface of her round blue eyes. "What do you mean?"

"Nothing. Really there is nothing." She jumped up from the table. "I must prepare the meal for the rest of the family. They will be here shortly."

She didn't want to talk at the moment. Ken could see that. That was her right. He went to the door.

The thunderheads he had seen earlier had grown and were now only a score of miles away, scudding up fast along the front of the mountain range. The bigger clouds were thick and boiling up with vigor. An especially large thunderhead was a very dark gray and shaped like a mammoth anvil. Its flatly beveled base stretched out farther than the width of the mountain range.

In the valley, the man on the mower had cut about one-half of his field of wheat. Ken could see him lifting his whip to hurry his team of horses. The women and children had made sheaves and shocked approximately one-quarter of the grain. They were hurrying at their task.

As Ken watched, the thunderheads continued to grow rapidly in the hot updrafts rising off the heated desert floor. To the south the land was disappearing, devoured by the cloud monsters. Deep within the churning clouds, yellow and orange lightning flashed back and forth like a witch's boiling caldron. Thunder rumbled.

Hearing the sound of the thunder, Johanna came to stand beside Ken. "Oh, my! The storm is coming straight at us and all the wheat isn't cut and shocked."

The people in the valley, at some signal Ken didn't see, began to leave their own land and hasten toward the wheatfield. They poured like a wave into the yellow grain from all sides. Some men had scythes and they went immediately to the standing wheat and began to swing the sharp blades. All the remaining people fell to binding sheaves and standing them in shocks.

"They'll never get it all done before the storm hits," Ken said, measuring the speed of the approaching mass of clouds.

"Yes they will," declared Johanna. "When all the people pull together, they never fail. However, I do believe Bishop Blackseter has waited until it's awfully late. I must go and help them."

She dashed across the yard and down a path toward the wheatfield. Ken tried to keep pace, but his heavy footfalls brought a thudding pain to his head and he slowed.

When he got to the field, Johanna was lost among the bending, hurrying people binding the wheat.

He stooped to the job, working as quickly as he could. Now and then he glanced at the line of thunderheads to check its nearness. Once when he looked up, Blackseter was watching him. Ken nodded to the bishop and went back to work.

Ken's hands were fast and the sheaves were quickly made. Yet each time he finished tucking the ends of the tying reeds under themselves to hold it tight, a little silver-headed boy was there to take the sheaf and race with it to a shock. Then back he darted to stand with his eyes wide with excitement as he waited for Ken to finish the next sheaf. Ken wondered why the lad had selected him to help.

Time was infinitely short to Ken, and yet also infinitely long. He was totally caught up in the communal effort and the electrical charge of the storm. For a long period, he lost track of everything except the stooping, gathering, and tying of the wheat. And the white-headed little boy waiting to grab a finished sheaf of the grain and dash off with it.

A throng of people moved with Ken over the field. One of the bent figures vied with him for the same golden wheat lying cut and waiting to be picked up and tied. Ken's shoulder struck the young woman, knocking her to the ground in the sharp wheat stubble. She cried out with pain.

Ken hastily helped her up. "I'm sorry," he said. "Are you hurt?"

"No. And it wasn't entirely your fault," she replied,

brushing some stickers from a bare arm. "I should have been more watchful."

Ken marveled at the beauty of the girl. She was about his age, slender and nearly as tall as he. Ken reached out to help her remove some straw from her clothing.

She drew back, but her eyes, large and green, held his for a moment. "Thank you, but I need no help."

"Hurry, mister," called the boy. "There's still a lot more wheat to shock."

"Who was that girl?" Ken asked, still enthralled by her beauty. He felt his heart beating a rapid tattoo high inside his ribs.

"That's Marjo."

"Marjo who?"

"Just Marjo." The boy began to dance up and down with nervous energy. "Hurry, mister."

Ken watched after the girl for a minute longer, then bent back to the task.

Ken heard Blackseter shouting. He stood erect to see what was happening.

The giant black thunderheads overhung the valley, throwing everything in deep shadow. Mighty blasts of wind rippled the patch of wheat still standing. The dresses of the women flared and flapped, pressing tightly against their bodies. The wind was filled with the scent of rain.

Blackseter called out loudly and pointed toward the village. The women and children dropped what they held and ran off in the direction of the houses. To Ken's amazement, in all the rushing hustle, families began to gather into distinct groups. The children, seeing, sensing, feeling which mother was theirs among all the blond-headed women, collected behind them like chicks behind the hen.

The men and the larger boys bore down with feverish

haste to save every head of wheat. Ken again bent his back. A few scattered drops of rain, tremendously large, began to pepper the ground. He smelled the water on the earth. Then he became lost in the work. Sheaf after sheaf formed in his hands and he stowed each safely in a shock.

Ken reached for a handful of wheat straws. A big hand scooped them up first. The man added the wheat to some he already held and deftly bound them in a tight bundle. The man began to laugh.

All around Ken, men took up the laugh and looked from one to another. They seemed not to feel the rain, which was now a cold, pounding torrent, soaking them quickly. Every stalk of wheat had been gathered. They had won, the storm beaten.

Wicked lightning flashed, blinding Ken, and thunder deafened him. The wind buffeted him, but his spirits soared with the energy of the storm. He turned his head up and laughed loudly with the men of Janos. God! What a grand feeling to be part of these people.

A hand fell on his shoulder. Joakim stood beside him. A happy smile crinkled his face. He chucked a thumb toward the village, indicating they should go.

A second man ran up close. Joakim said something and pointed at the newcomer. Thunder exploded at the same instant and the deafening cacophony drowned out his words. But Ken didn't care what the man's name was. He felt kin to every man in the valley. With Joakim's arm across his shoulders, they went off through the deluge.

Lightning seared the land as the stupendous anvil-shaped cloud discharged its electrical load like an erupting sun. The titanic bolt of raw power hammered the mountain, shaking its deepest roots. The super-charged air that the men breathed snapped and crackled with static. They burst into laughter again. The storm was angry that it had lost. But it couldn't harm the men, for they were indestructible.

The rain changed to hailstones, large as the rocks that boys throw. The men ran.

The three men halted at the door and removed their mud-caked boots. Then, dripping water, they entered the house.

Johanna came from the kitchen. She called out to Ken. "I told you the wheat would all be gotten in before the storm harmed it."

"And you were correct," Ken said. He flicked water from his eyebrows. He shivered with a chill. He grimaced as pain ran through his head.

Johanna's face clouded with concern. "How terribly thoughtless of me. Are you all right? You got out of a sickbed and then you worked as hard as any man. And now you're soaking wet."

The challenge and excitement of the battle with the storm had ended, and Ken felt his weakness. He really did need to sit down before he fell. He sagged into a chair.

"Joakim, give Ken some of your dry clothes and get him warm before he catches pneumonia," directed Johanna. "You and Asael change clothes too. While you're doing that, I'll prepare supper."

All three men turned away to do just as Johanna had said.

THE HOT SUN FELL BEHIND THE MOUNTAINS; shadows rose up from the cracks and crevices of the valley and hid Janos with shade. The heat of the day began to drift away into the heavens.

As if the disappearance of the sun had sounded a signal throughout Janos, people came out of doors from every house. They laughed and talked as they converged upon the town hall. Three men carried fiddles. One man twanged a Jew's harp between his teeth as he strolled along. Women had baskets containing cakes and cookies.

Several young women cranking on a rope windlass lifted up jugs of cider from where they'd hung chilling in the cold water of the deep public well. Others filled pitchers with the water. Then in a spritely, laughing group, they turned their sparkling faces in the direction of the town hall.

Ken walked with Johanna. Asael and Joakim had hastened on ahead and now were beside two girls, in lively conversation with them.

"Those are the Sunde sisters, Ina and Sophronia,"

174

Johanna told Ken. "Joakim and Asael are badly taken with them. Especially Joakim with Sophronia, the older one."

"She's very pretty. Will Joakim ask her to marry him?"

"She will be fifteen in two days. That's marriageable age here in Janos. Joakim would like to have her as a wife, but I don't think he will ask her. He owns no land except for an interest with Asael and me in the thirty acres our parents left to us."

Ken sensed the sadness in Johanna's voice. Did she fear for the future should her last two brothers marry? The parents of the Wilander brothers and sister had been killed by bandits several years before while on a trip to El Paso. The three brothers had raised their young sister. Now all were adults, or nearly so, and significant changes were happening.

Johanna tossed her head in that peculiar fashion that Ken had noticed she used when discarding an unpleasant thought. She looked up at him and smiled. "I will be fifteen in a little more than a year," she said.

Ken continued to stride along the street and didn't respond. He'd like to help Joakim acquire land so he would be equal to other men in the valley in competing for a woman.

"Will you dance with me first?" Johanna asked boldly.

Ken laughed out loud. "I was about to ask you for the first dance. And perhaps the second and third also, if some other fellow doesn't steal you away."

The people streamed into the town hall and in a flurry of activity speedily rearranged the furnishings of the big room. The tables were put end to end on the side opposite the door and the sweets and cold drinks placed upon them. The chairs and benches were placed along the remaining three sides of the room.

A small piano with its front to the wall was whirled around to face the people. Ken was surprised at the presence of the piano in such a remote place as Janos.

The three fiddlers and the man with the Jew's harp drew chairs near to the piano. One of the older women sat at the keyboard. The crowd found seats and all grew quiet as the fiddlers began to tune their instruments.

Ken surveyed the people of Janos. He judged the number present at a hundred or slightly more. He was struck by the color of their hair. Most were very blond. Even the darkest was only a light-auburn shade.

Never had he seen so many beautiful girls and women in such a small group of people. Most of them sat in family groups around an older man, their father. The women were very composed and their smiles subdued. The girls of the family, those on the young side of womanhood, seemed to be trying to do the smiling for all their kin.

Marjo sat on the periphery of Bishop Blackseter's huge family. She was one of the unsmiling women.

The musicians struck a chord to call the dancers to the floor. Immediately they launched into a lilting, happy tune.

Ken danced with Johanna, swinging her and promenading around the floor. She smiled up at him dimpled-cheeked and with a sparkle in her eye.

Blackseter was dancing with his wife. More couples thronged to the floor to dance to the second tune. They joked with one another as they swung by, and to accidentally bump into another person elicited only a happy, smiling nod.

Children gathered and began to dance in a corner of

the room. The little, shiny-faced boys and girls closely watched their elders and then imitated them to the best of their ability. Ken saw the white-headed boy who had helped him in the wheatfield. Too young to be self-conscious, he danced by himself, an elf doing a jig when the music was a waltz.

Ken noted an oddness about the family groups. Five middle-aged men had extremely large families with many women, varying in age from very young to those approximately the same age as the men. Half-a-dozen men in their twenties had smaller families. Many young men were by themselves and obviously unmarried.

The older men danced with the women of their families, one after the other. The bachelors, at least twenty-five in number, were concentrating their attentions on a select nine or ten of the youngest girls. These fortunate lasses—the Sunde sisters and Johanna included—radiant with smiles at their popularity, danced every tune with a different partner. The young men waited impatiently for their turn to hold the girls and guide them about the floor.

Other girls equally pretty and sitting with their fathers were never asked to dance by the bevy of eligible men. Ken saw the men deliberately pass them by without a glance. These girls followed the dancing couples with their eyes. Marjo was tapping her foot on the floor in rhythm with the music, Ken felt sorry for the girls the men avoided.

A fellow cut Johanna from Ken and spun her away among the other dancers. Ken stood stranded for a moment, then he took a glass of cold cider and went to sit with Joakim on a bench near the wall.

Joakim nodded acknowledgment of Ken's presence. Both sat and listened to the music.

Ken glanced here and there at the dancers. As his view roamed about, a lane opened and he could see the Blackseter family.

Marjo's eyes caught Ken watching her from across the room. For a brief length of time she returned his gaze. Ken felt that same rising tempo of his pulse that he had experienced upon meeting the girl during the wheat harvesting.

Marjo looked away.

Ken's disappointment quieted his excited heart. He stood up. He hadn't seen Marjo dance, not once.

"I'm going to ask one of Blackseter's daughters to dance," Ken told Joakim. "Why don't you come with me and ask one of them too. They are some of the prettiest girls here."

A strange expression passed over Joakim's countenance. He shook his head in the negative. "They . . . I . . ." Then he became silent.

"No wonder you're still a bachelor," Ken kidded. "You're afraid of these girls sitting close to their fathers." He slapped Joakim on the shoulder, crossed the floor, and stopped in front of Marjo. He bowed slightly. "Would you dance with me?"

Marjo's eyes widened in sharp surprise. She seemed rattled by the invitation. Why should she be? Ken wondered. She turned her head quickly and looked along the row of women to Blackseter. Ken glanced in the same direction.

Blackseter frowned, disapproval imprinted hard on his face. He remained motionless, as if making some kind of judgment. Then he nodded in the affirmative.

The girl rose and Ken took her by the hand. Her fingers were cold to his touch. For a moment he thought she was going to pull away from his hold, but then she relented and Ken led her onto the dance floor.

"I'm Ken Larrway," he told the girl as they picked up the rhythm of the music.

"I know. Everybody in Janos knows who you are."

"And what is your name?"

"My name is Marjo," she said. Then added, "Marjo Blackseter."

Marjo felt soft against Ken. He felt her flesh warming under his fingers. She glided in perfect, synchronized rhythm with him over the floor. Her breath fanned his face, gentle as thistledown on his cheek. He felt compelled to draw her closer, but when he tried, she stiffened and he ceased the effort.

The music ended, seemingly having lasted only a few seconds. Ken checked the musicians to see if they had a problem and had quit playing before the piece should have ended.

"I must go now," Marjo said. She started to move away.

"No." Ken's voice was rougher than he had meant it to be. His grip tightened and he held her. Something magical had happened to him. He knew that if she left him, his heart would be crippled. "One more dance, please. Mr. Blackseter won't mind."

"I think he may. You see . . ." Marjo hesitated and she looked intently at Ken. She didn't finish her statement, and her mouth set firmly.

Ken saw her struggle with some thought, then seem to make a decision. A new light came alive in the depths of her eyes. The light was dulled for a second by some uncertainty, maybe fear. Then Marjo took a deep breath and the daring glint returned.

"Yes. Another dance. The last one was most pleasant."

Ken laughed happily. He caught her by the waist and they whirled away to the new tune. He let his mind bask and revel in this moment with the woman and the music.

Ken danced with Marjo a third time. Then the music stopped.

Ken stood with Marjo waiting for the next tune to begin. When it didn't, he looked at the musicians.

The fiddlers, the Jew's-harp player, and the pianist sat staring at Ken and Marjo. When Ken turned to them, the young Jew's-harp player winked at him.

Every person in the room was watching Ken and Marjo. Blackseter was standing, his big hands balled into fists. Ken felt Marjo tremble.

With a sudden jerk, Marjo tore free of Ken's hand and ran from the dance hall.

Dumbfounded, Ken turned around slowly until he saw Joakim. He walked toward him. "What's wrong? Can't a man dance with a girl more than once in Janos?"

Johanna came into his view. She was pale, taut, her eyes moist, as if she was ready to cry.

The whole town is crazy, thought Ken. "Tell me what is going on," Ken said to Joakim.

"All right. Come with me."

Joakim walked to the door. Ken followed him outside and fell in beside him. They went into the night.

"Well?" Ken said. "What did I do wrong? What did Marjo do that was so bad?"

"Marjo is Bishop Blackseter's wife." Joakim's voice had an angry undertone.

"Wife! My God! I thought she was his daughter."

"I know you thought that. And so do all the other people, even Blackseter. Most of them won't hold what happened here tonight against you. Blackseter will, though. He's very possessive."

"But Marjo . . . she must have known the consequences. Why did she allow it to happen? I wouldn't have prevented her from leaving me."

"I don't know. It's very strange."

"I thought she wanted to dance with me."

"I think she did. I really can't explain her actions."

"If she's Blackseter's wife, then who are all the older women?"

"They are his wives. All the women around him are his wives. He has fifteen."

Ken halted and stood stock-still in the darkness. "Which one is Marjo?"

"The last one. Number fifteen." Joakim laughed, a guttural, growling sound. "He almost had a sixteenth, but my brother Nilo stole her from him within minutes after the wedding. He rode right up to Blackseter on this street as they left the church, lifted the bishop's bride up on his horse, and carried her off into the sand dunes. I hope they made it safely across to El Paso and onward to wherever he planned to go."

Ken peered at Joakim. "You must understand this better than I do. Why did Marjo do it?"

"I wouldn't think it's very pleasant being wife number fifteen."

"Will Blackseter punish her."

"Yes. He has to. She has been a disloyal wife. The first I've ever heard of in Janos."

"Will he beat her?"

"That would be the easiest punishment for her. But no, he won't do that. This must be a community punishment, a warning to all the young wives. She'll most likely be shunned for a long period."

"Shunned? What does that mean?"

"No one in the village will talk to her, or acknowledge in any manner that she exists."

"Damnation. I'll surely talk with her."

"No. I don't think you should do that. It would only make her punishment worse. And besides, how long will you be in Janos?"

Ken didn't answer. He had some thinking to do. "Do any of the other men have more than one wife?"

"Each of the five elders has several wives. All of them together have forty-seven wives. Then some of their sons have more than one wife. Those fellows were fortunate enough to have fathers who had land to give them and the water to irrigate it."

"Isn't it against the law to have more than one wife at a time?"

"In the United States it is. But we are now in Mexico."

"Why don't you have a wife?"

"There are reasons. We are the poorest family in the valley. Our father arrived last. All the water was claimed. But Blackseter and the other elders joined together and gave him thirty acres of land and enough water for it. Enough water unless it's a dry year like this one. Then we get little water to irrigate with.

"To make enough money to live, we try to run cows on the mountain. However, there's not much grass on those rocky slopes."

"So you need land before you can have a wife. Is that the rule in Janos?"

"It's not written that way. But no girl can get married without the consent of her father. The fathers listen to the bishop, and the bishop says a man must have enough land to support a family. And the competition is tough for the few eligible girls. There aren't enough for every man. You saw that tonight."

"I can see why, with some men having so many wives," said Ken.

"And the bandits steal the young women," Joakim said. "Since the kidnappings started about five years ago, we've lost twelve girls. Only Johanna was gotten back."

"I think I know what happens to those that are stolen. I saw a yellow-haired girl in Mexico City. She said her name was Anya."

"Anya! You saw Anya? Was her last name Borgeson?"

"I don't know. A Mexican woman stopped our talk before I found out."

"A girl of that name was taken from Janos last fall. Who has her? Is she all right?"

Ken again felt his shame for having left the girl a prisoner. "She's in the hands of a man named Zaldivar."

"That's the name of the man who would have bought Johanna from the bandits. One of those two you shot lived a couple of minutes and I questioned him. He told me Zaldivar dealt in slave girls and had sent the bandits here to steal one."

"A friend warned me Zaldivar was the most powerful military chieftain in all Mexico. From what you say he must also be in league with bandits. I had trouble with his sons. Now their father sends men out to kill me. I have fought them three times."

"You must have won, as you are here. I'm glad of that, regardless of what happened here tonight. How many of Zaldivar's men have you killed?"

"Too many. Far too many."

"You must be very skilled with guns."

"Luis Calleja was my instructor. I trained with him for nearly six months."

"I've heard of Calleja. They talk about him in El Paso. They say he's the best trainer in all Mexico."

"He's dead now," Ken said. He looked away to the south.

Music started up again within the town hall. Feet trod the floor. A girl laughed out above the music.

"Go back to the dance," Ken told Joakim. "I'm going to walk awhile. I've some thinking to do."

"Be careful if you go all the way to the mouth of the valley near the sand dunes. There's a guard at each side of the valley on the ridge points. They might take you for a bandit and shoot you."

"Right. I'll watch out for them if I go that far."

Feeling unsettled and troubled about Marjo, about Blackseter's wife, Ken walked into the darkness. He passed the big houses in the center of the town. Blackseter's was the largest. Ken now knew why. The man had the most wives.

Ken went down the sloping path toward the fields. At the short bridge that spanned the main canal, he stopped abruptly. Someone came out of the darkness toward him.

"Marjo, is that you?" Ken called.

"Yes, Ken. I've been waiting. I thought you might come outside. May I talk to you?"

17

EN STOOD WITH MARJO ON THE BRIDGE. HE
could hardly make out her form in the night.
The moon lay hidden below the rim of the
world and the faint starlight barely broke the darkness.

He felt pleasure at her presence, yet also concern that
Blackseter might find her with him. He didn't fear for
himself, but no more hurt should be brought down upon
the girl.

No. That wasn't correct. She wasn't a girl. Marjo was
another man's wife.

"Should you be here with me?" he asked.

"Perhaps not. Do you want me to leave?"

"I was thinking only of you."

"Then I'll stay." Marjo moved a little closer to him.
"Johanna told me you're going to a town called Los
Angeles in California."

"That is my home. I'll be leaving in a day or two."

"Do you like me?" Marjo's voice, hesitant and thin as
a ghost's, came out of the night's gloom.

Ken was silent for a few heartbeats. Then he answered
truthfully. "When I'm near you, I feel like smiling."

Marjo came with a rush into his arms. Ken held her
tightly against him. She turned her face up to him, and
her seeking lips found his in the darkness.

Marjo pulled gently away from Ken. "Please take me
to California with you. I have no money, but I'm strong
and would be no trouble."

"You're married to Blackseter."

"Yes," she said in an angry tone. "I should have run
away before I agreed to that. But I can't undo that here.
I ask you again, will you take me to California with
you?"

"I'd have to fight Blackseter. He'd never allow you to
go. I saw that in his face tonight. I might have to kill
him."

"We could simply slip away. We could leave right
now, this very moment."

"I don't think I should do that, Marjo. But let me
think about it."

"Think very hard. I can't stay here. With or without
you, I'll leave this place."

"A woman can't travel across the desert to California
alone."

Marjo started to answer, but before she could speak,
there was a sound of many voices as people came from
the town hall. The dance had ended much sooner than
normal.

Marjo turned and ran toward the village.

Ken awoke early with night still upon the valley. He
dressed and left Janos and made his way through the
brush and rocks that held strange shadowy forms. At the
top of the ridge north of town he stopped.

Far away in the south a star lost its moorings in the

immense sooty heavens and fell streaking toward the earth, where it disappeared in a final, winking flash.

Ken pondered Marjo's pleas to be taken to California with him. As he considered the probable conflict with Blackseter should he attempt to leave with the woman, Ken looked down into the valley. Not one trace of Janos was visible in the darkness, as if the village didn't exist, indeed had never existed. Was that an omen?

A thought crystallized in Ken's mind. Janos was doomed. He knew it with an iron certainty. The village was so outlandishly alien, a little white island of Americans surrounded by a nation of dark-skinned people speaking a different language. A village where a few men owned all the land and possessed most of the women. Such a place couldn't long exist. Already the strife had begun between the elders and the young men and women. Now the bandits had found the fair females. One day those ruthless men would grow dissatisfied with stealing one woman at a time and would come in force. They would capture and destroy Janos. The inhabitants would be terribly abused and killed.

A great sorrow touched Ken's soul. There were many good people in Janos. And he knew there was absolutely nothing he could do to prevent the coming death of the village.

The day arrived and hardened with hot sunlight. Two men rode from the town toward the mouth of the valley. Soon two different men returned. The lookouts stationed near the sand dunes had been relieved.

The bell in the church belfry began to ring. The people of Janos left their homes and wound a course toward the church. Ken saw Johanna come outside and stand scanning about in all directions. Ken thought she was looking for him. He headed back to town.

Ken entered the high-ceilinged church and stood against the rear wall. Nearly every pew was full, the members of each family sitting together as a group. Joakim, Asael, and Johanna were in the right rear corner. Marjo was with Blackseter's other wives in the front row of pews. She sat very erect, her chin raised. Though Blackseter's wives talked among themselves as they waited for the church service to begin, not one spoke to Marjo.

A scuffle of feet and a few whispers sounded from the open door of a room to the side of the altar. A rank of small boys and girls came marching into sight and formed a line between the pulpit and the seated adults. A man came last and took a position in front of his young choir. He raised his arms, blew a tiny pitch whistle, and brought his arms down. The children began to sing.

Ken listened to the children singing the hymn in sweet, high-toned voices. The silver-headed tyke was one of the choir. As he sang, he kept his eyes on Ken. The hymn ended and the children promptly turned and marched back through the door and out of sight.

As Blackseter rose and walked to the pulpit to start the religious service, Ken left the church and went to the Wilander corral. The gray horse watched with gold-flecked brown eyes as Ken lifted a saddle onto its back. The horse went off willingly, carrying its rider at a gallop.

Field after field was passed. Some were being irrigated, the water flowing in the furrows that ensured that every section of the land received its proper share.

At the lower end of the valley, Ken crossed the creek bed. The channel was nearly dry, the flow of water having been diverted from the creek by dams at several places. A half-mile later, the irrigated land ended, the water supply completely used up.

He looked back across the lush fields, then in the opposite direction at the arid, brush-covered desert. Without water the land had no value to a farmer. Ken swung to the south side of the valley and continued onward to the east.

In some ancient, unnumbered geologic epoch, a lava dike, a great igneous sheet of liquid rock, had been thrust vertically upward through the crust of the earth, cutting completely across the valley. That savage wound was now marked by a long black scar of solidified basalt.

Ken reached the dike and turned toward the creek channel. As he rode along, he examined the dense ribbon of durable basalt draped over the land and standing three to four feet above the soft, older rocks. He had seen such earth structures before and knew they extended deeply below the surface.

Ken halted where the stream that flowed down from the high mountains and past Janos had hammered a passageway through the dike. The channel, some thirty feet wide where it lay in the dike, was dry and dusty. He dismounted and walked down the creek bed looking at the deposit of sand and gravel carried there and dropped by the creek.

After a time, Ken returned to Janos. For the remainder of the day he sat and talked with the Wilander sister and brothers. They spoke of many things: of California, and Mexico City, and Ken's trouble with Zaldivar. They said nothing about the people of Janos, as if the subject was forbidden.

*   *   *

"Wherever Larrway goes there's fighting and men are killed," Tamargo said. He pointed at the corpses of the three *bandidos* lying near the spring.

"He's a tough hombre," said Quillón. "Up until now he has always killed all the other men. But this time he was hurt or killed."

"What do you mean?" asked Tamargo. The tracker had spent about an hour examining the tracks of horses and men in the narrow valley, especially around the spring.

"The gringo rode up over there and dismounted from his horse. He fought these men near the spring. Someone shot him and he fell there. See the blood." He indicated a patch of dry blood baked nearly black by the hot sun.

"There were other people here also," said Tamargo.

Quillón nodded. "A small person with flat-soled shoes. A man wearing boots was in the rocks over there. He shot twice. I have the empty casings. I can't figure out all that happened, but the man from the rocks and the smaller person took Larrway off with them. They'll be easy to trail. Do you want to take time to bury these dead men?"

"No. Let's go after the American."

"Right." Quillón stepped to his mount and swung astride. He lifted the animal to a trot along the tracks of the gringo's horse.

"That's the place called Janos, the gringo village where the men have many wives," said Quillón. His eyes roved over the cluster of houses in the distance. "I've been here once before. Not into the town, but to watch it from the dunes."

"I've heard Zaldivar speak of the place," said Tamargo. "He said the women are very beautiful with fair skin and

190

golden hair. The girl, Anya, that Melchor has came from here."

Tamargo lay behind a sand dune two miles east of Janos. He drew back out of sight and rolled onto his back. "They may have lookouts posted. We'll wait until dark and then slip in among the houses. They will have a graveyard near the church. I want to check it to see if there are any new graves that might contain Larrway's body."

"What will we do if there are no fresh graves?"

"We know Larrway has gone into the village, for we've trailed his horse here from the spring. We'll stay hidden and watch until he comes out. We'll have his head either from his corpse now, or after we have slain him ourselves. For now we'll divide the rest of the day into two watches. You take the first. Wake me when the sun is three fingers from the horizon."

"Yes, Captain."

Tamargo moved to a place where he would be in the shade, stretched out, and went to sleep.

Tamargo stood in the deep gloom between the two houses. He listened to the music and the steps of the dancers on the floor of the large building. The laughter and gay voices of the people drifted to him on the slow, warm wind.

He and Quillón had been spying on Janos for two days. They had found no new graves at the church and had settled down to wait for Larrway to leave the valley or at least show himself. This night Tamargo had grown restless and under cover of darkness had crossed the irrigated fields and crept in among the homes of the villagers.

The music stopped and an unnatural silence fell in the

191

building containing the dancers. Then abruptly a young woman ran from the lighted doorway and into the night. She slowed, looked over her shoulder, then veered to walk down the path a few steps in the direction of a bridge spanning an irrigation canal.

Barely a minute later, two men came from the dance hall. They talked for a moment, and then one reentered the building. The second man walked along the path to the bridge.

The girl stepped out of the darkness. The man called to her and they began to talk.

Tamargo came out from his hiding place and crept through the murk across the street closer to the man and woman. He hunkered low to the ground and listened to the conversation. He understood English sufficiently to make out that the man planned to go to Los Angeles. Tamargo chuckled wickedly to himself. He had found Larrway.

Tamargo pulled his pistol. Larrway had just come from a dance. He would be unarmed, and easy to kill. The girl was also very valuable. Tamargo would kill Larrway and take his head, and make the girl a prisoner. He could do that in the dark before the men of Janos could stop him. Tamargo would take two valuable prizes to Zaldivar. He would be doubly rich. He stood erect.

A clamor of voices erupted and people began to stream from the dance hall. The men, women, and children fanned out in many directions along the street. The girl with Larrway turned from him and ran up the hill to the street fronting the houses.

Tamargo drew hastily back between the buildings. He pressed tightly against a wall in the deepest darkness. He had hardly hidden himself when the girl rushed past almost within arm's length.

The last person from the dance finally went by and faded into the night. Tamargo left his hiding place. He walked leisurely and openly across the street and down the hill toward the bridge. Larrway, when he saw a man approaching, would think him one of the townsfolk.

Tamargo peered hard to pierce the gloom. The bridge took shape. It was empty. The gringo with the head worth so much gold was gone.

18

JOAKIM ENTERED THE HOUSE AND STOPPED just inside the door. He spoke to Ken who was seated at the breakfast table with Johanna and Asael. "Bishop Blackseter and the elders want to see you at the town hall."

"Is it about Marjo?" asked Ken. "Are they trying to decide her punishment?" At the thought of Marjo being hurt, his anger flared fresh and hot.

"No, her punishment has already been determined," replied Joakim. "She will be shunned for three months."

"Damnation," exclaimed Ken. "Three months without talking to another person will be a lifetime. I wish they would hold me responsible for what happened. Then I could ride away from Janos and Marjo's relationship with her husband and the other people would be like it was before I came."

"It can never be the same," said Joakim. "People here have long memories. Blackseter wouldn't mind if you broke your neck. You've caused him problems with Marjo and embarrassed him before the other men. But he doesn't

194

want trouble with you. Especially since I told him you studied the use of weapons under Luis Calleja."

"Why did you tell him about Calleja?"

"The bishop asked how you could so easily kill the two bandits that tried to carry off Johanna. I told him about your training and about the fights you've had because of Zaldivar."

"What do they want to talk to me about?" Ken asked.

"I don't know. Go and talk with them and find out."

Ken went to his room and buckled on his six-gun. He didn't trust Blackseter. The man must surely consider him a rival for Marjo and would try to destroy him in some manner. He walked outside and turned along the street.

People on their way to the fields passed him. Most of them returned his greetings. Their friendliness made Ken think of Marjo. To be shunned by every man, woman, and child in Janos, people she had known all her life, would be cruel punishment. Ken resolved to seek out an opportunity to talk with her.

The door of the town hall stood open when Ken arrived. He stopped in front, reluctant to enter. Bishop Blackseter spotted him in the yard and beckoned for him to come inside.

The furnishings had been restored to their normal position for conducting the business of the village. Blackseter sat behind a long table. Two elders flanked him on the left and two on the right. All of their expressions were grim.

"Please be seated," Blackseter said. He motioned at a chair on the opposite side of the table from him.

Ken had seen all the men before, but he recognized only one, the father of Sophronia and Ina. He spoke to the man. "Good morning, Elder Sunde."

"Good morning to you, Ken," said Sunde.

"I don't know these other men," Kent told Blackseter.

"They are Elders Fiersen, Borgeson, and Nystrom," Blackseter responded, pointing at each man as he said his name.

Ken nodded briefly at the introduction. He spoke to Borgeson. "You are Anya's father?"

"I've heard that you saw a girl in Mexico City who might be my Anya. Joakim told me how you described her."

"I saw a white girl with yellow hair in the house of a man named Zaldivar."

"Did she seem well?" asked Sunde.

"No," Ken replied truthfully. "She was badly frightened. I'm sorry that I couldn't rescue her." He knew that even if he had gotten the girl away from the guards at Zaldivar's hacinda, Zaldivar and his *pistoleros* would have killed him on the road to Tacubaya and again taken the girl captive.

Ken shoved the thoughts of Anya aside and focused his keen attention on the group of men. They wanted something from him, something no one else in the village could give them. He would watch them carefully, for they were used to having their way, even if it harmed others. They ruled the people of Janos, making the laws, enforcing them, and punishing that person, man or woman, who should break a rule. They took many wives for themselves. Blackseter was the most powerful of all. And he had the most wives. A grasping, selfish man, thought Ken.

"Are you well and strong?" questioned Blackseter.

"Yes, quite well. My strength has returned and I'll soon be leaving to continue on to my home in California."

"How soon?" asked Blackseter.

"Within a day or so."

"We had hopes that you might stay a few weeks in Janos," Sunde said.

"I must leave very soon. I've already been gone from home too long. There are crooked men in California trying to destroy my family's business. They're shrewed, and the law hasn't been able to help us. But there are other ways to fight an enemy."

"So you went to Mexico City to be trained by Luis Calleja and acquire the skill to slay your foes?" Blackseter said.

"Simply put, yes. Calleja was a friend of my father's. He agreed to teach me what he knew."

"He must have taught you very well," said Blackseter. "Joakim told us about your battle with the bandits that took Johanna."

"Luis Calleja was the best weapons instructor in all Mexico. Probably in all North America. It's too bad he's now dead. He grew old and lost part of his strength, so Zaldivar's son, Melchor, was able to kill him."

"Joakim said you had several fights with the *pistoleros* of this Mexican named Zaldivar," Blackseter said. "Do you think this is the same man who sends bandits to take our young women?"

"The very same, I believe," replied Ken. "He has a long arm. He is a caudillo, a military chieftain with his own private army. He put a reward of ten thousand pesos in gold on my head and sent many soldiers to kill me. I had to fight them, or die."

"How many men have you killed?" asked Blackseter.

That's the second time I have been asked that, thought Ken. "Far too many," he said stiffly, his eyes grinding into the elders.

"Let's get on with our proposition to him," said Fiersen.

"He seems well-qualified to do what we need to have done."

"All right," said Blackseter. He looked intently at Larrway. "We're in a foreign land and have outlaws that attack us. It's getting worse. For the first few years, we weren't bothered. More than likely because not many people knew we were here. But now all that has changed. Twice within six months, men have come and ridden away with one of our women. We are farmers, and not skilled with rifle and pistol. However, you're an expert. We want you to train all the young men of Janos. Make them into a group of fighters who can defend us against the bandits."

Ken was surprised at the request. "I'm not a teacher like Calleja. It takes a certain type of man to instruct others on how to use weapons and, more difficult still, on how to kill."

"We'll pay a reasonable sum of money," Fiersen said. "We must be able to protect ourselves. We have plenty of rifles and pistols and ammunition for them."

"It takes weeks of constant practice to become an expert with a gun."

"Our men don't have to be masters with firearms, only skilled enough to drive off any enemies that attack the village or try to slip close to steal a woman."

"Once you begin to fight the bandits, they'll start coming in larger numbers to overrun your defenses," said Ken.

"Perhaps," said Fiersen. "But we have no other alternative. Our women mustn't always be afraid that every time they leave the house someone will carry them off."

"Soon even being in the house won't keep them safe," said Sunde. "The bandits are getting braver all the time."

The bandits will eventually destroy Janos, thought

Larrway. And the greediness of these five men for land and women would in large part be responsible for that destruction.

"How would you protect a village when the people must scatter over a four-square-mile area to work the fields?" Ken asked.

"We must devise a plan to do that very thing," said Blackseter. "I think we can, once we have men who know guns and will use them."

"I'll consider your offer," Larrway said. He stood up. "When will you let us know?"

"Before the day is done, say midafternoon."

Ken found Joakim directing water with a shovel to irrigate a field at the lower end of the cultivated portion of the valley. He turned off the main road and rode on the narrow path beside a ditch toward the villager.

Joakim saw Ken approaching. He put his shovel across a shoulder and walked over the field to meet Ken.

"I see the elders didn't do you in," Joakim said. "What did they want?"

"They think I'm some kind of expert with guns," Ken said. He dismounted and leaned his back against the horse. "They want me to train you young fellows of Janos to fight the bandits."

"So the women belonging to the bishop and the elders will be safe," said Joakim harshly.

Ken was surprised at the bitterness in the man. "What's the problem?" he asked.

Joakim flung an arm to point out across the field. "Look! My crops are burning up. All I get is the tail-end water that is left after all those farmers above me are finished irrigating. This year the flow in the creek is low, so I'm getting precious little water."

199

"Why don't you leave here? There's land for the taking in many places back in the United States."

Joakim looked at Ken. "All I know is Janos. I was brought here as a very small boy. I'd be lost anywhere else."

"Why is there a settlement of Americans in such an unlikely place as Janos? How did all this get started?"

"You might call it a sanctuary," said Joakim.

"From what? It seems like a very dangerous place to me."

Joakim faced to the north. "The American government made a law in 1862 that a man could legally have only one wife. Well, some men already had two or several wives, and there were many children. What were they to do? Kick the women and children out the door? Some men decided to leave the States and go into Mexico. Bishop Blackseter and eight other men with their families came to the valley and settled Janos in 1863.

"Look, Ken, at what they have created in fourteen years." His hand swept around to indicate the lush fields nestling in the arms of the desert valley. "The land is rich and productive. The houses are built of stone and will last a hundred years. It was unfortunate that my father came late and there wasn't a goodly supply of water for him. He had two wives. Johanna is my half-sister."

"Your brother Nilo broke away. And he took a woman with him."

"I'm not Nilo. I don't like my station here, but I won't leave. This is my home."

Ken thought he'd like to meet Nilo Wilander. "Joakim, I'm going to tell you something I believe very deeply. I think Janos is doomed to die."

"What do you mean?" Joakim asked in shocked surprise.

"There isn't enough irrigation water to allow the town

to grow to a size where it would have enough men to defend it. At the same time the bandits grow bolder. The elders, and their sons who have been given land, take all the women. Under these conditions, a town of white people can't survive in this country for long. Mexicans will one day soon be living in those stone houses and farming the fields."

"You're wrong. The people of Janos are strong and can endure great hardship. They would never leave here. I know that I never will."

"You're a stubborn man, Joakim. But I understand you." Ken became quiet, studying the man he had grown to like. Then he spoke, "Bring your shovel and come with me."

With a perplexed expression, Joakim fell in beside Ken and they walked down the valley together. The gray horse tagged behind without being told.

"Joakim, what do you see?" Ken asked, halting in the stream channel where it cut through the basalt dike.

"Gravel in a creek bed and lava rock and some willows there along the banks."

"Right. Now, back up the valley at the higher elevation, a large amount of water is used to irrigate several square miles of land. Part of that water is used by the plants, part evaporates, but much of it goes into the soil. That which goes into the soil flows along the bedrock to an underground basin. Here in this valley I'd say the natural way for it to flow would be out there under the sand dunes.

"Usually what goes into the ground is lost. This time that may not be so." Ken pointed at the basalt half-buried beneath the gravel. "That dike goes deep. It's hard and dense. Just maybe it's acted like an underground barrier, damming the water and forcing it up. Those willows could be telling us that there's lots of water just below our feet. At least, a place I saw like this in California had water below ground."

"If we find water, it's ours," Joakim said. "That's the law of the valley."

"Then use your shovel. Find out what's down there."

Joakim worked swiftly, gouging and tearing at the creek bottom. Ken helped, throwing the larger stones from the growing hole. At a depth of two feet, the gravel was damp. At three the gravel was wet.

Joakim began to hum to himself. He wiped at the sweat that coursed down his face and dripped from the tip of his nose. He glanced at Ken and grinned a broad grin. "It's there. I feel it in my bones."

He lifted up a shovel full of sand and gravel and tossed it aside. At the bottom of the excavation, a tiny trickle of water flowed out toward the mouth of the valley.

Working furiously, Joakim deepened the excavation. The trickle grew to a small rivulet of clear, clean water.

He increased his pace even more, his muscles bulging and the tendons taut as wires. A few minutes later the hole had been broadened substantially. A stream of water some three inches deep and a foot wide rushed across the floor of the creek bed.

Joakim turned his face up to the sun, opened his mouth, and shouted out a wild, keening cry of joy. He dropped his sight to Ken. "You were right. Look at that powerful current of water."

"We're seeing only a small part of the total flow," Ken replied. "I'm betting that if we had all this sand and gravel dug out down to the solid lava dike, there'd be a full-sized creek.

"Then all we'd have to do is dam it up and divert the

water out onto the benches on both sides of the stream channel," said Joakim. He scrambled up from the excavation and ran to an elevated place from where he could see and evaluate the flatness of the land.

"The soil is good and the surface won't need a lot of work to make it flat and level enough to irrigate. We're suddenly men of property, Ken. Each of us could farm a hundred acres or so."

"You're rich. I don't want any of the land. I'm soon going to California. What will you do now?"

"Sweet Sophronia Sunde will be mine. I know she likes me and I'm pretty sure she'll say yes to my proposal."

Joakim sprang back into the excavation and, ignoring the flow of water that soaked his boots, began to labor mightly at moving aside more of the creek debris.

"All the blisters are yours too," Ken said. He went to the gray horse and climbed up into the saddle.

"Where are you going?" Joakim said, looking up.

"I've been asked to tackle a tough task. I have to decide if I will do it." Ken reined the horse toward the sand dunes lying beyond the mouth of the valley.

He glanced back. Joakim's head was already down as he bent to his work.

I wish you good fortune here in Janos, my friend, thought Ken. But I feel you'll die before your time.

19

THE MAN ON SENTRY DUTY IN THE BOULDERS and brush on the north side of the valley lifted his hand in salute. Ken returned the greeting and rode on into the sand dunes.

Blackseter had posted a man at each side of the valley where it met the sandy wasteland. Ken judged the lookouts did nothing to protect the people. A distance of more than a mile and a half separated the two sentries. During the night, bandits could easily steal between the men and up on Janos without the slightest fear of being discovered. If the enemy wanted to travel on foot, they could enter the valley by an even more deserted route, by crossing the long lava ridges flanking both sides of the valley.

Bishop Blackseter and the elders must realize how ineffective the lookouts were. Ken shrugged his shoulders. He didn't have a better plan. He wasn't sure he even wanted to think about the problem or get involved in any manner at all.

Ken rode slowly as he mulled and speculated upon the

proposition the village elders had put to him. His course was to the northeast so that the fireball sun still low on the morning horizon wouldn't shine directly into his eyes and blind him. Already the air was hot and beginning to shimmer. The day would be a scorcher.

A quarter-mile into the desert, Ken found a string of horse tracks coming from the south and heading north. He didn't think the sign had been made by a villager. Rarely did the men enter the barren wasteland. He reined his mount to a halt and stepped down to examine the tracks.

The hoof prints curved about to follow the low swales between the tall dunes. At no place had the rider crossed a point of land high enough that he could be seen from the valley.

Ken estimated the sign had been made a few hours before, probably in the very early morning. He cast a sharp look about. A man with a rifle could be within easy shooting range behind any one of a dozen dunes. He sighted along the line of tracks and marked the spot in his memory where the aligment would intersect two points on the mountain range.

Ken leapt upon the gray horse and spurred east at a full run. A half-mile deeper into the sand where the dunes were very large, he turned due north. He held the horse at the fast pace, swerving the animal left and right to avoid cresting a dune and becoming framed against the sky.

Two miles fell away behind, then three. Ken swung the running cayuse to the west. As the beast tore along, Ken searched for tracks on the ground and watched the mountains to the north.

The two marker points that he had selected to show the course of the unknown rider came into alignment, and then were passed. The only disturbance he found was the pad prints of a lone, wandering coyote. Ken continued west to a place where the sand sea lapped against the base of the mountain. Still there were no tracks of man or horse.

Ken halted and let his mount blow and catch its wind. He had the rider located south of him somewhere within a three-square-mile area.

He pulled his rifle and rode south. Now he would find the man and see if he was one of Zaldivar's soldiers, or a bandit, or merely a traveler who had lost his way.

Sergeant Quillón sat behind the peak of a tall dune and studied the land to the west. The base of the mountain with its great jumble of angular lava boulders was a couple of hundred yards away beyond several windrows of sand dunes. The entrance to the valley was twice that distance to the southwest.

Larrway, when he left the settlement of the Americans, would come from the valley and head toward Ciudad Juárez on the border of the United States. Quillón felt sure of that. Such a course would bring the gringo directly in front of Quillón's rifle. In the event that Larrway held close to the foot of the mountain, thus making the kill more doubtful, Quillón could drop down to the bottom of the dunes and move forward unseen to a better vantage point from which to fire his rifle.

The sergeant fondly rubbed the wooden stock of his long-range killing weapon. This time there would be no wild chase during which unexpected avenues of escape might suddenly appear. Instead, Quillón meant for Larrway to die, an execution, quick, and certain.

The Mexican watched and waited. He was a patient man. Now and then he looked to the south for Tamargo.

Soon the captain would arrive and add his rifle to Quillón's to kill Larrway.

Tamargo and Quillón had spotted the lookout stationed at the north edge of the valley. The captain believed there would be another Janos man guarding the south border. Tamargo was looking for that man's hiding place. The task wouldn't take the experienced fighter long.

Quillón's horse stirred at the bottom of the hollow. The Mexican caught the animal's movement in the corner of his eye and twisted to glance over his shoulder. The horse was staring at something behind Quillón.

With quick alarm, the Zaldivar soldier looked in the same direction. He froze to a motionless statue on the side of the dune. A man on a big gray horse had stolen close, riding on the soft, noiseless sand to within forty yards or so. The rider held a rifle in front of him across the saddle. His eyes were riveted on the Mexican.

Quillón recognized the gray horse and knew the young man sitting so easily upon the animal's back was Larrway. The sergeant was amazed at the youthfulness of the fellow. Yet this boy had killed many men in the past few days.

Quillón felt a terrible dread at the unprepared and awkward position that he now found himself in. He would have to spin halfway around before he could fire at the gringo. Larrway would merely have to raise his rifle to shoot. Quillón tensed. He had no choice but to try.

The young American began to shake his head in the negative. He called out quickly, "You can never beat me!"

Quillón spun, sweeping up his rifle. As he turned, he heard Larrway shouting, "Don't do it!"

The sergeant felt the shock of the bullet hitting, like a

horse kick to the chest. The rifle, only partially raised, fell from his suddenly nerveless hands. He lurched erect, then blackness swarmed over him and he collapsed onto his side. His slack body rolled and tumbled down the steep face of the dune.

Quillón came to groggy consciousness lying on his stomach and choking with a mouth full of dust. He lifted his head and coughed violently, expelling a blast of the grit. He breathed painfully and coughed again. The taste of blood was salt and cooper in his mouth. He felt the blood rising, clogging his throat.

Feebly Quillón turned his head to look in the direction the shot had come from. Larrway had ridden nearer. He climbed down from his horse and came to stand over the fallen man.

Quillón blinked to clear his eyes and stared up at the American, starkly silhouetted above him against the clean blue sky. Larrway, I see you close at last. But it's a sad sight for me. I've lost. And losers die.

But, gringo, why do you look so sad? You've won and you're alive.

Ken knelt beside the Mexican, a man with ropelike muscles and in the prime of life. "Why didn't you listen to me? I didn't want to shoot you."

"I'll see you in hell and we shall fight the battle again," said Quillón. He breathed, and it was like a shudder. Red bubbles burst on his lips. His eyes rolled up in his head.

"I want no more battles," Ken said. He spoke quickly, for he knew he held the man's thoughts by only a spider's thread. "Tell me who you are."

"It makes no difference who a dead man is," said the Mexican in the faintest of whispers. "But I tell you, you have no choice but to fight more battles. Zaldivar will

208

never let you live. If Captain Tamargo doesn't kill you in Mexico, Zaldivar will send men to Los Angeles to slay you and your family as revenge for what you did to his sons."

Quillón's lungs expanded as he tried to breathe. But his lungs were full of blood and there was no space for air. His muscles strained as if he were lifting a tremendous weight. His throat swelled. Blood streamed from his mouth. Total, unending darkness enveloped him.

Ken believed what the dead man had said, that Zaldivar would never cease trying to take his revenge. But who was this Tamargo he spoke of? Another man intent upon killing him for the reward?

Ken looked to the south. There, a thousand miles away beyond many days of hard travel across desert and mountains, his true foe Ramos Zaldivar, plotted Ken's death, and the death of his family. All of Ken's battles and the men who had died had resolved nothing, because Zaldivar still lived.

I've tried to leave Mexico in peace, but you won't let me. I can't let you destroy my family. With a gut-wrenching certainty Ken knew he had to return to Mexico City.

Ken went to Quillón's horse, a large black animal. He had taken the soldier's life. Now he would take his horse as a second mount for the long ride back into Mexico.

He yanked himself astride the gray with one pull of his arms. Towing the dead man's horse, he rode directly for Janos. He didn't see the Mexican horseman in the sand dunes behind him.

Captain Tamargo hurried north through the sand. He had located the Janos man on lookout. The man wasn't a threat. What made Tamargo spur his steed and worry was the rifle shot he had heard a few minutes before. Had Sergeant Quillón and Larrway met and fought?

The captain reined his mount to a stop. A rider directly west of him and traveling at a fast gallop was entering the mouth of the valley. The man led a black horse. Quillón rode a black. The man passed behind the lava ridge flanking the valley.

Tamargo ran his horse to the northwest. He shortly encountered the fresh tracks of the unknown man's horse. As Tamargo feared, the course of the hoof prints came straight from the spot where Quillón should have been waiting in ambush for Larrway.

Minutes later Tamargo found Quillón. He squatted near the bloody corpse of his sergeant. In a guttural, hate-filled voice he began to curse the goddamned gringo. For the first time, Tamargo wanted to kill the American just to see him die.

Ken returned speedily to Janos. He had decided what he must do. He would ride straight to Mexico City. He would leave at once.

He entered the rear door of the Wilander home and went toward the bedroom. It wouldn't take long to pack his meager belongings.

Johanna, carrying water from the irrigation canal to fill the bathtubs, heard Ken's arrival and caught a fleeting glimpse of him as he went into the house. She quickened her step, splashing water from the buckets onto her dress. She ignored the dampness. She set the water buckets down at the front door and intercepted Ken in the living room.

"Hello, Ken," Johanna said.

Ken looked at the smiling girl, her eyes luminous with the pleasure of some inner thought that he didn't comprehend. As always when his sight rested upon her, he was astounded at her fairness. Today she was more lovely than ever, for he knew that this was the last time he would ever see her. Sadness welled up at that knowledge, adding to the gloom already in him from killing the Zaldivar soldier.

Johanna observed his dejection. Something bad had happened. "What is the matter?" she asked.

"I found one of my enemies in the sand dunes. He tried to shoot me. I had to kill him."

Johanna shivered. She remembered the skull-faced bandit that had captured her and fondled her with bony hands as he rode. "Why don't they let us live our lives in peace?"

"These soldiers and the bandits are doing what Zaldivar will pay them much money for—my death, or one of you women as a slave. He's our real enemy. I'm returning to Mexico City to try to put a final stop to his attacks."

"You told us that Zaldivar has thousands of soldiers looking for you. How can you expect to make your way through them and reach Mexico City? And won't he have many guards protecting him?"

"All that you say is true. But I'll devise a plan. I made it to this place alive. Perhaps I can travel back over that route safely. I'll have plenty of days to think of a way to get through Zaldivar's soldiers and to him."

"You're a fool to try." Johanna caught herself and fell silent. She bit her lip and blinked rapidly to keep the moisture that was rising in her eyes from growing into tears.

"Where's Joakim and Asael? I want to tell them good-bye."

"Joakim went to register his claim to the new water that you and he found. Then he planned to ride up the mountain and tell Asael about the good fortune. Joakim said there was enough water to irrigate maybe two hundred acres. He told me how you helped him. I give you my most heartfelt thanks for what you did. But don't you want some of the water rights for yourself? You could return here after Mexico City."

"I have to go on to Los Angeles to help my family," replied Ken. "When will Joakim ask Sophronia to marry him?'

"Probably never."

"What do you mean? He'll have plenty of land to support a wife."

"I've heard Elder Fiersen has already spoken with Elder Sunde for Sophronia. Elder Sunde seems agreeable. Or so I've heard. Usually the rumors in the village turn out to be true."

"And what has Sophronia said?"

"Fiersen hasn't asked her yet. He's still meeting with the other elders at the town hall."

"Do you think Sophronia would choose Joakim over Fiersen?"

"Oh, yes! I'm certain of that."

"Then would you help me get Sophronia for Joakim?"

"You tell me what to do and I'll do it." A daring brilliance came into Johanna's eyes.

"Come with me." Ken took her by the hand. They left the house and hurried off along the street.

Ken stopped before they reached the open door of the town hall. The voices of the elders in the building could be heard as a murmur.

Ken spoke in a low tone to Johanna. "Wait here. After I'm inside and have talked with Bishop Blackseter and the elders for a couple of minutes, then you go out on the bridge crossing the irrigation canal. Stop there where you can be seen through the door and windows of the hall. Act like you're just enjoying the day and the water in the canal. You must be standing where we can see you from inside."

"What are you going to do? Tell me. I have to know."

Ken grinned with an angry twist to his lips. "I'm going to get Joakim a wife."

"But, I mean, I want to know exactly what you plan to do."

"No time to explain now. We mustn't be seen together by the elders."

Ken strode away. He reached the front of the town hall and entered the open door.

BLACKSETER WAS WARY AND ON GUARD. KEN Larrway had returned much earlier than he had said he would. He had stalked in and now stood in front of the bishop and the elders. His hand rested on the butt of his pistol and his face was bleak.

Larrway spoke in a tight voice. "Less than an hour ago, I shot one of Zaldivar's soldiers. He had followed me here to Janos. Another man hunts me and will also try to kill me. And there'll be many more after him. So I'm leaving immediately to travel to California and put another thousand miles between Zaldivar and me. He'll stop his men at the United States border and not follow me farther."

"What of our proposition for you to train our men?" asked Blackseter.

"Tomorrow there could be a dozen, or maybe a hundred bandits outside the valley waiting for an opportunity to attack. Zaldivar will have sent them. I can never train your men so that they can keep you and your women safe. But I have a suggestion for you if you want to hear it."

"What is that?" questioned Fiersen.

"Leave Mexico forever. Abandon Janos and return to the United States. You'll be safe there. Zaldivar wouldn't dare attack you north of the border."

"We'll never abandon Janos." Blackseter's voice was harsh. "This is our town. We have no other home."

The four elders nodded in quick agreement, their faces stern and unyielding.

"Then you have only one choice: you must destroy Zaldivar. He's your true enemy. As long as he lives, there will always be men who will come to steal your young women to sell to him."

"He's correct," said Fiersen. "This Zaldivar is responsible for our trouble."

"But how do we destroy Zaldivar?" asked Blackseter. "He sits far away in Mexico City. He's surrounded by an army of men to protect him."

"Do as he does," Ken said. "Hire a man to go to his home and strike him when he doesn't expect it."

Fiersen looked sideways to Blackseter. Ken saw silent communication pass between them. These two men were the strong and dominant ones of the group. What they agreed upon would be approved by the remaining three elders.

"Would you go and stop this man Zaldivar from further bothering us?" asked Blackseter.

"And bring my Anya home," added Borgeson.

Ken rubbed his chin in a thoughtful gesture and let his gaze drift over the five elders of Janos. He had already decided, for his family and his own safety, that he must fight Zaldivar. But he had wanted to put the rulers of Janos in his debt. Now they had requested that he fight Zaldivar for them. The first part of his plan had been achieved.

"I'll go to Mexico City and try to put a stop to Zaldivar. It just may be possible. I've traveled the route twice and have been in his hacienda."

Ken twisted halfway to the side and glanced out the open door. Johanna was on the bridge, idly tossing pebbles into the flowing water of the canal. The bright sunlight was yellow fire in her hair. The young woman was beautiful and it shouldn't be hard to make these men believe that he desired her.

He faced the elders and the bishop again. "You offered to pay me for helping you make Janos safe from attack," he said.

"How much pay do you want?" asked Blackseter.

Ken deliberately turned his back to the men and again stared out the door at Johanna. She was bending to pick up more stones. When she straightened, she flung back her long hair and combed it once with her fingers. She threw a stone. Ken saw the silver splash where it struck the water. He continued to watch the young woman for several seconds longer before he once more looked at the five men.

"I want one of your women," Ken said.

The four elders glanced at the bishop. Ken read their minds with ease. They were wondering if he meant Marjo. Or was the outsider thinking of the Wilander girl so close there on the bridge? She was also very pretty, but still young.

Blackseter saw the steely purpose in the hard line of Larrway's jaw, and the eyes staring back at him were those of a man who knew what he wanted. More than that, a confident animal, unafraid, and sure of its skill to kill. But Blackseter would never give up his latest wife. The pleasure of young women in his bed was his well-earned reward for all his hard work in creating Janos, and then guiding it and maintaining it through drought, storm, and now bandits.

Ken grinned wickedly as he let his view wash over the men who possessed many wives. Their growing hostility toward him was evident, but he didn't give a damn.

Blackseter's edginess about Larrway was growing. The fellow seemed most interested in the Wilander girl. She would make a suitable woman for him in a year or so. However, Blackseter must be careful. He still sensed something hidden, some unknown objective in Larrway's actions.

"We can't just give you a woman," said Blackseter. "They have the right to say no to a proposal."

A low, mocking laugh came from Ken. "You can influence their decision," he said.

Blackseter would protect what was his. "The woman must be unmarried," he said.

"Then I may have a woman if she is single? And you will help me get her?" Ken looked at each man in turn, holding his eyes until he nodded in the affirmative. Ken looked at Fiersen last, and got his signal of approval.

"Good," said Ken. "Now I warn you, I will get damned awful mad if you should try to back out of our agreement." He was quiet, waiting for his threat to be fully understood.

Ken spoke. "I want Sophronia Sunde."

Fiersen leapt from his chair. "No! Not Sophronia," he shouted out in a wrathful voice.

"She's single, isn't she?" questioned Ken.

"Yes, but I have spoken to Elder Sunde about her. He's agreeable for her to come to my house as one of my wives. She shall not be part of this deal with you."

"What did Sophronia say? Have you asked her to be your wife?"

Fiersen's mouth shut with a grim snap. His eyes bulged with his hate for this outsider. He tensed, on the verge of hurling himself at the man who had tricked him.

Ken smiled a daring smile, his lips pulling back and his teeth showing cruelly white as he stared into Fiersen's malignant face. If there was to be a fight, then let it begin now.

"Fiersen! No!" Blackseter's voice cut at the angry elder. "We made a promise to Larrway. You have no contract with Sunde and his daughter. Now sit down."

With a strangled oath, Fiersen obeyed, falling heavily back into his seat.

Blackseter now knew the trap had been set for Fiersen and not for him. Fiersen would get over his loss. The bishop spoke, "Sunde, what do you say as the father of Sophronia?"

"I have no objections. It will be her decision," replied Sunde.

"Then if she says yes, we'll all abide by it," said Blackseter. "Sunde, go and talk with your daughter."

"Elder Sunde, I shall come to your home this evening to speak to Sophronia," said Ken. "I understand a girl must be fifteen before she may marry. Sophronia will be fifteen tomorrow. The wedding will take place one hour past sunrise."

"Why so soon?" said Sunde.

"I'll be leaving for Mexico City tomorrow," Ken said. He spoke to Blackseter. "Will you perform the wedding ceremony?"

"Yes," said the bishop. He wanted this man gone from Janos, never to return.

"So the deal between us is made. Wish me good luck and that I live long enough to kill Zaldivar."

Ken left the town hall. Johanna hurried to him. He told her what had happened.

"Now go tell Sophronia to say yes to getting married to me. When the call is made for the bride and groom to come forward, Joakim will take my place. I believe Blackseter will go ahead and perform the ceremony."

"He's probably happy that you didn't choose Marjo," said Johanna. She left in the direction of the Sunde home.

The desert evening had turned dark and absolutely silent. Ken and Joakim sat on chairs in the yard of Joakim's home. They were quiet. The talking had been finished for some time.

A light burned in Johanna's bedroom window. She hadn't come outside to join her brother and Ken. Joakim wondered if Ken knew how strongly Johanna felt about him.

Ken raised his sight to see the great clock in the northern sky. The Big Dipper had appeared, hanging there near Polaris. Once each twenty-four hours the Dipper revolved around the pole star, ticking off the passing of the hours with a precision of measurement more exact than any clock man could ever construct. The heavenly clock told him the time had arrived.

"I'll go now and see Sophronia," said Ken. "It's best that I go alone. Our changing places at the wedding must be a complete surprise. If we're lucky, Fiersen won't be there to raise any objection."

"I agree. I'll wait on you to find out her answer," Joakim said.

"Johanna said Sophronia seemed pleased at the plan for you to be the groom. So the answer will be yes."

"I hope so. But this is a strange way to get married."

"The end result is what counts," said Ken. He walked from the yard and into the street.

"Will the bride and groom come forward?" Bishop Blackseter said. He stood at the front of the church with a bible in his hands. He glanced expectantly at Sophronia with her father at the rear of the church, and then at Ken standing with Joakim off to the side near the wall.

"That's you, my friend," said Ken. "Today sweet Sophronia Sunde, as you call her, becomes your wife."

"Thanks for everything, Ken," said Joakim. He moved toward the bishop.

Blackseter's face stiffened with surprise when he saw Joakim coming forward and Ken remaining near the wall. His eyes locked on Ken with a questioning expression.

Ken nodded and chucked a thumb at Joakim. This was the test. Would Blackseter continue the ceremony?

Blackseter closed the bible and gripped it in his big callused hands. Now he understood. Larrway wasn't finished with his tricks. Yesterday's calling for Sophronia as a wife, had been but the first. Blackseter looked at Sophronia Sunde.

Elder Sunde was speaking to his daughter in a low, agitated voice. Sophronia's head bobbed as she answered her father. And she smiled. Father and daughter continued forward. Sophronia took the last two steps alone and stopped by Joakim's side.

A murmur of whispered amazement ran through the church. Then all fell silent, every eye on the bishop.

Blackseter studied the bible in his hands for a moment. Then he opened it and began the marriage ritual.

Ken relaxed. Fiersen's pew stood empty. He and his family hadn't appeared. There would be no more obstacles to Joakim's marriage.

The ceremony ended and bride and groom hurried to the exit. Ken fell in with the crush of people that followed close behind. Once outside the townsfolk crowded about Joakim and Sophronia to give them their best wishes.

Ken turned and headed for the Wilander's house. His departure had been delayed a day to help Joakim. Now Ken felt a great urgency to be traveling south. As Luis Calleja had once said, it was best to get a battle over with as soon as possible.

"Ken, wait," someone called after him.

He turned. He recognized Marjo's voice. She had separated from Blackseter's throng of wives and was walking swiftly in Ken's direction.

He was astonished that she would so openly approach him. But he was pleased at her courage. However, she would pay dearly, for in the eyes of these people, her action was an unthinkable and wanton deed.

Marjo came very close before she halted. "I heard the women talking, saying you were going to marry Sophronia. I didn't believe it. Now I know that you did all this to help Joakim."

"I consider him a friend."

"Make me your friend also. Take me to California with you."

"I'm going south to Mexico City and not to California."

"I know about your plan to fight Zaldivar. But when you come back north, come past Janos. I'll be waiting."

Ken knew he would help Marjo, should he live long enough. "The Mexican is a tough man. I may not win against him. If I do not return within a month, don't wait any longer for me. I'll be dead."

"No. You won't die. I'll pray for you."

"Blackseter is coming," Ken said quickly as he looked past Marjo.

"I can take his punishment, and everyone else's too, until you come to take me away."

"Marjo, get back with the women," Blackseter's voice cracked like a whiplash. "Do it this very second," he thundered. Veins were ridged like purple cords on his forehead.

He whirled upon Ken. "Damn you, Larrway. Don't ever talk to my wife again. Do you hear me? You have played your last underhanded trick here in Janos."

Ken didn't reply to the enraged husband. He stood ready to defend himself against the larger man.

"Never return to Janos," continued Blackseter in his strident harangue. "Or you shall die here."

Ken's eyes flattened in anger and he retorted. "Your threats are puny compared with what Zaldivar has in store for me. He's a thousand times more dangerous. But I go to fight him. So, tell me Blackseter, why should I fear you?"

Ken twisted away from the ugly, ageless hatred in Blackseter. He caught Marjo's questioning, fearful expression. Had Blackseter scared Ken so that he wouldn't help her? Ken stared steadily back at her. Then he turned and, leaving Blackseter in the street glaring after him, stalked off.

Behind him, Johanna's eyes roamed their tender touch over his departing figure. Then they filled with a young girl's sadness.

Ken removed his American clothing and donned the vaquero outfit. Dressed as a Mexican, he would draw less attention to himself. All his spare gear and bedding were rolled into a tight bundle and fastened behind the saddle on the black horse of the dead Mexican. He added two canteens and a packet of food.

He mounted the gray horse and guided it from the Wilander yard. At the mouth of the valley, he set a course southeast across the broad sandy wasteland. Chihuahua lay there, less than two days away. In that town, provisions for the first long leg of the journey might be quietly purchased, if he could avoid the reward seekers.

The sun increased the intensity of its heat. A slow hot wind came alive and blew directly into Ken's face. Sweat leaked from under the band of his hat and coursed down his cheeks. But finally the burning sphere of the sun aged and weakened and the world turned black.

Ken dismounted and leaned against the gray horse in the darkness of the night. He felt, just for a moment when his guard fell, the primal melancholy of possible death waiting for him ahead. He shoved the thought of death away. But he couldn't conquer an overwhelming feeling of aloneness in this foreign land.

He stirred himself to care for his mounts. He split the water in one of the canteens between the two horses, pouring it into his hat and holding it for them to drink. Ken drank deeply from the second canteen, ate a few bites of food, then stretched out on his blankets.

For a long time he lay listening to the wind talk in ragged, sullen sounds around the sand dunes. He brooded about Zaldivar, a man who would spend a fortune to kill him. He tried to devise a plan to safely recross a thousand miles of rugged land filled with hostile men searching for him. No good plan came to him.

Ken went to sleep in the blackness, lying in the middle

of the wasteland of sand. His last thought was the memory of Luis Calleja falling to the ground with a sword protruding from his back. You died well, Ken thought. I hope I can do the same, if it should come to that.

21

KEN AROSE WITH THE COMING OF DAYLIGHT. He ate nothing, simply gathering up his gear and climbing astride the gray horse. He again took up a course to the southeast.

The horses warmed to their work and Ken let their pace grow swifter. Run, you mustangs, carry me to Zaldivar, he thought. I'm tired of being hunted and chased. I want an end to it, and only a killing will do.

The desert sun captured the heat, repeated, magnified, and threw it back at Ken and the horses. The laboring beasts dripped sweat. Ken slunk low in the saddle, hiding his face in the shadow cast by the brim of his sombrero.

He left the land of sand dunes and entered a rocky zone under the shoulder of the Sierra El Nido. The iron shoes of his mounts made a constant clatter against the stones for several miles.

The stony area fell to the rear and he came out onto the outwashed plains lying east of the mountain. He struck El Camino Real north of Chihuahua shortly after noon.

225

An hour later Ken came abreast of the federal military garrison on the edge of Chihuahua. He heard pistol shots and saw a crowd of some three hundred soldiers and civilians in the field outside the tall adobe walls of the fort.

He guided the gray horse toward the assemblage of people. He should be safe in such a large group.

The people were gathered in a large half-circle. In the center of the curvature and facing the open end, a young American stood with a Colt revolver in each hand. At his signal, an older American threw a glass ball high into the air. The American with the pistols lifted the gun on his right hand and fired, shattering the small, three-inch target.

He nodded at the thrower. A second glass ball sailed up against the blue sky. And was instantly broken into fragments.

Two targets arched high at the next signal. The pistol-wielding American shot one with the gun on his left and the last with the gun on his right.

The gunman pivoted swiftly, thrust the pistols into the air, and fired both at the same instant. With that finale to his exhibition of shooting skill, he began to call out to the crowd in excellent Spanish.

"*Señores,* you have just seen the famous Colt six-shot revolver doing its fine work. There was not one misfire and I shot many times. In fact, one of these weapons will fire thousands of times and still be in perfect condition. Now you gunsmiths here know that I tell the truth. Without a doubt, this pistol is the best handgun in the world.

"The Colt Company wants representatives to sell its renown firearm. My partner and I have the authority to make such a contract with you. In addition, we have guns for sale here today. Or we will take orders for later delivery.

"You who have bandits to fight, come buy these great guns. And you, army officers, what better weapon could you take into battle? Buy two for yourself. Have the army supply officer order one for each of your soldiers. Equip them with the best weapon in the land, and at a very reasonable price."

Ken watched the two Americans lead a bunch of interested army officers and civilians to a canvas-covered wagon. The tall wooden sideboards of the vehicle contained large red letters stating "Colt Arms Company. Russel Kincaid and Dave Tarpon, Agents." The Americans began to sell guns and take orders for the weapon they bragged about so highly.

The crowd around the Americans gradually thinned, and then the last man drifted away. Leading his horses, Ken walked up to the gun salesmen.

"Very fine shooting," Ken said in Spanish. "It appears you have sold a lot of guns."

The Colt agents ran their eyes over Ken's dusty vaquero clothing and the Colt six-gun in the holster on his hip.

"A fair number," said the younger man, also speaking in Spanish.

"How many pistols do you have with you?" asked Ken. A plan had formed in his mind.

"We started our trip into Mexico with two hundred guns that we had shipped from El Paso. We've sold nearly half of them. We have given a few away as gifts. But we still have plenty to sell you all that you might want to buy."

"Gifts are needed in Mexico if a person is to do business here," said Ken. "Are all the guns packed in their individual wooden cases?

"They surely are," said the older American. He gestured into the bed of the wagon. "Take a look."

Ken stepped closer and peered down into the wagon. The guns in their cases were wrapped in lots of ten, in canvas. Each covering was stamped on the side in bold black letters, "Colt Arms Co."

The man reached into the wagon and lifted out one of the flat, square boxes from an open batch of the guns. He opened the lid. The Colt revolver lay embedded in red satin. "Now isn't that a beautiful sight?"

"I heartily agree," said Ken. "I'd like to buy five of them from you. How much for the guns?"

"Will you be paying in pesos or American dollars?"

"American dollars."

"That will be two hundred dollars."

"All right," said Ken. He unbuttoned the front of his shirt and, taking off his money belt, counted out the proper number of golden double eagles.

"Give me one of those pieces of canvas with the writing on it to wrap the guns in," Ken said. "And I'd like to buy a hundred rounds of ammunition."

"Dave, dig this hombre out some cartridges," said the older man. "A gun can't shoot unless it's got bullets to fire." He held out his hand for the money.

Russ and Dave watched the American in the vaquero clothing ride away with the tightly bound packet of pistols balanced in front of him.

"Dave, that man intends to kill somebody."

"Or get himself killed," replied Dave. "But why does he need five pistols?"

*   *   *

Captain Tamargo sat in the shade of the cantina patio. He had been there almost an hour watching the small hotel across the street where Larrway had gone.

Two days earlier, the gringo had left the valley of Janos and veered southeast. Tamargo was surprised that his course was not to the north toward the border of the United States. He rode in pursuit, holding far to the rear out of sight and following the tracks of the American's horses.

The first night, Tamargo crept up on Larrway's camp. But the gringo's gray horse sensed his approach and nickered an alarm. The gringo rose up in the moonlight with his rifle in his hands and stared searchingly around him.

The captain had drawn back. He would delay his attack on the gringo until the kill was certain.

The next day he trailed Larrway into Chihuahua. There the American had purchased several pistols from a Colt dealer and then left his horses at a livery stable, paying for thirty days' care and feeding. Tamargo had stabled his horse and, carrying his rifle, followed along.

Tamargo grew tense and leaned forward in his chair. Larrway was leaving the hotel. He had changed from his vaquero clothing and was now dressed as an American. He carried his bedroll and the packet of pistols he had purchased earlier. With a glance left and right, he moved along the street.

Tamargo picked up his rifle and fell in behind. It was strange that the man had come to Chihuahua and now walked in plain view down a busy street. He should have been running to California.

Tamargo began to grin under his beard as he closed the distance with Larrway. His finger slid inside the trigger guard of his rifle. He followed the gringo into the stage station. The American was trapped.

Ken left the street and entered the stage-station compound. The enclosure consisted of an acre of land surrounded on three sides by a chest-high stone wall. A corral in the rear held several horses. The station, a flat roofed adobe building, stood near the street.

As Ken crossed the yard, he cast an eye at a stagecoach, stoutly built of iron and wood, standing in front of the station house. A man was backing the last of three teams of horses into position, straddling the tongue of the coach. He yelled at the horses to stand and swiftly hooked the trace chains onto the singletrees. Finishing his task, the man went inside the ticket office.

Ken hastened his step to the door of the station. The coach appeared ready to leave. He wanted to be aboard when it rolled. A stage traveling day and night, with frequent changes to fresh horses, could transport him to Mexico City in a fraction of the time it had taken him to ride north.

He stopped in front of the ticket agent sitting behind a counter holding tickets and a cash box. Ken spoke to the man. "The hotel manager said there was a stage traveling south this afternoon."

"That's it, *señor*," replied the man, and pointed out the door.

"Do you have any seats left?"

"Yes. Where do you wish to go?"

Ken laid his bedroll and packet of pistols on the floor. He was careful to place the guns so that the Colt Arms Co. name was visible to the agent and the stagecoach driver standing nearby and watching.

"I'm a representative for the makers of Colt pistols. I

want a ticket to Mexico City. I'm going to sell our famous handgun to your army. How much is the fare?"

"When you're finished here, bring your baggage out to
the coach," interjected the driver. He raised his voice
and called out, "All passengers aboard." He led the way
from the station.

Ken paid for his passage and gathered up his belongings. He glanced at the tall vaquero who had come up
behind him. The man held a rifle in one hand and was
reaching into his pocket with the other.

"A ticket to Mexico City," Tamargo told the station
agent, and handed him some gold coins.

At the last instant, Tamargo had held his finger from
pressing the trigger and blasting apart the gringo's spine.
When the man had asked for passage south, a beautiful
thought had come to the captain. Why kill the man in
Chihuahua and then carry his head preserved in tequila
all the long distance to Mexico City? Why not let the
man carry his own head there? Then Tamargo would
take it from him.

Still, Tamargo wondered why Larrway was returning
to the stronghold of his greatest enemy. Surely he knew
that an army of men hunted for him. Larrway must have
a plan, but it would never save his life. Tamargo turned
and went outside.

"The boot's full," the driver told Ken. "Your baggage
will have to go on top."

"That all right for my bedroll, but I'll take these good
Colt pistols inside with me."

"Okay," said the driver. "You'll be the one crowded.
Give me your bedding and I'll tie it down so it won't be
lost."

Ken handed the bundle to the driver to stow away. He climbed into the coach. There were four bench seats situated crossways in the vehicle. The two in front faced each other, and the pair in the rear did likewise. The coach had space for twelve passengers. Most of the seats were occupied. Ken took a window spot near a slender old Mexican with silver buttons on his dark jacket and a long-barreled pistol strapped to his side.

As Ken evaluated the other occupants of the stage, the Mexican in vaquero clothing who had been behind him in the station climbed up into the coach. He found a seat with his back to Ken at the opposite end of the vehicle.

The driver secured the door and climbed up the front wheel of the stage into the high driver's seat. He yelled at the horses, and his long bullwhip cracked. The fresh horses left the station at a run. A billowing brown tail of dust trailed the coach from the town.

The driver soon pulled the teams down to a trot and went directly south on the worn Camino Real. The coach lurched and rattled as it struck the ruts in the road, or dipped down into the dry rocky gullies. No one tried to talk in the heat and the dust that swirled in from the rear.

In midafternoon the stage halted at Horcasitas. Rested horses replaced the tired ones. The passengers barely had time to grab a drink of water before the driver was yelling for them to get aboard the coach.

At Saucillo the stage slanted down to cross the Río Conchos, a shallow flow of yellow water. A rider was crossing from the south. As the horseman came abreast of the coach, the tall vaquero began to shout for the driver to stop.

The driver continued on across the water, then with a

curse pulled his teams in. "What do you want?" he asked
in an angry voice.

Tamargo ignored the driver. He leaned out the window and called to the rider. "Fuentes, come with me,"
he ordered.

Cuadrado saluted the Zaldivar captain who knew him
as Fuentes. He reined his mount through the water and
up beside the coach. He tied the horse to a strap on the
boot and climbed into the stage.

The driver popped his whip and the stage rushed onward. Tamargo and Fuentes talked briefly in low voices,
then sat back in their seats and said not another word.

Ken closely scrutinized the two vaqueros. They had
given not one sign that they knew who he was.

The stage reached Ciudad Camargo in the scant light
of a low, distant moon. The vehicle stopped in front of
the yellow-lighted doorway of the local station. Some
passengers took their baggage and went off in the darkness down the street.

"Food's ready," a woman called from the door of the
station.

Ken dined with the other passengers on thin tortillas,
roast beef, beans, and boiled eggs. The two vaqueros
continued to studiously avoid looking at Ken, and that
began to worry him. They should have some interest in
an American with a bundle of Colt revolvers.

The driver for the next leg of the journey came to the
station door. "I'm loading baggage now," he said. "The
stage leaves in ten minutes."

There was a last foray upon the food, and the passengers filed outside. The stage coach left the town and
plunged south beside the Sierra Las Pampas and onward
beyond that rocky mountain into the desolate desert of
the Bolsón de Mapimí.

Ken lost track of the names of the stage stops and the little desert towns where the coach halted to change horses and the passengers sought a moment of relief.

His weariness grew with the long hours and the constant jolt and sway of the vehicle. He dozed when he could. He thought that even if the vaqueros meant to harm him, they wouldn't do it while the crowded coach roared along.

The night died and gave way to day. Then the day faded back to night. Only Ken and the tall vaquero remained of the original passengers, the others having reached their destinations or left the stage to sleep and rest and catch a later scheduled vehicle. Ken noted that the two vaqueros didn't both doze at the same time.

In the long black hour just before day came again, the coach crossed the Río Nazas and rumbled into Torreón. At the call of the driver giving the name of the town, Ken came instantly alert. This was Zaldivar's main stronghold, the most dangerous place along the route to Mexico City. Should the vaqueros on the coach with him be part of Zaldivar's soldiers, they could summon hundreds of men to help them kill Larrway.

A new coach and driver awaited the arrival of the stage from the north. A thirty-minute stopover was announced to allow the arriving passengers time to eat.

The two vaqueros ate at a long table with Ken and made no move to leave the station. Upon completion of the meal, all the passengers walked outside.

Ken was amazed, for in the light shining from the door of the station, he saw a larger and nearly new coach. It was painted red, its undercarriage a brilliant yellow. There were splendid, thick cushions on the seats. The vehicle was barely half-full and Ken appropriated a full row of seats for himself.

The big coach departed Torreón, moving swiftly behind the trotting horses. It rode easily, rocking on its leather through-brace shock absorbers.

Ken's exhaustion overwhelmed him. He couldn't stay awake any longer and he was safely past Torreón. He stretched out and slept as best he could as the coach dived through the black night on the Bolsón de Mayran.

Ken reached Zacatecas a day and a half after leaving Torreón. Woolly-headed, he collected his possessions from the stage and staggered off on the midnight street to a hotel. He slept until daylight came.

Ken assembled with other people to await the morning stage. He had hardly arrived when the tall vaquero who had traveled with him from Chihuahua came, carrying his rifle and bedroll. The man called Fuentes accompanied him. They too had lain over to rest. Or had they stopped because Ken had left the stage?

Ken's wariness increased at the coincidence of the two men's continued presence on his trip. He found a seat on the coach where he could watch them.

The stage hurried south. The towns were closer together. Children and adults gathered at the stations to watch the activity of the loading and unloading of the passengers and their baggage. People in the fields beside the road straightened up from their work to watch the brightly colored vehicle dash past behind the sweating horses. Now and then the driver would halt at the edge of the infrequent streams to allow the horses to drink a few swigs of water and the passengers to wash the dust from their faces.

San Luis Potosí was reached in the middle of the night. The stop to exchange horses and passengers was brief. In the first, frail light of dawn, they passed the Sierra Guanajuato and shortly thereafter the Mesa del Sordo.

Ken saw the dead walnut tree where the headless corpse of the bandit Ortiz had hung. He glanced at the vaqueros who had traveled such a long distance with him. Had they been part of the band of men that took Ortiz's head? Were they scheming to take his?

Ken knew that he must stay ever more alert as he drew closer to Mexico City. To remove part of his weariness, he would stop in Querétaro for a few hours' rest. The sharp eyes of the blacksmith must be avoided.

⟫ 22 ⟪

"**C**APTAIN TAMARGO INTENDS TO KILL YOU HERE in Querétaro."

Ken was startled by the words. The man Fuentes had drawn close, moving with the crowd of passengers disembarking from the stage in the night. He had uttered the words without looking and walked on.

Why would Fuentes warn Ken when obviously the man worked for Tamargo? What trap were the two about to spring on him?

He recalled the dying bandit in the desert near Janos. That man had spoken of a Captain Tamargo searching for Ken. Now the Zaldivar captain had been identified for him.

He picked up his belongings and walked into the night. He must somehow control the time and place of the fight with Tamargo. Ken had observed how the man moved, with a smooth, flowing motion. He would be very quick with a gun.

Ken looked down the dimly lit main street of Querétaro. The blacksmith's shop was closed.

237

Ken went out onto the street. He walked on, passing a streetlight, and arrived at another, the last one in that direction. Glancing over his shoulder, he saw the two vaqueros followed, and quite openly. Tamargo carried his rifle. Fuentes had told the truth.

Ken breathed a sad sigh. God! He was so very tired of the battles with Zaldivar's men. But this one must be fought. And should he survive, then the one with Zaldivar himself, the final battle.

He continued onward for twenty paces and then pivoted swiftly, letting his load tumble to the ground. He had led the vaqueros far enough away from other people.

His hand loosened the pistol in its holster. He kept hold of the butt of the weapon. His enemies must be given no advantage over him.

Larrway stood in the edge of the faint island of light cast by the street light. His back was to the blackness of the night. However, his sudden stop had caught Tamargo and Fuentes in the full glare of a light.

"Halt," Ken called harshly. "Tamargo, what do you want with me?"

Damn the gringo, thought Tamargo. A few more steps and he would have raised his rifle and killed Larrway, without danger to himself. Now there would be a fight. Still he and Fuentes could beat the lone man.

"I want your head," replied Tamargo.

"As you took Ortiz's?"

"The very same. Will you die as bravely as that lowly bandit did?"

"Fuentes, do you stand with Tamargo?" Ken challenged the man.

Cuadrado knew the deception and his days as a spy for Díaz in Zaldivar's army were over. "I warned you of Tamargo because I too am a foe of Zaldivar." Cuadrado twisted about and darted off hastily at an angle. He halted out of the line of fire. For his own survival, he must know who remained alive after the conflict.

Ken saw Tamargo jerk with surprise at Cuadrado's unexpected action. Then the captain collected himself. "It makes no differences that Fuentes has betrayed me. I'll kill you and then deal with him." With a sudden movement, Tamargo lifted his rifle.

Ken pulled his pistol with a swing of his hand. Tamargo was sharply etched by the streetlight, a bright target. Ken fired at the heart of the man.

Tamargo was slammed backward by the punch of the bullet. As a great pain surged through him, he recalled the premonition that he had felt when he had read Zaldivar's notice of the ten-thousand-peso bounty on Larrway. Tamargo had thought he would catch the gringo and collect the golden reward. Now Tamargo knew that he had misinterpreted the premonition. He had trailed Larrway two thousand miles to collect only the reward of black death.

All day and far into the night the miles slid past beneath the rumbling wheels of the stagecoach tearing along the King's Highway. As the night aged, the wind stiffened and shadows rippled the darkness as clouds chased one another across the heavens. The clouds and the moon fought for possession of the sky. The clouds won, thickening rapidly, and a dense overcast came in across the moon.

After the shooting of Tamargo, Ken had hurried to the opposite end of Querétaro. The local law officials mustn't delay him in reaching Zaldivar. He rented a room and tried to sleep. After only a few hours of fitful tossing, he had risen and returned to the stage station.

The man Fuentes was there ahead of him. They boarded the stage. Not one word passed between them.

The coach rolled up the black volcanic mountain and then through the even darker, night-blanketed forest on the highland. A patter of rain ran over the coach, rattling on the wood and the slicker of the driver. The road tipped in a long, sliding downgrade into the valley of Anáhuac. The rain followed the stage down from the mountain and into Mexico City.

The stage halted on the stone-paved Zócalo, the Grand Plaza, and disgorged its passengers. Ken took his packs, and wearily, stiff-legged like a sleepwalker, he aimed his steps from the plaza toward the home of Lucas Alamán. Lucas, of all the people in the city, might be one who would help him.

"Melchor died this afternoon," said Lucas. "Canosa couldn't stop the internal bleeding and he died a slow and lingering death. Ramos Zaldivar seems half-insane."

"Then Zaldivar is still in Mexico City," Ken said.

"Yes. He's at his hacienda and will surely stay there until Melchor's funeral."

"Then he'll be easy to find."

"Do you intend to fight him in his own fortress?"

"That's the last place he'd expect to see me."

"It's said that Ramos is the fastest and most accurate *pistolero* in all Mexico. I saw him fight a duel once and I do not doubt his skill. You'd be a fool to face him."

"Perhaps so. But I must do it. Would you lend me a horse? I came in on the stage and am on foot."

"Certainly, my friend. I have an outstanding horse that I'll give you."

"I also have a gift for you. There are five Colt revolvers inside this canvas covering. They're yours. Now I must change into my vaquero clothing and be going. Daylight is not far off."

"You may change in there," said Lucas, pointing to an adjoining room. "Then come to the stables with me. I'll show you your mount, and I'll go partway to Zaldivar's hacienda with you. But I can't help you fight Ramos Zaldivar, for that would be suicide."

The streetlights were yellow stains on the drizzily night as Ken and Lucas crossed over the Zócalo. All the avenues were deserted. The horses' hooves reverberated dull echoes between the black buildings.

The city was left behind and the sour, damp darkness of the countryside wrapped itself close about the two riders. Ken checked the position of the Big Dipper in the sky. Dawn lay an hour ahead. Not much time to steal upon Zaldivar.

He urged his mount to a trot on the Belén Causeway toward Tacubaya. Alamán kept pace beside him. The rain slackened and quit as they drew close to Chapultepec hill.

Ken saw the ghost-ridden cypress woods where Luis Calleja had died. He had been a brave man.

With cold logic, Ken began to design a plan. His enemy had to be killed or Ken would die in this foreign land of Mexico. His parents in Los Angeles would feel Zaldivar's vengeance. He knew he was also fighting for the slave girl, Anya, and for his friends in Janos.

He felt his logic slipping from his grasp. There came the tingle and slither of his anger, like the coil of a great snake unwinding in his belly.

The two riders swung onto the private road leading up to Zaldivar's hacienda. They slowed their mounts to a

241

noiseless walk on the wet earth. At the top of the grade, they halted and sat staring at the massive home and the single lighted window on the ground floor. Ken detected movement in the yellow square.

"Must you go through with this plan?" asked Lucas.

"Yes." Ken's voice was sharper than he intended.

"Then, good fortune to you. I'll wait here. I hope you live to see the dawn."

Ken stepped down from his mount. "By dawn it'll surely be all over." He moved off in the Stygian gloom of the cloud-covered night.

He had wanted darkness. But this was too much, like wading through a pit of total blackness. He stole forward, the lighted window drawing him as if it were the only light in all the world.

His outstretched hand encountered the high wall surrounding the fortress home. He jumped up and grabbed the rough stone top of the wall, muscled himself up, and dropped inside. He hunkered low, his ears reaching out for some noise made by a guard.

There was no sound close by, but the muted voices of men came from the hacienda. Ken crept forward. Getting into Zaldivar's stronghold might be easy. Getting out alive could be impossible.

Lieutenant Cuadrado followed Larrway to the hacienda of Lucas Alamán. When the two men rode away into the night, Cuadrado ran behind them until he was confident he had guessed their destination. He then hurried to the quarters of General Castillo.

Castillo came into his office, rumpled from sleep but alert. The lieutenant wouldn't be here in Mexico City and awakening him at this hour of the night unless very important events were happening.

Cuadrado saluted his general. Without preamble he said, "The American Larrway is in the city. At this very moment he is riding toward Zaldivar's home. Lucas Alamán is with him."

Castillo sat at his desk. "So Larrway has come to the conclusion he must kill Zaldivar or he will always be in danger of the man's vengeance. Is that a correct assumption on my part, Lieutenant?"

"Yes, General. I can think of no other reason for him to return. He was north of Chihuahua and could have escaped to the American border. But instead, he comes back here. He killed Sergeant Quillón, one of Zaldivar's soldiers, in the sand desert. Perhaps he learned something from him."

"Can Larrway beat Zaldivar in a fight or a formal duel?"

"I saw him kill Tamargo. He's fast, But Zaldivar's a better *pistolero* than Tamargo. Larrway is very tired. I traveled with him for many miles on the stagecoach and I'm exhausted. He's a brave one, but he'll be slower than if he were well-rested. I believe Zaldivar will win any contest tonight."

"We can't sit idly by and wait while this battle occurs." The general sprang up land went swiftly to the door. He jerked it open and shouted out to his orderly. "Lieutenant, wake the duty officer, Captain Suazo. Tell him I want a hundred lancers armed and mounted in front of the palace in fifteen minutes. No, in ten minutes."

"Yes, General," said the orderly. He started down the hall.

"On the double-quick, Lieutenant," snapped the general. "Hurry your ass."

*   *   *

"I bid six thousand pesos," said the brothel owner, Melgares. Though his face was impassive, he was smiling inside his head. The white woman with the fine golden hair was worth twenty thousand pesos. However, he was confident he would purchase her for much less than that. He would place her in his most expensive whorehouse. She would make him a fortune before she became diseased and died.

Melgares looked at his competitors Zovala and Lejanza. They were timid, stingy men and would soon stop bidding against him. Zaldivar had made a large mistake in limiting the number of bidders. He seemed to be in a big hurry to complete the transaction.

"Come! Come! Hombres, make your bid." Zaldivar's voice was hard and his eyes stabbed at the men.

Zovala continued to examine the fair-skinned woman in the center of the room. She had been stripped of all her clothing except for the thinnest, barest of garments to better show her beauty. His pulsed raced. This woman shouldn't be made a whore. She was worthy of a man's private bed.

"I bid seven thousand pesos," said Zovala.

"Seven thousand and three hundred pesos," said Lejanza.

"Eight thousand," Melgares called out.

Anya stood frozen in the center of the room as the men bid for her. She didn't look at them. Instead, she stared straight ahead, her eyes blue pools of torment.

Melchor had died that morning. The remainder of the day, Ramos Zaldivar had stalked the house like a caged animal. Often he looked into the room where the body of his son lay. Anya had hidden in her room. Still, Ramos' curses and rantings could be plainly heard.

244

In the late hours of the night, Anya had been routed from her bed and roughly brought here before the men by the female guard, Rosa. Zaldivar was carrying out his threat to sell her as a harlot. She trembled in her fear of these men who had such total control over her.

She wanted to beg them not to do this thing. But she knew such a plea would lead to nothing. Her head lifted. Her back stiffened and her eyes burned with defiance. Her hate overcame her fear.

Ken stole from the perimeter wall to the side of the hacienda. Once there, he pulled his sombrero low over his eyes and briskly and openly walked through the gloom in the direction of the front entrance.

"Who goes there?" questioned a voice from directly ahead.

"Vicente," Ken mumbled. He hoped the guard would see the vaquero outfit and not become alarmed before Ken could get within striking distance.

The indistinct form of the man became visible. It was impossible to make out his features. Ken walked straight at him.

"Who are you?" the guard asked again, his voice full of suspicion.

Ken was three steps from the sentry. He leapt forward with all his quickness, pulling his pistol, swinging it swiftly. The vibrations of the iron striking the bone in the guard's head ran pleasantly up his arm. The man crumpled to the ground. Ken ran past three horses hitched to buggies and entered the front door of the hacienda.

"Eleven thousand pesos," Melgares bid. He thought this bid would buy the blond American girl.

The room became quiet, waiting. Zovala and Lejanza

looked one last time at Anya, then at Zaldivar. They said not a word.

"I bid my life for Anya," came a voice from the open door of the adjoining room.

Zaldivar pivoted. His hand swung to float over his six-gun. He knew who spoke without seeing him.

Other voices began to call to Ramos, the ghostly whispering voices of Melchor and Martín. Kill him, the whispers said urgently, kill him for us.

Larrway stepped out into the candlelight illuminating the room. Zaldivar was surprised at the sight of the gaunt body of the gringo. His features were strained, taut, as if from a very great weariness.

Zaldivar's face became an evil mask, splitting open to smile horribly. His eyes sharpened and filled with a merciless glitter. He heard Melchor's whisper again: Kill him!

Ken sensed the hate in Zaldivar, an unreasoning hate that allowed no room for fear of death. Only one desire: to slay him.

Just for a moment, the force of Zaldivar's single-minded purpose created a germ of fear in Ken. Then a cold wind blew through his mind and whisked the fear away. He too had no alternative except to kill. In a ferocious sort of way, he looked forward to the battle.

Ken saw the minute, almost imperceptible tensing of Zaldivar preparing to draw his weapon. Ken's hand plunged down for his pistol. He swung the gun up. As he fired, he twisted to the side to put the thin edge of his body toward the expert *pistolero*.

The two pistols erupted, shattering the night with fire. The candle flames flickered out at the mighty concussion of two cartridges exploding simultaneously in the room.

Then the hot wicks reignited and the flames burned brightly.

Ken flinched as Zaldivar's bullet tore across the front of his chest. A soaring pain seared the nerve endings of his damaged flesh. He brought his pistol back into alignment with the Mexican.

Zaldivar was spinning slowly, a dead man dancing. The spinning stopped and he leaned backward at an impossible angle, seemingly leaning on the air. He crashed down on his back on the stone floor.

The barrel of Ken's gun swung to point at first one, then another of the three brothel owners, like some deadly snake's head searching for something to strike. None of the men moved.

"Anya, let's go," cried Ken. His chest was constricted with pain and his breath came shallowly.

"To the front door. It's open. Hurry!" He grabbed the girl by the hand and ran from the room.

"Can we make it?" came Anya's frightened voice.

"We must, or we are dead."

23

GENERAL CASTILLO HEARD THE DOUBLE PISTOL shots, one piled upon the other, as he reached the turnoff to Zaldivar's hacienda. He shouted at his lancers to follow and sent his horse into a full run.

In the pitch darkness on the hill, a score of lights came to life and began to bob and rush about. Men's voices roared, a storm surf of alarm, that swiftly changed to anger.

The charging troop of lancers piled up against the wall of Zaldivar's fortress. Castillo looked over the wall to survey the gathering of lights centered midway in the compound.

"Go over the wall and open the gate," the general ordered the nearest rider. "Don't let anyone stop you."

The man reined close to the obstruction. He pulled himself from the saddle, up and over, and down inside. The gate swung open. The lancers spurred through behind Castillo.

"Form one rank abreast," barked Castillo. "Pull carbines. Stand ready for my command." He led his lancers forward.

THE SLAVERS

* * *

Ken felt the cold fingers of threatening death touch him. Half a score of guards had caught Anya and him before they could reach the gate. So many guards that he knew that he couldn't kill them all. They had roughly disarmed him and now held him tightly. In the light of the torches and lantern, their faces appeared savage and animallike.

Vicente had directed the guards to hold Ken and had gone into the house to determine what had happened. Now he returned. The three brothel owners hesitantly followed him outside.

"Zaldivar is dead," Vicente called to the guards. He pulled his long-bladed knife and stalked toward Ken.

"You murdering bastard," Vicente cursed Ken. "I'm going to kill you. And the girl shall yet be sold."

The thudding hoof falls of many horses sounded from the gate. A long file of riders advanced on the gathering of guards.

"This is General Castillo," the man in the lead shouted out. "What is happening here? Where is Señor Zaldivar? I want to warn him of an American coming to kill him."

"That is Larrway near the girl," Cuadrado said under his breath to the general. He stared hard at the American. "He seems to be hurt and bleeding badly."

"You're too late with your warning, General," Vicente said. "The American has killed Don Ramos. Now we will execute him."

"I regret that I'm late. But murder must be punished by the federal authorities." Castillo stepped down to the ground.

He advanced on the group of men holding Larrway. This one gringo, by shooting the powerful caudillo, had helped Díaz to solidify his power over all Mexico. He didn't deserve to die. But how could Castillo save him without the people thinking Larrway was an assassin in the pay of Díaz?

"No," cried Vicente. "I must be the one to punish him. It's my right, for he murdered my *patrón*." He whirled upon Larrway.

"Captain Suazo, disarm all these men," commanded the general. "Shoot any man that resists."

"First squad forward," ordered Suazo. "Take those men's weapons."

The squad of lancers spurred their mounts toward the guards and surrounded them. Reluctantly the guards handed up their firearms and knives.

The general called out in a loud voice so that all could hear. "Justice shall be done, and done quickly. I will personally execute the American. Hold your lights high so that I can see the sights of my gun."

He pulled his pistol and marched with a military step to Ken. He spun the injured man around and prodded him to an open area away from the guards and his lancers.

"Turn and see your death coming," the general said, again in a loud voice. Immediately after, he spoke in a whisper to Ken. "When I fire, fall as if you're dead. Or you soon will be." The general pivoted and marched ten measured steps away from Ken.

"He deserves a trial before a judge and jury," shouted a man hurrying up from the open gate. "He had a proper reason for fighting Zaldivar."

"Who are you?" questioned Castillo.

"Lucas Alamán."

"Are you a friend of this American?"

"Yes."

"Then you shall have the task of burying him," said

the general. "Captain Suazo, see that Alamán doesn't interfere with the execution."

Castillo aimed down the barrel of his pistol at the thin young American. You don't look like a Mexican hero, the general thought. But he must hurry on with the hoax. The light of the false dawn had already arrived.

The general shifted the point of his aim and fired. Ken grabbed his chest, whirled around, and fell. Castillo walked forward and knelt over Larrway. He whispered, "Don't move, no matter what happens."

The general stood erect. "Larrway is dead. Now, Alamán, you can be of service. Bring up one of those buggies tied by the entrance of the hacienda and I shall personally help you load your friend's body."

"You have done a terrible wrong," cried Alamán.

"Get the buggy," sternly ordered Castillo.

Alamán climbed up into the nearest vehicle and drove it close to Ken's slack body. Castillo caught Ken by the shoulders and, with Lucas lifting the feet, placed the body on the floor of the buggy.

"Take the girl and see that she gets safely back to her people," said Castillo. He motioned for Anya to come to them. "Go with this man. He'll help you."

Castillo spoke quickly to Alamán. "Leave now."

Vicente had pushed free of the ring of lancers and was drawing near.

Castillo stepped to the horse hitched to the buggy and slapped the animal smartly on the rump with his hand. Then, with his back to all the men, he watched the buggy draw away.

Castillo would wait three days for the death of Zaldivar to become known to all his soldier and to the remaining caudillos. But then he would swiftly attack President Díaz's enemies before they could select a new leader and organize around him. Mexico would have no more revolutions for a hundred years. A thousand years.

Lucas halted the buggy on the road and retrieved Ken's and his horses. Sadly he tied them to the tailgate near Ken's head.

Ken stirred and sat up slowly. He groaned with the effort.

"Madre de Dios," ejaculated Lucas. "But you are dead."

"Not yet, my friend."

"I saw the general shoot you."

"The good general is a trickster. I don't know why he risked so much to help me, but I'm glad he did."

Anya reached out and touched Ken's hand. "You're not dead, but you're badly hurt. We must find a surgeon to stop your bleeding."

Alamán sprang up into the buggy. "The surgeon Canosa is the one."

"Yes, Canosa," Ken said. "Then Anya and I have a long journey to make. To Janos."

Author's Note

JANOS TRULY EXISTED—FOR A FEW SHORT years.

    The first United States law prohibiting polygamy was passed in 1862. Men with plural wives soon began to migrate south to settle in northern Mexico—a place they hoped would be a sanctuary from persecution. Janos was settled in 1863.

A second and more stringent federal law was passed in 1882. The flow of polygamists into Mexico accelerated.

An even tougher law against the practice of one man having several wives became the rule in the United States in 1887. The number of émigrés to Mexico grew greatly. In total, several thousand American men and women founded twenty settlements.

President Porfirio Díaz extended his protection to these thrifty, hardworking Americans. He ordered the Federal Rural Police and the army to assist the Americans in resisting the attacks of bandits. For thirty-three years, until 1910, the Americans were relatively safe, by order of this strong Mexican ruler.

The most bloody of Mexican revolutions began in 1910,

and Díaz was driven from power. During the military phase of the revolution, battles between the opposing forces were fought almost everywhere. One million people were slain out of a national population of fifteen million.

Many rebel chieftains sprang into being. Soldiers deserted the federal army and formed marauding bands. Bandits rode all over the back country.

The American settlements, where each man had several wives, were prime, tempting targets for the large bands of men moving about the country. The gangs invaded the towns and raped the women, forcing "favors," as they called it.

A rapid exodus of the American polygamists began. They streamed north, abandoning years of labor and fertile land, to settle in secluded valleys in the desert Southwest of the United States.